The Underworld
The story of Robert Sinclair, miner

by

James C. Welsh

Double9
BOOKS

The Underworld
The story of Robert Sinclair, miner
by James C. Welsh

ISBN: 978-93-68093-77-0

Published by

DOUBLE 9 BOOKS
2/13-B, Ansari Road
Daryaganj, New Delhi – 110002
info@double9books.com
www.double9books.com
Tel. 011-40042856

ABOUT THE AUTHOR

James C. Welsh (2 June 1880 – 4 November 1954) was a prominent Scottish miner, trade unionist, novelist, and politician affiliated with the Labour Party. His political career as a Member of Parliament spanned from 1922 to 1931 and from 1935 to 1945. Beginning his work in the mines at just 12 years old, Welsh's experiences profoundly shaped his literary voice, evident in his novels "The Underworld" (1920) and "The Morlocks" (1924).

Welsh is an author celebrated for his exploration of labor, community, and the human experience, particularly within industrial settings. His works often focus on the lives of individuals facing challenging professions, such as miners, and highlight the physical and emotional struggles they endure. Welsh's storytelling combines vivid characterizations with social commentary, offering insights into the bonds formed among workers in difficult environments. Ultimately, his works reflect a profound understanding of the struggles for dignity and connection in the face of adversity, resonating with readers who appreciate authentic narratives.

CONTENTS

PREFACE

I have tried to write of the life I know, the life I have lived, and of the lives of the people whom, above all others, I love, and of whom I am so proud.

My people have been miners for generations, and I myself became a miner at the age of twelve. I have worked since then in the mine at every phase of coal getting until about five years ago, when my fellow workers made me their checkweigher.

I say this that those who read my book may know that the things of which I write are the things of which I have firsthand knowledge.

JAMES C. WELSH.
DOUGLAS WATER,
LANARK.

CHAPTER I
THE THONG OF POVERTY

"Is it not about time you came to your bed, lassie?"

"Ay, I'll no' be very long now, Geordie. If I had this heel turned, I'll soon finish the sock, and that will be a pair the day. Is the pain in your back worse the nicht, that you are so restless?" and the clicking of the needles ceased as the woman asked the question.

"Oh, I'm no' so bad at all," came the answer. "My back's maybe a wee bit sore; but a body gets tired lying always in the yin position. Forby, the day aye seems long when you are out, and I dinna like to think of you out working all day, and then sitting down to knit at nicht. It must be very tiring for you, Nellie."

"Oh, I'm no' that tired," she replied with a show of cheerfulness, as she turned another wire in the sock, and set the balls of wool dancing on the floor with the speed at which she worked. "I've had a real good day to-day, and I'm feeling that I could just sit for a lang while the nicht, if only the paraffin oil wadna' go down so quick. But the longer I sit, it burns the more, and it's getting gey dear to buy now-a-days."

"Ay," said the weary voice of the man. "If it's no' clegs it's midges. Folk have always something to contend against. But don't be long till you stop. It's almost twelve o'clock, and you ought to be in your bed "

"Oh, I'll no' be very long, Geordie," was the bravely cheerful answer. "Just you try and gang to sleep and I'll soon finish up. I'll have to try and get up early in the morning, for I have to go to Mrs. Rundell and wash. She always gi'es me twa shillings, and that's a good day's pay. The only thing I grudge is being away all day, leaving you and the bairns, for I ken they're no' very easy to put up with. They're steerin' weans, and are no' easy on a body who is ill."

"Ay, they're a steerin' lot, lassie," he answered tenderly. "But, poor things, they must hae some freedom, Nellie. I wish I was ready for my work."

"Hoot, man," she said with the same show of cheerfulness. "We might have been worse, and you will be better some day, and able to work as well as ever you did."

For a time there was silence, broken only by the loud ticking of the clock, the clicking of the needles, and occasionally a low moan from the bed, as the injured miner sank into a restless sleep.

There had been an accident some six weeks before, and Geordie Sinclair, badly wounded by a fall of stone, had been brought home from the pit in a cart.

It was during the time known to old miners as the "two-and-sixpenny winter," that being the sum of the daily wage then earned by the miners. A financial crisis had come upon the country and the Glasgow City Bank had failed, trade was dull, and the whole industrial system was in chaos. It had been a hard time for Geordie Sinclair's wife, for there were four children to provide for besides her injured husband. Work which was well paid for was not over plentiful, and she had to toil from early morning till far into the night to earn the bare necessities of life. There were times like to-night, when she felt rebellious and bitter at her plight, but her tired eyes and fingers had to get to the end of the task, for that meant bread for the children in the morning.

The silence deepened in the little kitchen. No sound came now from the bed, and the lamp threw eerie shadows on the walls, and the chimney smoked incessantly.

Her eyes grew watery and smarted with the smoke. She dropped stitches occasionally, as she hurried with her work, which had to be lifted again when she discovered that the pattern was wrong, and sometimes quite a considerable part had to be "ripped out," so that she could correct the mistake.

The dismal calling of a cat outside irritated her, and the loud complacent ticking of the clock seemed to mock her misery; but still she worked on, the busy fingers turning the needles, as the wool unwound itself from the balls which danced upon the floor. There was life in those balls of wool as they spun to the tune of the woman's misery. They advanced and retired, like dancers, touching hands when they met, then whirling away in opposite directions again; they side-stepped and wheeled in a mad riot of joyous color, just as they were about to meet: they stood for a little facing each other, feinting from side to side, then were off again, as the music of her misery quickened, in an embracing whirl, as if married in an ecstasy of colored flame, many-shaded, yet one; then, at last, just as the tune seemed to have reached a crescendo of spirit, she dashed her work upon the floor, as she discovered another blunder, and burst into a fit of passionate weeping.

Suddenly there was a faint tap at the window, and she raised her head, staying her breath to listen. Soon she heard it again, just a faint but very deliberate tap, which convinced her that someone was outside in the darkness. Softly she stole on tiptoe across the room, so as not to disturb her sleeping husband, and opening the door quietly, craned forward and peered into the darkness to discover the cause of the tap.

"It's just me," said a deep voice, in uneasy accents, from the darkness by the window, and she saw then the form of a man edging nearer the door.

"And who are you?" she asked a little nervously, but trying to master the alarm in her voice.

"Do you not ken me?" replied the voice with an attempt to speak as naturally as possible; yet there was something in the tone that made her more uneasy.

Then the figure of the man drew nearer, and he whispered "Are they all sleeping?" alluding to the inmates of the house.

"Ay," she answered, drawing back into the shelter of the doorway. "Why do you ask? And what is it you want?"

"Oh, I just came along to see how you were all getting on," was the reply. "I ken you must be in very straitened circumstances by this time, and thought I might be able to help you a bit," and there was an ingratiating tone in the words now as he sidled nearer. "You must have a very hard battle just now, and I would like to do something to help you."

"Come away in," said the woman, with still an uneasy tremor in her voice, yet feeling more assured. "Geordie is sleeping, but he'll not be hard to waken up. Come away in, and let us see who you are, and tell us what you really want."

"No, I'm no' coming in," he whispered hoarsely. "Do you no' ken me? Shut the door and not let any of them hear. I'm wanting you!" and he stepped into the light and reached forward his hand, as if to draw her to him.

Mrs. Sinclair gasped and recoiled in horror, as she recognized who it was that stood before her.

"No," she cried decisively, stepping further back into the shelter of the house, her voice low and intense with indignation. "No, I have not come to that yet, thank God. Gang home, you dirty brute, that you are! I'll be very ill off when I ask anything, or take anything, from you, Jock Walker!" For it was well known in Lowwood that Jock Walker's errands to people in distress had always in them an ulterior motive.

He was the under manager at the pits, and his reputation was of the blackest. There were men in the village of Lowwood who were well aware of this man's relations with their wives, and they openly agreed to the sale of the honor of their women folk in return for what he gave them in the shape of contracts, at which they could make more money than their neighbors, or good "places," where the coal was easier won. In fact, to be a contractor was a synonym for this sort of dealing, for no one ever got a contract from Walker unless his wife, or his daughter, was a woman of easy virtue, and at the service of this man.

"Very well," replied Walker with chagrined anger. "Please yourself. But let me tell you that you'll maybe no' ay be so high and mighty; you'll maybe be dam'd glad yet of the chance that I have given you."

"No, no," protested Mrs. Sinclair. "Go away—"

"Look here, Nellie," he said, his voice changing to a low pleading tone, "you're in a hole. You must be. Be a sensible woman, and you'll never need to be so ill-grippet again. I can put Geordie in a position that he'll make any amount of money as soon as he is able to start. You are not a bit better than anyone else, and for the sake of your bairns you should be sensible. And forby," he went on, as if now more sure of his ground, "what the hell's wrang in it? It's no' what folk do that is wrong. It's in being found out. Now come away and be sensible. You ken what is wanted, and you ken that I can make you well off for it."

"No, by heavens," she cried, now tingling with anger at the insult. "Never! Get out of this, you brute! If Geordie Sinclair had been able this nicht, I'd have got him to deal with you. Get out of here, or I'll cleave your rotten body, and let out your rotten heart." And she turned in, and closed and bolted the door, leaving Walker fuming with anger at the repulse of his advances. Nellie Sinclair had never felt so outraged in all her life before. She was trembling with anger at the insult of his proposals. She paced the floor in her stockinged feet, as if a wild spirit were raging within her demanding release; then finally she flung herself into the "big chair," disgust and anger in her heart, and for the second time that night burst into a passionate fit of weeping, which seemed to shake her body almost asunder. For a long time she sat thus, sobbing, her whole being burning with indignation, and her mind in a fury of disgust and rebellion.

Then there was a faint stirring in the bed where the children slept, and a little boy's form began to crawl from amongst the rough bedclothes, his eyes gazing in amazement at the bowed figure of his mother. She was crying, he concluded, for her shoulders were heaving and it must be something very bad that made his beautiful mother cry like this. He crept across the bare wooden floor, his bare sturdy legs showing beneath the short and meager shirt, and was soon at her side.

"What's wrang wi' you, mother?" he asked, as he put his soft little hand upon her head. "What's wrang wi' you? Will I kiss you heid and make it better?" But his mother did not look up—only the big sobs continued to shake her, and the boy becoming alarmed at this, also began to cry, as he placed his little head against hers. "Oh, mother, dinna greet," he sobbed, "and I'll kiss your heid till it's better."

At last she lifted her head, and seeing the naked boy, she caught him in her arms and crushed him to her breast, as if she would smother him. This was strange conduct for his usually undemonstrative mother; but it was nice to be hugged like that, even though she did cry.

"What made you greet, mother?" he queried, for he had never before, in all his four years, seen his mother cry. For answer she merely caught him closer to her breast, her hair falling soft and warm all over him as she did so.

"Was you hungry, mither?" he tried again.

"No' very," she answered, choking back her sobs.

"Are you often hungry, too, mither?" he persisted, feeling encouraged at getting an answer at last.

"Sometimes," she replied. "But dinna bother me, Rob," she continued. "Gang away to your bed like a man."

He was silent for a time at this repulse, and lay upon her knee puzzling over the matter.

"Do you greet when you are hungry?" he enquired, with: wide-eyed earnestness and surprise.

"There noo," she answered, "don't ask so many questions, Daddy'll not be long till he is better again, and when he is at work there'll be plenty of pieces to keep us all from being hungry."

"And will there be jeely for the pieces?" pursued the boy, for it seemed to him that there had never been a time when there was plenty to eat.

"Yes, we'll get plenty o' jeely too," she replied, drying the remaining tears from her eyes, and hugging him again to her breast.

"Oh, my," he said, with a deep sigh. "I wish my father was better!" and the little lips were moistened by his tongue, as if in anticipation of the coming feast.

Another silence; and then came the query—"What way do we not get plenty o' pieces when my daddy's no' working? Does folk no' get them then?"

"No, Robin," she answered, "but dinna fash your wee noddle with that. You'll find out all about it when you get big. Shut your eyes and mother'll sing, an' you'll go to sleep." And he snuggled in and shut his eyes, while Mrs. Sinclair gathered him softly to her breast and began to croon an old ballad.

As she sang it seemed to the boy that there were no such things as "jelly-pieces" to bother about. He liked his mother to sing to him, for he seemed to get rolled up in her soft, warm voice, and become restful and happy. Gradually the low crooning song grew fainter in his ears, the flicker of the fire danced further and further away, until long streaks of golden thready light seemed to reach out, straight from his eyes to the fireplace, and all the comfort that it was possible to have flowed through his soul, and at last he slept. Mrs. Sinclair placed him beside his brothers and sisters in the bed and went back to finish her knitting. The night was far gone before she accomplished her task, and she stood and surveyed her humble home with weariness in her heart.

Through the dim smoke which hung like a blue cloud along the roof, and made more seemingly thick by the small lamp upon the table, she looked at her husband lying asleep, and so far free from pain. Then her eyes traveled to the children in the other bed, and they filled with tears as she thought that she had had to put them supperless to bed that night, and again rebellion surged through her blood as she thought of all the misery of her life. Was it worth living and going on in this way? Was it worth while to continue? What had she done to reap all this suffering?

She was hungry and weak and exhausted. Perhaps if she could sleep she would forget it, and in the morning the socks she had finished would bring her a few pence, and that would mean food.

She decided to go to bed, and in passing by the shelf at the window, her eye caught sight of a plateful of potato skins, the remains of the meager dinner of boiled potatoes which the children had had; and clutching them, she began greedily to devour them, filling her mouth and cramming them in in handfuls, until it seemed as if she would choke herself. Then, licking the plate clean of every crumb, she undressed and slipped quietly into bed, to lie and fret and toss, as she thought of the insult which Black Jock had offered her, and pondered over the unhappy lot of her children and their injured father.

CHAPTER II
A TURN OF THE SCREW

On the Friday following Jock Walker's visit to Mrs. Sinclair, a notice was put up at the pit by Peter Pegg and Andrew Marshall, to the effect that a collection would be taken next day on behalf of Geordie Sinclair. The notice was posted up before Andrew and Peter descended the pit for the day.

"Black Jock," as Walker was called by the miners, saw the notice before it had been ten minutes posted, and deliberately tore it down. He then visited Peter Pegg and Andrew Marshall at the coal face.

"I suppose you an' Andrew are goin' to gather for Geordie Sinclair the morn?" he said, addressing Peter.

"Ay," Peter answered, "we were thinkin' it was aboot time somethin' was done. There's four bairns an' their two selves, an' though times are no' very guid for ony of us now, it maun be a lot worse for them. Geordie has been a guid while off."

"Do ye think, Peter, they are in such need?" asked Walker, with a hint in his voice that was meant to convey he knew better.

"Lord, they canna be aught else!" decisively returned Peter. "How can they be? I ken for mysel'," he went on, "that if it was me, I wad hae been in starvation lang syne."

"Weel, wad ye believe me when I tell ye—an' it's a fact—they're about the best-off family in this place, if ye only kent it."

"What!" cried Peter in surprise, "the best-off family in the place! Lord, I canna take that in!"

"Maybe no'," said Walker, "but I ken, an' ye're no' the first that's been taken in by Nellie Sinclair. If ye notice, she never tells any thin' to anybody; but she lets ye carry the notion in your mind that she's in great straits. She's a cute one, Nellie."

"Weel, Nellie does keep hersel' to hersel'," admitted Peter. "She's no' given to clashin' and claverin' about the doors like some o' the rest o' the women; but I canna' for the life o' me see where she can be onythin' but ill aff at this time."

"Weel, I ken when folk are bein' imposed on," said Walker, in a knowing tone, "an' I tore down your notice this mornin'. I didna want to see you mak' a fool o' yersels. I ha'e been considerin' for a while," he went on, speaking quickly, "about puttin' a stop to this collectin' business at the office on pay Saturdays, for it just encourages some men to lie off work when there's no' very muckle wrong wi' them; after they get the collection they soon start work again. Ye had better no' stand the morn, for I might as well begin at once and put a stop to it."

Up till now Andrew Marshall had not spoken; he was a silent man, given more to thought than speech, but this was a way of doing things he did not like.

"But ye might let us tak' the collection first, and then put up a notice yersel sayin' that a' collections have to be stopped. It wad be best to gi'e the men notice."

"No," said Walker, "there's to be nae mair collections taken. I might as well stop it this time as wait. So ye'll no' stand the morn."

"Will I no'?" returned Andrew challengingly. "How the hell do ye ken whether I will or no'?"

"I ken ye'll no'," replied Walker, with quiet menacing tones; "the ground at the office belongs to the company, and is private. So ye can do it if ye like, but ye'll be weel advised no' to bother."

"I don't gi'e a damn," cried Andrew explosively, "whether the ground is private or no'. I'll take that 'gathering' for Geordie Sinclair the morn, though ye ha'e a regiment o' sodgers at the office."

"Very well," said Walker, as he departed, "if ye do, ye can look out."

Peter took his pipe out of his mouth and spat savagely on the ground; he then replaced it with great deliberation and looked gloomily at the stoop-side. He was a man about thirty-five, tall, bony and angular; his neck was long and thin, and his head seemed always on the point of turning to allow him to look over his shoulder. His right eye was half closed, while his left eye looked big and saucer-like, and never seemed to wink; one eye was ready to laugh and the other to "greet," as his comrades described it. He had been badly disfigured in a burning accident in the pit when he was a young man, and a broken nose added still more to the strangeness of his appearance. Andrew, on the other hand, was stout and broadly built, with a bushy whisker on each cheek, and a clump of tufty hair on his head.

"What do ye mak' o' that, Andrew?" enquired Peter, after a few minutes, as he again spat savagely at the stoop-side.

"What do I mak' o't?" echoed Andrew, as he glowered across the little bing of dross at his mate, "it's just in keepin' wi' the rest o' his dirty doin's, the dirty black brute that he is!"

"I wonder what's wrong wi' him?" mused Peter as he sucked quietly at his snoring pipe. But there was no answer from Andrew, who was sitting silent and glum, gazing at his little lamp.

"What are ye goin' to do about it, then?" broke in Peter again.

"Just what I said," returned Andrew with quiet firmness. "I'll take that collection the morn, some way or another, if I should be damned for it. Does he mean to say that we can let folk starve?" He lifted his pick and began to hew the coal with an energy that told of the passion raging within him.

"Does he mean to think I'm goin' to see decent folk starve afore my e'en?" he asked after a while, pausing to wipe the sweat from his eyes. "No' damned likely! Things ha'e come to a fine pass when folk are compelled to look at other folk starvin' an' no' gi'e them a crust."

"Do ye think there's onything in what he said about them bein' weel-aff?" asked Peter cautiously, while his big eye tried to wink. "Nellie is a wee bit inclined to be prood an' independent, ye ken, an' disna say muckle about her affairs. An forby we don't ken very muckle about her; she's an incomer to the place, and she might ha'e been weel-aff afore she married Geordie, for aught we ken."

"It disna matter," replied Andrew, "I dinna care though they had thousan's. What I don't like is this 'ye'll-no'-do-this-an'-ye'll-no'-do-that' sort o' thing. What the hell right has ony gaffer wi' what a man does? It's a' one to him what I do. I'm nae slave, an' forby, I dinna believe they are weel-aff. They maun be hard up."

"But he'll maybe sack ye," suggested Peter, "if ye take the collection."

"Well, let him," cried Andrew, now thoroughly roused, "the bastard! I would see the greyhounds o' hell huntin' him roun' the rocks o' blazes afore I'd give in to him!"

Nothing further was said of the matter until well on in the day, when it suddenly occurred to Andrew that Peter, who had a large family, might not care to incur the displeasure of Walker by taking the collection the next day.

"Of course, Peter," he said, after he had thought the matter over, "if ye don't care to take the collection wi' me, I won't press ye. I'll no' think ony worse o' ye if ye don't. Ye ha'e a big family, while I ha'e only the wife to look after. Sometimes I think it's lucky we ha'e nae weans; I can flit, and ye might no' be able to rise an' run. But I mean to take the collection onyway, for I don't like a man to order me what I ha'e to do."

"Oh, I wasna mindin' that, Andra," replied Peter, trying to make Andrew believe that he had not guessed the truth. "I'll take the collectin wi' ye, an' Black Jock can gang to hell if he likes."

"No, Peter, ye'll do naethin' o' the kind. I'll take it mysel'." And Andrew would not move from that decision.

Next day everybody was curiously expectant; it had got noised abroad that Walker had defied Andrew Marshall to take a collection at the office, and had threatened him with arrest. There were wild rumors of other penalties, and when pay-day came everybody was surprised to see Andrew draw his pay and walk home. They concluded that Andrew had thought better of it, and had been cowed into submission. When darkness began to fall, however, Andrew sauntered out and visited every home in the village, soliciting aid on behalf of Geordie Sinclair. There were few houses from which he did not get a donation, though the will to give was often greater than the means. In each house Andrew had to give in detail the interview between Black Jock and himself in the pit.

"The muckle big, black, dirty brute that he is!" the good-wife would cry in indignation. "It's a pity but he could ken what starvation is himsel'. It might make him a bit mair like a human bein'."

"That's true," Andrew would agree.

In one or two houses he met with a blank refusal, but in these he was not disappointed, for he knew that the men would not risk Walker's disapproval by contributing. Again, some were wholly hostile. They were the "belly-crawlers," as Geordie Sinclair had once dubbed them at a meeting, those who "kept in" with the management by carrying tales, and generally acting as traitors to the other men.

"No, I'll no' gi'e ye onythin'," would be the reply; "he can just be like me an' gang an' work for his bairns. Forby, look at yon stuck-up baggage o' a wife o' his. She can hardly pass the time o' day wi' ye—she thinks hersel' somethin'."

"Very well," Andrew would reply, "maybe ye ha'e mair need o't for other things." And he would pass on to the next house.

He had gathered between three and four pounds, contributed sometimes even in pennies, and going to Geordie's house, he knocked at the door. This was the most uncomfortable part of his work, and he stood shifting from one foot to the other, wondering what he would say when he entered. Mrs. Sinclair was busy washing the floor and cleaning up, after having been at work all day washing for someone in the village. She wiped her hands and opened the door.

"How are ye a' keepin' the night?" inquired Andrew, as he stepped inside at Mrs. Sinclair's invitation, feeling more and more uncomfortable. It was a hard enough matter to go and ask others whom he knew had little to spare, but now, having got the money, he did not know how he was going to hand it over to Nellie. He ruminated for a time as to how he would break into the subject. He knew that Nellie Sinclair must have heard of the collection, and guessed his errand, for he saw that she, too, was uneasy and agitated.

"How are ye a' the night?" he again enquired, to break the silence.

"Oh, I'm no' so bad at a', Andra," replied Geordie. "I'm feelin' a wee bit easier the night. How's yersel'?"

"No' so bad," answered Andrew, putting his hand in his pocket for his pipe.

"Dash it! I'm away without my pipe," he said with a show of annoyance. "Can ye len' me yours, Geordie, to get a smoke? I ha'e my tobacco and matches. Ye see," he went on, speaking more rapidly, "I thought I would just slip round to see how ye was keepin'."

Andrew knew that Geordie would not have had a smoke for a long time, and this was his way of leaving him with a pipeful of tobacco.

"I think my pipe's on the mantelshelf," returned Geordie, "but I doot it's empty."

Andrew took down the pipe, filled it generously, set it alight, and sat for a few minutes trying vainly to keep up a connected conversation. After he had puffed a few minutes at Geordie's pipe he laid it down, dived his hand into his trousers pocket as he made for the door. He pulled forth the money, which was in a little bag, and laid it down on the table, saying: "I'm no' guid at this kind of thing, Geordie. There's something for ye from the men. Guid nicht!" and he was off, leaving Nellie in tears and Geordie in glum silence.

Mrs. Sinclair's tears were tears of rebellion as well as of gratitude. She was touched by Andrew's delicacy, but her independent spirit was wounded at having to take help from anyone. She thought of the children and of her husband, who needed nourishment, and taking up the little bag she poured its contents into her lap, while her hot tears fell upon the money.

Little Robert, who was sitting watching, and who had never in all his life seen so much money, ran to his mother with a cry of delight.

"Oh, mammy, will I get sweeties noo?" and the boy danced with glee, as he shouted, "I'll get jeely-pieces noo, hurray!"

That night there was happiness in Geordie Sinclair's house, for there was food in plenty, and it seemed as if the children would never be able to appease their hunger.

The "jeely-pieces," or slices of bread with jam on them, disappeared with amazing rapidity, and Geordie had some beef-tea, which seemed to improve him almost as soon as he had taken it. For the first time for many months Mrs. Sinclair and the children went to bed with satisfied appetites; and the children's dreams were as the incidents in the life of a god, exalted and happy, and their mother's rest was unbroken and full of comfort.

But on Monday morning Andrew Marshall had to pay the price of the happiness he had been instrumental in giving them, for he was informed by one of Walker's henchmen that his place was stopped. The excuse given was that it was too far in advance of the others. Andrew knew what that meant, and as he went home, fierce rebellious feelings stirred within him. Peter Pegg, he was glad to know, had got started on "oncost" work, and Andrew felt he had done right in not allowing Peter to take the collection with him.

CHAPTER III
THE BLOCK

"I see Andra Marshall's back again," observed Sanny Robertson to Peter Pegg one evening three months later.

"Ay," said Peter, "he was at Glampy, but his place was stopped, an' there wasna anither for him."

"Got the sack again, I suppose," said Sanny. "Weel, he maun learn, Peter, that gaffers are no' gaun to put up wi' his nonsense. If a man will no' do what he's telt, he maun just take the consequences."

"Ay," said Peter, very dryly, and as Peter knew his man, no more was said.

Later the same night Matthew Maitland observed to Peter, as they sat on their "hunkers" at the corner:

"Andra's back again, I suppose."

"Ay," was the answer, "he was telt his place was stopped."

"Imphm," said Matthew, "it's a damn fine excuse. It's a pity but somethin' could be done."

"It's the Block," said Peter. "I'm telt that a' the managers roun' aboot ha'e an understandin' with one another no' to gi'e work to onybody they take a dislike to."

"Ay," agreed Matthew, "I ha'e heard aboot it, but I would soon put a stop to it."

"Ay, Matthew, it's a union we need up here badly. I'm telt that that chap Smillie has managed to start one down in the West Country, an' it's daein' weel. He's got some o' their wages up a hale shillin' a day since he took it in hand."

"Is that a fact, Peter? The sooner we ha'e him up here the better then. Black Jock needs a chap back onyway," and Matthew looked like a man who had suddenly discovered a great truth.

Andrew Marshall had never been allowed to forget his action in defying Walker; everywhere he went it was the same story—no work for him. The

"Block" system among the managers was in good working order, and could easily starve a man into docility. Andrew became more desperate as time passed, and he knew that he and his wife were nearing the end of their small savings. He returned home one evening from his usual fruitless search for employment, and threw himself into the arm-chair by the fireside.

"No work yet, Andra?" asked Katie.

"Nane," was the gloomy response.

"We have no' very mony shillin's left noo, Andra. I dinna ken what we'll do."

Savage, revengeful feelings surged through Andrew, and found vent in a volley of oaths which terrified his wife.

"Dinna talk like that, Andra," she pleaded. "It's no' canny, an' forby, the Lord disna like ye to do it."

"If the Lord cared He could take Black Jock by the scruff o' the neck an' fling him into hell oot o' the road. It's Black Jock that's at the bottom o' this, an' I could twist his dirty neck for him."

"Weel, Andra, it's the Lord's doin', an' maybe things'll soon men'."

"If it's the Lord's doin', I dinna think muckle o' His conduct then," and Andrew lapsed into sullen silence.

On Monday morning he was up at five o'clock, desperately resolved to lay his case before the men. He walked to the end of the village, knowing the colliery would be idle, for Tam Donaldson was to be "creeled." This was a custom at one time very prevalent in mining villages. When a young man got married, the first day he appeared at his work afterwards he was taken home by his comrades, and was expected to stand them a drink. It generally ended in a collection being made, after they had tasted the newly-married man's whiskey, and a common fund thus being established, a large quantity of beer and whiskey was procured, and all drank to their heart's content.

Andrew heard the men calling to each other as they made their way to the pit, the lights from their lamps twinkling in the darkness of the winter morning.

"Is Tam away yet, Jamie?" he heard wee Allan ask, as he overtook old Jamie Lauder on his way to the pit.

"Ay, I saw to that," replied Lauder, "I chappit him up at five o'clock, so that he wadna sleep in. I hinna missed a creelin' for thirty-five years, an' I wasna' gaun to miss Tam Donaldson's. I heard him goin' oot two or three minutes afore me. We're in for a guid day, for he telt me he had in two bottles for the spree."

"That's a' right, then; I was afraid he wad maybe sleep in," and the two trudged on together towards the pit.

A group of dark figures stood on the pithead, waiting their turn to go below. The cage rattled up from the depths of the shaft, the men stepped in, and almost immediately disappeared down into the blackness. Arrived at the bottom, they walked along towards the different passages, chaffing and jesting with Tam Donaldson, the newly-married one.

"Ye'll be gaun to do something decent the day, Tam, when we take ye hame?" said Jamie Allan. "I hear ye ha'e two bottles ready for the occasion."

"Ay, but I'm damned shair there's no a lick gaun unless ye take me hame," answered Donaldson. "If I ha'e to be creeled, I'll be creeled right, an' every one o' ye'll gang hame wi' me afore ye get a taste."

"Oh, but we'll see to that, chaps," said old Lauder. "Here's a hutch, get him in an' aff wi' him."

The victim pretended to resist, and stoutly maintained that they should not creel him. He was seized by half a dozen pairs of arms, and with much expenditure of energy and breath, deposited in the hutch. Some considerate person had put some straw and old bags in the "carriage" to make it more comfortable, and a few of the wags had chalked inscriptions, the reverse of complimentary, all over it.

"There, noo', boys," said old Lauder, who had been busy hanging lighted pit lamps round Tam's cap, "gi'e him a guid run to the bottom, and see that he gets a guid bump in the lye."

The men ran the hutch to the "bottom" straight against the full tubs ready to be sent to the surface.

"Come on, Sourocks, let us up," called Allan to the old man who acted as "bottomer."

"Hell to the up will ye get!" replied the old fellow, "I'm gaun to put on these hutches first."

"No, ye'll no', an' if ye do, you'll gang into the 'sump,' an' we'll chap the bell oorsels" — the sump being the lodgment into which the water gathered before pumping operations could start.

"Sourocks" thought discretion the better part of valor in this case, and swearing quietly to himself, he signaled to the engineman at the top to draw them up.

"He's no gaun to walk hame," said Allan, as they all gathered again on the pit head. "We'll take the hutch hame wi' Tam in it. Put a rope on it, and we'll draw the damned thing through the moor, an' maybe Tam'll mind the day he was creeled as lang as he lives."

This proposal was jumped at, especially by the younger men, to whom an idle day did not mean so much worry on pay-day as to their married elders.

Andrew Marshall had waited at the end of the village, knowing that the creeling was to take place, and that he would get the men on their way from the pit. Presently old Lauder, who had taken a short cut across the moor, came up, and Andrew accosted him.

"Will ye wait here, Jamie, so that I can try an' get a meetin' held wi' the rest o' the men when they come alang?"

"I will that, Andra," replied Jamie, taking the lighted lamp from his head, and sitting down at the corner on his "hunkers." "They're a' comin' hame anyway, for we're creelin' Tam Donaldson."

Soon the procession appeared, the hutch jolting along the rough street, the men shouting and singing as they came. The village had turned out to see the fun. Andrew and Jamie found themselves in the midst of a crowd of women and children, as the foremost of the men came to a halt at the corner.

Andrew quietly stepped out and addressed the men, asking them if they would wait a few minutes—as they were idle in any case—to have a meeting. All were agreed.

"Here's Sanny Robertson," said Tam Tate, peering into the breaking light, "he'll no' likely wait, but we'll see what he says aboot it," and all waited in silence until Robertson approached. He seemed to guess what was in the air, and hurriedly tried to pass on, but Andrew stepped out with the usual question.

"No," he replied uneasily, "I'll ha'e no part in ony mair strife. Folk just get into bother for nothing. Men'll ha'e to keep mind that gaffers now-a-days'll no' put up wi' disobedience."

"Ay, but ye maun mind," said Tam Tate hastily, "that men maun be treated as human bein's, even by a gaffer."

"I can aye get on with the gaffer," replied Robertson, "an' I dinna see what way ither folk canna do the same."

"That's a' richt," put in old Jamie Lauder, "but a' men are no' just prepared to do as ye do," and there was a hint of something in his voice which the others seemed to understand.

"I ha'e no quarrel," sulkily replied Robertson, "an' I dinna see what way I should get into this one. I can get plenty o' work, an' ither folk can get it too, if they like to behave themselves."

"Ye're a liar," roared Tam Tate angrily, his usual hasty temper getting the mastery. "It's no' you that gets the work, it's Mag!"

The others laughed uproariously, for it was common knowledge that Sanny got his good jobs because of Walker's intimacy with his wife.

"Ye leave the best man in the house every mornin' when ye gang oot!" roared another amid coarse laughter, whilst Andrew turned to tackle the next comer.

A few refused to wait, but it was generally known that these were the men whose houses were always open to Walker by day or night. When they were all gathered, Andrew Marshall stood up, and for the first time in his life spoke at a meeting.

"Weel, men," he began, "ye a' ken the position o' things. Ye ken as weel as me that I got the sack for gatherin' for Geordie Sinclair. Weel, I ha'e been oot o' work three months; the Block is on against me, an' it seems I ha'e to starve. I canna get work onywhere, an' I stopped ye a' the day to ask ye to make my quarrel yours, an' try and put an end to this business."

That was the whole speech, but its simple sincerity appealed to all, and many expressed approval and determination to stand by Andrew in his fight.

"I think it's a damn'd shame," said old Lauder.

"I'll tell ye what it is," said Matthew Maitland, "it's a downricht barefaced murder, an' I would smash this damn'd cantrip o' Black Jock's. I ken that he'll get a' that is said at this meetin', an' maybe I'll get the same dose; but I think it's aboot time somethin' was done to put an end to his capers," and so Matthew floundered on.

"Ay, an' let us see what can be done for Geordie, too," put in Peter Pegg, and his long neck seemed to get longer at every syllable, while his big eye made a great attempt to wink and to look backward, as if he expected to see someone coming from behind. "We a' ken," continued Peter, "that Geordie is ready for work noo', this fower week syne, but Black Jock says he has no places, an' forby two strangers got jobs just yesterday."

"I ken for yae thing that there's fower places staunin' in Millar's Level," said Jamie Lauder, "an' I'm telt there's five or six staunin' in the Black Horse Dook. It's a' a bit of humbug, an' I think we should try an' put an end to it."

"Weel, I think we're a' agreed on that," said Tam Tate. "Has ony o' you onything to suggest?"

For a few minutes there was silence, while they sat or stood deep in thought, trying to find a solution. It was an eerie gathering, with the gray dawn just beginning to break, while on every head the indispensable lamp burned and flickered. Men expectorated savagely upon the ground, staring hard at the stones at their feet, thinking and wondering how they might serve their comrades.

"It's about time we had a union," said one.

"Ay," replied another, "so that some bigmouthed idiot can pocket the money an' get a guid saft job oot o' it."

"We've had plenty of unions," put in another. "The last yin we started here—ye mind Bob Ritchie gaed aff to America wi' a' the money. It was a fine go for him!"

"Oh, ay, but let us see what can be done wi' this case," said Jamie Lauder. "Hoo' wad it do if we appointed a deputation to gang an' lay the hale thing afore Mr. Rundell?"

Jamie was always listened to with the respect due to his proved good sense, for everyone knew that he was a man who would not intentionally hurt a fellow creature by word or deed.

"I believe it wad be a guid plan," agreed Tam Tate. "He maybe disna ken the hauf that gangs on. What do ye a' think o' it, men?"

This was before the days of limited companies and coal syndicates, and the proprietor of the pits in Lowwood, Mr. Rundell, lived about two miles out of the village. He was not a bad man, as men go; he was fiery and quick-tempered, but had a not ungenerous nature withal, and was usually susceptible to a reasoned statement. Just as they were about to decide on a course of action, Andrew spoke: "I dinna want ony mair o' ye than can be helped to get into bother, so, if ye like, Jamie Lauder—if he's agreeable— could gang wi' me and Geordie Sinclair, and we'll put the hale case afore him an' see what he mak's o't."

This was received with approval, and it was agreed that Andrew, Jamie and Geordie should form the deputation.

But Black Jock soon heard of the decision, and, as usual, acted with alacrity; for, had the men only known it, they had decided on a course which he did not want them to adopt. He visited Jamie Lauder, and told him that the day before Rundell and he had agreed that the places in the Black Horse Dook should be started at once, and that he was angry at the course taken by the men. He believed that Mr. Rundell would also be very angry, and if only Andrew and Geordie had come to him the night before, they could have been working that day. He represented Rundell as being in an explosive mood, and that he was furious at the men taking the idle day, and that he had threatened that if they were not at work next day, he would lock them out. So plausibly did he speak, and so sincere did his concern appear, that Jamie, who was withal a simple man, and aware that the circumstances of his comrades would not admit of a very long fight, began to think it might be as Black Jock had said.

"I think ye'd better ca' a meetin' o' the men, Jamie, and put the hale case afore them. Let them ken that Rundell decided just yesterday to start the places, and that Andra and Geordie can start the morn. I ha'e no ill wull at ony o' the twa o' them, and I'm vexed that things ha'e been as bad as they've been, but I couldna get the boss to start the places, and what could I do? They can a' be back at their work the morn if they like to look at it reasonably. Of course, ye can please yersel'," he went on, "it's a' yin to me; but if Rundell tak's it into his head to ha'e a fight, well—ye ken what it means, an' I wouldna like to ha'e ony strife the noo', for times are very hard for us a'."

Simple and honest as Jamie was, Black Jock's plausibility appealed to him, and he began to think that Walker perhaps was not so bad as he was made to appear. Again, Jamie knew that Rundell was a man of hasty temper and impulsive judgments, and could not brook trouble, and he began to think that perhaps it might be better to hold the meeting as suggested and tell the men what he had heard, and appeal to them to go back to work.

"All right," he said to Walker, "I'll call a meeting to-night and put the case as you have said, and ask them to go back. But mind, you've not to go back on your promise. You'll have to start Andrew and Geordie within twa days, or the men will no' continue to work. Mind, I'm taking a lot on myself to do this, and you'll have to carry out your part and start them."

"I'll fill my part, never fear," was the answer, and there was relief in Walker's voice. "See, there's my hand," he said, extending a big black limb as he spoke, first spitting on his palm to ensure due solemnity. "There's no dryness about that, Jamie. I mean it. I'll start Geordie and Andrew all right. You get the men to go back to work to-morrow, for I'm afraid Rundell will make trouble if you remain idle anither day. Noo' I promise." And Jamie took the extended hand in token of the bargain and returned to summon the meeting, which was duly held, and, as Walker had anticipated, the men were appeased, and returned to work the next day.

Sure enough, within two days Andrew Marshall and Geordie Sinclair were both started to work, and matters went smoothly for a time.

But though they had had a lesson, it did not stop their activities as agitators for the establishment of a union, for they knew that there was no protection for any of them if they remained unorganized.

"Men never were meant to work and live as colliers do," said Geordie, thoughtfully. "Life should be good, and free, and happy, with comfort and enjoyment for all. Look at the birds—they are happy! So are the flowers, or they wouldn't look so pleased. God meant a' men and weemin to be glad, even though they have to work. But hoo' the hell can folk be happy and worship God on two and sixpence a day? It's all wrong, Andrew, an' I'll never believe that men were meant to live as we live."

"That's true, Geordie," agreed Andrew soberly. "I only wish we could get everybody to see it as we see it. There's plenty for a' God's creatures— enough to make everybody happy, an' there need be no ill-will in the world, if only common-sense was applied to things; but I'm damn'd if I can see where even the men can be happy who are making their money oot o' our lives. They're bound to ken surely that what comes from misery can not make happiness for them."

"True, Andrew, true, and we maun just go on working for it. Sometimes I have the feeling that we are on the point of big changes: just as if the folk would awaken up oot o' their ignorance, with love in their hearts, an' make all things right for everybody. A world o' happiness for everybody is worth workin' for. So we maun gang on."

And so they talked of their dreams and felt the better for it.

CHAPTER IV
A YOUNG REBEL

About two years after these events little Robert Sinclair went to school. It was a fine morning in late spring, and Robert trudged the seemingly long road, clasping an elder brother's hand, for the school lay about a mile to the north-west of the village, and that seemed to the boy a very long way.

It was a great experience. Robert's clothes had been well patched, his face had been washed and toweled till it shone, his eyes sparkled with excitement, and his heart beat high; yet he was nervous and awed, wondering what he would find there.

"By crikey," said wee Alec Johnstone to him, "wait till auld Clapper gie's ye a biff or twa wi' his muckle tawse. Do ye ken what he does to mak' them nippy? He burns them a wee bit in the fire, an' then st'eeps them in whusky. An' they're awful sair."

"Oh, but I ken what to do, Rab, if ye want to diddle him," put in another boy. "Just get a horse's hair—a lang yin oot o' its tail—and put it across yer haun', an' it'll cut his tawse in twa, whenever he gie's ye a pammy."

"That's what I'm gaun to do, Jamie," replied another. "I'll get some hairs frae Willie Rogerson. He's gettin' me some frae his father's when he's in the stable the morn, an' ye'll see auld Cabbage-heid's tawse gaun in twa, whenever he gie's me yin." And they all looked admiringly at this little hero who was going to do this wonderful thing so simply.

"I got four yesterday," said another, "an' I wasna' doin' onything. By criffens! it was sair, an' gin I had only had a horse's hair, I'd soon ha'e putten his tawse oot the road."

"I got four yesterday too," said another, "an' a' because I was looking at yon new laddie wha cam to the schule yesterday. By! they were sair. I never heard auld Cabbage-heid till he cam up an' telt me to put oot my haun."

"It's Peter Rundell's his name," chimed in another. "He's the Boss's laddie. My! if you just saw what fine claes he has on. A new suit, an' lang stockings, an' a pair o' fine new buits."

"Ay, an' a white collar too," said another, "an' hundreds o' pooches in his jacket."

"He has a waistcoat wi' three pooches in it—yin for a watch—an' a braw, black, shiny bonnet."

"He had a white hankey too, an' sweeties in yin o' his pooches."

Robert felt a certain amount of resentment as he listened to the description, and he grudged Peter Rundell his new suit for he himself had never known anything of that kind, but had always worn "make-downs" created by his mother's clever fingers out of the discarded clothes of grown-ups.

"Auld Cabbage-heid didna' like me looking at Peter Rundell an' that's the way he gied me four, but I'll get a horse's hair too, an' his tawse 'll soon get wheegh. He's awful cruel, Rab," he said, turning to Robert, "an' ye'd better look oot."

Each and all had some fearful story to tell of the cruelty of the headmaster, and all swore they'd get even with him. These stories filled Robert with a certain fear, for he was an imaginative and sensitive boy. Still he knew there was no escape. He must go to school and go through with it whatever the future might hold for him.

So far he had grown wild and free, and loved the broad wide moor which began even at the end of the row where he lived. It seemed to him that there never had been a time when he did not know that there was a moor there. Nothing in it surprised him, even as a child. Its varied moods were already understood by him, and its silences and its many voices appealed to and were balm to his soul. The great blue hills which fringed it away in the far distance were for him the ends of the world, and if he could go there some day, he would surely look over and find—what? The thought staggered him, and his imagination would not, or could not, construct for him what was at the other side. All day, often, he had lain stretched full length upon the moor, watching the great white clouds sailing past, seeing himself sometimes sitting astride them, proudly surveying, like God, the whole world. At times it was so real that he bounded to his feet when by some misadventure he slipped from the back of the cloud. He listened to the songs of larks, the cries of curlews and lapwings and all the other moorland birds, and became as familiar with each of them as they were with one another.

But this going to school was a break in his freedom, and it stirred him strangely. He felt already that he would rather not go to school. He had always been happy before, and he did not know what lay ahead.

In the schoolroom that morning, Robert was called out by the headmistress to her desk, and while she was jotting down in her register particulars as to his age, etc., it happened that Peter Rundell was also on the floor. Robert looked so wonderingly at the white collar and the shining boots, that Rundell, to fill in the blanks and keep himself cheerful, promptly put out his tongue. Robert, not to be behind in respectfulness, just as promptly put out his, at the same time making a grimace, and immediately they were at it, pummeling each other in hearty glee before the teacher could do anything to prevent them. It was their first fight. The whole class was in immediate uproar and cries of—"Go on, Rob!" and "Good Peter!" were ringing out, as the supporters on either side shouted encouragement. Both went at it and for a couple of minutes defied the efforts of the teacher to separate them; but in response to calls for help, Mr. Clapper, the headmaster, came in, and taking hold of Robert soon had him across his knee, and was giving him a taste of the "tawse" he had heard so much about that morning, and Robert went back to his seat very sore, both physically and mentally, and crying in pain and anger. Thus his first day began at school, and the succeeding months were full of many such incidents.

Life ran along in the ordinary ruts for three or four years, but always Peter and Robert were antagonists. If Rundell happened to get to the top of the class, Robert never rested till he had excelled and displaced him; and then it was Peter's turn to do likewise till he too succeeded.

Robert, when in the mood, was eager and brilliant, and nothing seemed able to stay him. At times, however, he was given to dreaming, and lived through whole days in the classroom quite unconscious of what was going on around him. He worked mechanically, living in a strange world of his own creation, usually waking up to find himself at the foot of the class with Peter smiling at the top.

Often he went hungry, for times were still hard, and the family had increased to six. It was a bitter struggle in which Mrs. Sinclair was engaged to try and feed—let alone clothe—her hungry children. Patient, plodding, and terrible self-sacrifices alone enabled her to accomplish what she did. It was always a question of getting sufficient food rather than aiming at any particular kind. It was quantity rather than quality that was her biggest problem, for the children had sharp appetites and could make a feast of the simplest material. A pot of potatoes, boiled with their "jackets" on, tumbled on to the center of the bare, uncovered table and a little salt placed in small heaps at the exact position where each person sat, a large bowl of butter-milk when it could be got, with a tablespoon for each with which to lift a spoonful of the milk, and thus was set the banquet of the miner's family.

"Mither, Rob's taken twa sups of milk to yae bite o' tattie," little Mary would say.

"Ay, an' what did you do?" Robert would reply. "When you thought naebody was lookin', you took three spoonfu' to yae wee tattie. I was watchin' you."

"Now that'll do," the mother would admonish them. "Try and make it gang as far as ye can. Here you!" she would raise her voice to another, "dinna be so greedy on it. The rest maun get some too." At this the guilty child would frown and look ashamed at being caught taking more than his share.

Robert's dreams, however, were always satisfying, and even the sordid surroundings of the home were gilded by the warmth and glow of his imagination. Some day, somewhere he seemed to feel, there was a place for him to fill in the hearts of men. Vague stirrings told him of great future events which no one could dominate, save the soul that filled his body.

One day, during the dinner hour, when the school children were all at play, Robert and Peter again came into conflict. Some girls were playing at a ring game, and Robert and a few other boys were shamefacedly looking on. He was by this time at the bashful age of ten, and already the sweet, shy face of Mysie Maitland had become familiar in every dream. Mysie's modesty and grace appealed to him and the strange magnetic power of soul for soul was continually drawing them together, even at this early age. No voice was like Mysie's voice, no name like her name to him. If only she chanced shyly to ask if he had a spare piece of pencil Robert was happy; he'd gladly give her his only piece and forthwith proceed to borrow another for himself. He saw that Mysie did certain things, used, for instance, to clean her slate with a bit of rag, and he instantly procured one, and this kept his jacket sleeve clean and whole.

> "Choose, choose wha' ye'll tak',
> Wha' ye'll tak', wha' ye'll tak',
> Choose, choose wha' ye'll tak',
> A laddie or a lassie."

So sang the girls, as with hands joined they walked round in a ring, with Mysie, blushing and sweet, standing in the center—a sweet, shy, little rosebud—a joy in a cheap cotton frock.

"Come on, Mysie," urged the girls, who had now come to a standstill with the finish of the song. "Choose an' dinna keep us waiting." But Mysie stood still, her little heart beating at a terrible rate, her breath coming in short, quick gasps, and a soft, glowing light of nervous intensity in her eyes.

"Oh, come on, Mysie Maitland," cried one girl in hurt tones, "choose an' dinna spoil the game."

"Come on," urged another, "the whistle will be blawn the noo."

"She's feart," said one, "an' she disna need, for we a' ken that she wants to choose Bob Sinclair."

Something sang uproariously in Bob's ears at this blunt way of stating what they all felt; a hot wave surged over him, and his whole being seemed to fill with the energy of a giant. He shifted uneasily, his senses all acutely alert to pick up even Mysie's faint gasp of shame, as the hot blood suffused her face. Would she choose him before all these others? He hoped she wouldn't, and he tried to summon a smile to hide his uneasiness. Still Mysie hesitated. She wanted to choose Robert, but if she did, perhaps the other boys and girls would tease them afterwards.

"Oh, come on, Mysie. It's no' fair," cried one of the girls, getting more and more impatient. "Choose an' be done wi' it. It's only a game."

Thus urged Mysie stepped forward, and, excited out of all judgment, her face covered with shame, her heart thumping and galloping, she grabbed the first hand she saw, which happened to be Peter Rundell's, and something seemed to darken the day for all. Robert, now that he had not been chosen, felt murder in his heart. His body felt charged with energy, a flood of passion poured over him and he lost all discretion. He saw only Peter's shining collar, his fine boots and good clothes, and above all the smile, half of shame, half of triumph, upon his face. In passing Peter staggered against Robert, who let drive with his fist, and there was a fight before anyone really knew what had happened.

"What are ye shovin' at? Can ye no' watch folk's toes?" And he was on Peter like a whirlwind. There was the hatred of years between them, and they pummeled each other heartily.

"A fight, boys!" yelled the others. "Here's a fight!" and a crowd rapidly gathered to watch operations, while little Mysie, who had been the cause of it all, shrank back into a quiet corner, the tears running from her eyes and a sore pain at her heart.

"Go on, Bob! Gi'e him a jelly yin," cried Bob's supporters.

"Watch for his nose, Peter," cried those who pinned their faith to the coal-owner's son. Amid a chorus of such encouragement, both boys belabored each other and fought like barbarians.

"Let up, Peter," cried Bob's admirers, "an' gi'e him fair doo," as the two rolled upon the ground, with Peter, who was much the bigger boy, on top. "Come on now, he let you up when you was doon," and so they kept the balance of fair play. But the fight raged on in a terrible fury of battle, sometimes one boy on top, sometimes the other. Bob was the more active of the two, and hardier, and what he lacked in weight he made up in speed. One of Peter's eyes was bruised, while Robert's lip was swelling, and each strained to plant the decisive blow that would end the fight.

"Nae kickin', Peter! Ye're bate," yelled one watchful supporter of Bob, as he noticed the former's booted foot come into violent contact with Bobbie's bare leg.

"Big cowardie!" cried another, as Peter, crying now with rage and vexation, hit out with his foot. "Fight fair an' nae kickin'!"

Bob managed to dodge the kick, and flinging himself in before Peter recovered his balance, planted a heavy blow upon his opponent's nose.

"Ho! a jelly yin! a jelly yin!" roared the crowd in admiration. "Gi'e him anither yin," and even Peter's supporters began to desert him. Bob, thus encouraged, laid about him with all the strengthened "morale" of a conscious victor, finding it comparatively easy now to hit hard—and often. Peter, blinded by tears and choking with passion, could not see, but struck aimlessly, till one resounding smack upon his already injured nose brought the eagerly looked for crimson blood from it, and that of course, in schoolboy etiquette, meant the end of the fight. Peter was now lying upon the ground, his handkerchief at his nose, and roaring like a bull, not so much because of his injured nose, as because of the hurt to his pride and vanity.

"Haud back yer held," advised one boy, "an' put something cauld doon yer back."

Suddenly there was silence, and everyone looked awed and shamefaced as Mr. Clapper, the headmaster, strode into the midst of them. He had heard the noise of the fight, and had stolen up unobserved just in time to see Peter get the knockout blow.

"What is the meaning of this?" he demanded sternly, his eyes traveling all over the children, till they rested finally on Robert. No one answered, and so he proceeded to question Peter, who had struggled to his feet. Peter, like many other boys in similar circumstances, poured forth a great indictment of his adversary, and Mr. Clapper then turned to Robert.

"What have you to say, Sinclair?" he asked. "Speak out, and give me your side."

But Robert said nothing. His rebellious spirit was roused, and he resented the tone of the headmaster's voice. Again Mr. Clapper tried, but Robert remained silent.

"Come now, tell me what led to the fight? Why were you fighting with Peter?"

Robert would not speak, and Mr. Clapper, being of an explosive temperament, with little tact, was fast losing his temper. He turned to question some of the other boys, finally calling them all into the school, and putting Robert into the teacher's room, so that he might "get to the bottom of it."

Mr. Clapper, whatever good points he may have possessed, was not at all fitted for the teaching profession, for he lacked the sympathy necessary in dealing with children, and he was a rigid believer in the doctrine of punishment.

After a time he came into the room where Robert sat, and began once more to question him. But Robert was still obdurate, and stolidly kept silent. Mr. Clapper recognized at once that this was a clear case of a dour nature in the wrong. It needed correction, and that of a severe kind. That spirit he felt must be broken, or there would be trouble ahead in after years for Robert Sinclair. Mr. Clapper was determined to do his duty, and he believed that Robert in later life would probably feel grateful for this thrashing. He thrashed the boy soundly and severely upon the most sensitive parts of his body, so that the pain would help to break his spirit. He saw no indignity heaped upon a high-spirited, sensitive soul. It was all for the boy's own good, and so the blows fell thick and heavy upon the little back and hips.

Robert bit his lip to repress the roar of pain that wanted to escape. He would not cry, and this was another spur to the efforts of Mr. Clapper. The boy's flesh twitched and quivered at every blow, yet never a cry came from him. It but served to feed his rebellion, and he struggled and fought with fury until completely exhausted.

"There now," declared Mr. Clapper, flinging down the "tawse" upon the table, panting from his exertions and wiping his brow, "I shall leave you for a time until you decide to speak. If you will not speak when I return, I shall thrash you again," and he went out, locking the door, leaving the boy, still proud and unsubdued, but aching in every muscle and bone of his little body.

Left to himself, Robert very nearly cried, but he dashed the gathering tears from his eyes, angry at the weakness, and resolved, as he adjusted his garments, that he would die rather than speak now. He looked round, and seeing the window raised a little from the bottom, sprang to it, a sudden resolve in his heart to run away. Just as he got astride the sill he spied a piece of chalk and the "tawse" on the table, so turning back he put the "tawse" in his pocket, and with the chalk wrote on the table:—

"You are an ould pig and I'll not speak, and you'll never put your hands on your tawse again."

Then he was out of the window, dropped easily to the ground, and was away to the moors. He ran a long way, until finding that he had not been detected, he skirted a small wood, dug a hole in the soft moss, put in the "tawse," and covered them up. There they may be lying to this day, for no one ever learned from him where they were buried.

The spell of the moor took possession of him, and his wounded soul was soon wrapped in the soft folds of its silence. The balm of its peace comforted him, and brought ease and calmed the rebellion in his blood. He was happy, forgetting that there ever had existed a schoolmaster, or anything else unpleasant. Here he was free, and no one ever misunderstood him. He gave pain to no one, and nothing ever hurt him here.

He flung himself down among the rank gray grass and heather, while the moor cock called to his mate in an agony of pleading passion, the lapwing crooned upon a tuft of grass as she prepared a place for her eggs, the whaup wheepled and twirled and cried in eerie alarm, the plover sighed to a low white cloud wandering past; while the snipe and the lark, the "mossie," the heather lintie, and the wandering, sighing winds among the reeds and rushes of the swampy moss, all added their notes to soothe and satisfy the little wounded spirit lying there on the soft moorland. Already he was away upon the wings of fancy in a world of his own—a world full of dreams and joys unspeakable; a world of calm comfort, where there was no pain, no hunger, no unpleasantness; a world of smiles and warm delights and love.

Thus he dreamed as he watched the white clouds trailing their draperies along the sky, till the shadows creeping over the hills, and the cries of the heron returning to his haunts in the moor, woke him to a realization of the fact that the school was long since out, and probably another thrashing awaited him when he got home. Sadly and regretfully he dragged his little aching body from its soft mossy bed, felt that his limbs were still sore, and that he was very, very hungry. Rebellion again surging within him as he remembered all, he trudged home, fearful yet proud, resolved to go through with the inevitable.

CHAPTER V
BLACK JOCK'S THREAT

That same day Walker intimated to Geordie, when he was at work underground, that a reduction was to be imposed on his ton rate, which meant for Sinclair that it would be more difficult to earn a decent wage. Geordie had always had it in his head to confront Walker about his very unfair treatment of him, and on this occasion he decided to do so.

"What way are you breakin' my rate?" he asked, when Walker told him of the reduction.

"Oh, it's no' me," replied Walker. "It's Rundell. He thinks it can be worked for less than it's takin', and, of course, I've just to do as I am tell'd."

"Weel, I don't ken," said Geordie. "But I've thocht for a lang while back that you had a hand in it. Have I done anything to ye, for I don't ken o' it?"

"Ye've never done me any harm, Geordie," replied Walker with a show of sincerity. "What mak's ye think that?"

"Weel, for a lang time noo', I've ay been kept in hard places, or places wi' nae air, or where there was water to contend wi'. There's ay been something, an' I ha'e come to the conclusion that there's mair design than accident in it."

"I dinna think so," was the reply. "But maybe it's because you're ay agitatin' to have a union started."

"An' what about it," enquired Geordie, getting a bit heated. "If I ha'e been advocatin' the startin' o' a union? It seems to me to be muckle needed."

"Oh, I've nothing to say aboot it," replied Walker. "It's the boss, an' I was merely givin' ye a hint for yer ain guid."

"It's a' richt," exclaimed Geordie, getting still more heated. "I can see as far through a brick wall as you can see through a whin dyke. The boss has naething to do wi' it. It's you, an' I'm quite pleased to get the chance to tell ye to yer face. Ye could, many a time, ha'e given me a better place, if you had cared. But let me tell you, if there was a union here, it would soon put an end to you an' yer damn'd cantraips."

"Very weel. Gang on an' start yin. Man, though ye were a' in a union the morn, I could buy an' sell the majority of them for the promise of a guid place, or a bottle of whisky—Ay, if they jist thocht they were in wi' the gaffer, I'd get all I wanted frae the maist o' them. A clap on the shoulder, a smile, or even a word would do it. The one hauf o' the men can ay be got to sell the ither. Ye daurna' cheep, man, but I hear of it."

"Damn'd fine I ken that," replied Geordie, "an' it's mair the peety. But that's no' to say that men'll ay be like that. If they'd be true an' stick to yin anither, they'd damn'd soon put an end to sic gaffers as you."

"Maybe ye'll be the first to be put an end to," said Walker, rising to leave. "I might ha'e something to say to—"

"You rotten pestilence o' hell," cried Geordie, now fairly roused, and jumping over the coals on the "roadhead" after him. "I'll cleave the rotten heart o' ye if I get my fingers on ye, you an' yer fancy women, yer gamblin' an' yer shebeens!"

But Walker was off; he did not like to hear these matters of his private life mentioned, and so Geordie, left to himself, lit his pipe, and sat down to cool his temper.

A few minutes later Matthew Maitland came round to borrow a shot of powder, and Geordie unburdened his mind to him.

"He's a dirty brute," said Matthew, "an' it's time we had a union started. I hear great stories aboot how Bob Smillie's gettin' on wi' the union that he started doon the west country."

"I ken Bob fine," said Geordie. "He's a fine fellow. I worked next wall to him doon there a while, an' a better chap ye couldna' get."

"I hear that he's gotten as muckle as tippence on the ton to some o' the miners who ha'e joined. I'm gaun to join whenever it can be started."

Geordie agreed that it would be good to have a union, but he knew that whoever led in the matter would very likely have to pay for his courage. There was the "Block" to consider, and he could not see how they might start a union just then in such hard times.

He sat and thought after Matthew had gone away, and was still sitting when Matthew's shot went off. His lot, he knew, was hard. He could not afford to "flit," even though he did find work somewhere else. His six children depended upon his readiness to swallow insult and injustice, and he could see no way but to submit. If only his first boy were ready for work, it would soon make a difference in the house. It was only a few months now till that time would come, and perhaps things might change.

All day he was sullen and angry, and he tore at his work like some imprisoned fiend, a great rebellion in his heart, and a fury of anger consuming him. Everything seemed to go wrong that day, and at last when "knock-off" time came, he felt a little easier, though still silent and angry. His last shot, however, missed fire, just as he was coming away home; and that, added to all the other things that day, made him feel that his whole life was clouded, and was one long trial.

On the way home from the pit he heard the story of Robert's rebellious outburst at school, and when he came into the house his wife saw by his face that something had upset him. She proceeded to get him water to wash himself, and brought in the tub, while he divested himself of his clothes, flinging each garment savagely into the corner, until he stood naked save for his trousers. Most miners are sensitive to the presence of strangers during this operation, and it so happened at that particular time the minister chose to pay one of his rare visits among his flock in the village.

"Wha the hell's this noo?" asked Geordie, when he heard the tap at the door, as he looked up through soapy eyes, his head all lathered with the black suds. "Dammit, they micht let folk get washed," he said angrily.

When he heard the voice of the minister, he plunged his head into the tub, and began splashing and rubbing, and lifting the water over his head.

"Oh, you are busy washing, I see, Mr. Sinclair," observed the minister, looking at the naked collier.

"Ay," said Geordie shortly, "an' I dinna think you'd ha'e thankit me for comin' in on the tap o' you, when you were washin' yerself," he said bluntly—a remark which his wife felt to be a bit ill-natured, though she said nothing.

"Oh, I am sorry," replied the minister. "I did not mean to intrude. I'll not stay, but will call back some other time," and his voice was apologetic and ill at ease.

"I think sae," retorted Geordie, splashing away and spitting the soap from his mouth. "Yer room's mair to my taste than yer company the noo."

"My! that was an awfu' way to talk to the meenister," said Mrs. Sinclair when the door was again closed. "You micht aye try to be civil to folk," and there was resentment in her voice.

"Ach, dammit, wha can be bothered wi' thae kind o' folk yapping roun' about when yer washin' yerself. He micht ken no' to come at this time, when men are comin' hame frae their work," and he went on with his splashing. "Here, gi'e my back a rub," and he lay over the tub while she washed his back from the shoulders downward, making it clean and free from the coal dust and grime. Then she proceeded to dry him all over with a rough towel, after which he put on a clean shirt, and taking off his pit trousers, stepped into the tub and began to wash his lower limbs and make them as clean as the upper part of the body.

"Ach, folk should ha'e a place to wash in anyway," he grumbled, as if to justify his outburst, for secretly he was beginning to feel ashamed of it. "The folk that ha'e the maist need o' a bath are the folk wha never get the chance o' yin," he went on. "Look at that chap wha was in the noo. He never needs to dirty a finger, an' look at the hoose he has to bide in, wi' its fine bathroom an' a' things that he needs. Och, but we are a silly lot o' blockheads!" And so he raved on till he sat down to his frugal dinner of potatoes and buttermilk, after which he relapsed into silence again, and sat reading a newspaper.

It was in this mood that Robert found him when he returned from the moors. Nellie had noticed that something was worrying her husband, and she suspected some fresh trouble at the pit, though she asked no questions.

"Where hae ye been?" asked Geordie very calmly, as Robert entered furtively, and sat down on a chair near to the door. The boy did not answer. He dreaded that calmness. He seemed to feel there was something strong, cruel and relentless behind it. But he had something of his father's nature in him, so he sat in silence.

"What kind o' conduct's this I hear ye've been up to?" was the next question, with the same studied calm, seemingly passionless and pliable. Still no answer from the boy, though when he looked at his father he felt afraid. He turned his eyes appealingly to his mother, but her face betrayed nothing, and a feeling of hopelessness entered Robert's heart. There was nothing else but to go through with it.

"Tak' aff yer claes," quietly commanded the father, and the boy reluctantly began to peel off his scanty garments one by one, till he stood naked on the bare floor. He was glad that no one except the baby was in to see his humiliation, his brothers and sisters being all out at play.

The father rose and went to the corner where his working clothes lay in a heap. Selecting the belt he wore round his waist at his work, he grasped it firmly, and with the other hand took the boy by one arm, saying:—

"Are ye going to answer my question noo', and tell me where ye ha'e been?"

But Robert did not answer, so down came the hard leather belt with a horrible crack across the naked little hips, and a thick red mark appeared where the blow had fallen. A roar of pain broke from the boy's lips, in spite of his resolution not to cry, as lash after lash fell upon his limbs and across the little white back. Horribly, cruelly, relentlessly the belt fell with sickening regularity, while the tender flesh quivered at every blow, and an ugly series of red stripes appeared along the back and down across the sturdy legs.

"Oh, dinna' hit me ony mair, faither," he pleaded at last, the firm resolution breaking because of the pain of the blows. "Oh, dinna hit me!" and he jumped as the blows fell without slackening. "Oh, oh, oh! Mother, dinna' let him hit me ony mair!" roared the boy, while the grim, set face of the parent never relaxed, and the belt continued to lash the quivering flesh.

Mrs. Sinclair, who by this time was crying too, feeling every blow in her mother-heart, began to fear this grim, cruel look on her husband's face. He was mad, she felt, and there was murder in his eyes; and at last, spurred to desperation, she jumped forward, tore at the belt with desperate strength, and flung it into the corner, crying, as she gripped the boy in her arms.

"In the name of Heaven, Geordie, are ye gaun to kill my bairn afore my een?"

She tore the boy fiercely from his father's grasp and shielded him from her husband, exclaiming at the same time with indignation, "Ha'e ye nae humanity aboot ye at a'? Hit me if ye are goin' to hit any more. It's murder, an' I'll no' stand ony longer an' let ye do it."

Geordie, surprised and amazed at her action, and the fierceness in her voice, looked up, and immediately reason seemed to steal back into his mind. A flush of shame overspread his face, and he sat down, burying his face in his hands.

"Wheesht, sonny. Wheesht, my wee man," crooned the mother soothingly, as she began to help Robert to get on his clothes, the tears falling still from her own eyes, as she saw the ugly stripes and bruises upon his back beginning to discolor. "Wheesht, sonny! Dinna' greet ony mair. There noo', my wee son. Daddy's no' weel the nicht," she excused, "an' didna' ken what he was doin'." Then breaking into a louder tone: "I wonder what in Heaven's name puir folk are born for at a'. There noo'. There noo'. Dinna greet, my wee man, an' mither'll gi'e ye yer denner."

Sinclair could stand it no longer, so slipping on his boots and reaching for his cap, he went out, never in all his life feeling more ashamed of himself.

Left to themselves—for all the other children were still out at play— Nellie soon had Robert quietened and sitting at his dinner of cold potatoes and buttermilk. Bit by bit she drew from him the story of the fight at school; divining for herself the reason for Robert's attack upon Peter Rundell, she soon was in possession of the whole story with its termination of revolt against the headmaster and even the confession of what he had written on the table.

"An' what did ye do wi' the tawse, son?" she enquired, her dark eyes showing pride in the revolt of her laddie. She was proud to know that he had sufficient character to stand up to a bully, even though he were a headmaster.

"I buried them in the muir," he replied simply, "but I dinna' want to tell naebody where they are. I'll never gi'e them back."

"Oh, weel, if ye dinna' want to tell me, dinna' do it," she said. "I'll gang with ye to the school the morn, an' I'll see that ye're no' meddled wi'. But, Robin, while I like to see ye staunin' up against what is wrong, I dinna want ye to dae wrang yersel. An' I think ye was in the wrang to strike Peter. He staggered against ye, an' I dinna think he wad try to tramp on yer taes. An' always when ye're in the wrang, own up to it, an' make what amends ye can."

Robin did not reply to this, but she could see that he knew she was right. Before he could say anything she added, "Come awa' noo', if ye ha'e gotten yer denner, son, I think ye should gang awa' to yer bed. Ye'll be the better o' a lang sleep. Dinna' think hard o' yer faither; he's feelin' ashamed o' hittin' ye. There must be something botherin' him, for I dinna' mind o' him ever leatherin' one o' ye like that."

This was true, for Geordie Sinclair was rather a "cannie" man, and had never been given to beating his children before. She felt that something had happened in the pit, and whatever it was it had made her husband angry.

Robert again stripped off his clothes and crept into bed, while his mother seemed to feel every pain once more as she looked upon the soft little body with the ugly black stripes upon it. She placed him under the rough blankets as snugly as possible, telling him to lie well over near to the wall, for there were five of them now who lay abreast, and there was never too much room. He was soon asleep, and Mrs. Sinclair put fresh coals on the fire, and began to tidy up, so as to have everything as cheerful as possible when her husband should return. It was no easy matter to keep a house clean, with only a single apartment, and eight individuals living in it.

The housing conditions in most mining villages of Scotland are an outrage on decency. In Lowwood there were no sanitary conveniences of any kind, and it was a difficult matter for the women folk to keep a tidy house under these circumstances. But it was wonderful, the homeliness and comfort found in those single apartment houses. It was home, and that made it tolerable. In such homes fine men and women were bred and reared, but the credit was due entirely to our womenfolk; for they had the fashioning of the spirit of the homes, and the spirit of the homes is always the spirit of the people.

CHAPTER VI
THE COMING OF A PROPHET

Another year passed, and Robert was now eleven years of age. Though full of hardship, hunger and poverty, yet they were not altogether unhappy years for him. There were joys which he would not have liked to have missed, and in later life he looked back upon them always through a mist of memory that sometimes bordered on tears.

He had grown "in wisdom and stature," and gave promise of being a fine sturdy boy; but lately it had been borne in upon him that no one seemed just to look at things from his point of view. He was alluded to as "a strange laddie," and the gulf of misunderstanding seemed to grow wider every day. Old Granny Frame, the "howdie-wife" of the village, always declared that he would be a great man, but others just took it for granted that he would never see things as they saw them.

He was already too serious for a boy, and his joys were not the joys of other children. Sensitive, and in a measure proudly reserved, he took more and more to the moors and the hills. All day sometimes he roved over them, and at other times he would lie motionless but happy, for the moor always understood. If he were hurt at anything which happened, the moor brought him solace; if he grieved, it gave him relief; and if he were happy, it too rejoiced. He loved it in all moods, and he could not understand how its loving silence was dreaded by others.

His parents now found that their battle, though not much easier, certainly was no worse, and hope shone bright for them in the future. The oldest boy was already at work and one girl was away "in service." Robert, too, would soon be ready, and in quick succession behind him there were three other boys. Geordie Sinclair was often told by his workmates that he would "soon ha'e naethin' to do but put in wicks in the pit lamps." But Geordie merely smiled. How often before had he heard that said of others who had families like his own and he knew that he would never see them all working. Fifty years was a long time to live for a collier in those days of badly ventilated and poorly inspected pits and many men were in their graves at forty.

Walker still indulged in petty persecution, whilst Geordie agitated for the starting of a union, and many a battle the two had, until the enmity between them developed into keen hatred.

"I wonder what Black Jock really has against me," he had said over and over again, unable to understand his persistent hostility, but his wife had never dared tell him.

One night, however, after he had been out of work a week, because, as Black Jock had said, "there was nae places," she decided to tell him the real reason of Walker's antipathy.

"Man, it's no' you, Geordie, that Black Jock has the ill will at," she ventured to say, "it's me, an' he hits me an' the bairns through you."

"You," said Geordie in some surprise, "hoo' can that be?"

Bit by bit, though with great reluctance, she told her husband how and when Black Jock had attempted to degrade her. When she had ended, he sat in grim silence, while the ticking of the clock seemed to have gained in loudness, and so, too, the purring of the cat, as it rubbed itself against his leg, first on one side and then the other, drawing its sleek, furry side along his ankle, turning back again, and occasionally looking up into his face for the recognition which it vainly tried to win.

The fire burned low in the grate as Nellie busied herself with washing the dishes; while outside the loud cries of the children, playing on the green, mingled occasionally with a clink, as the steel quoits fell upon each other, telling of some enthusiastic players, who were practicing for the local games. Loud cries of encouragement broke from the supporters, and Geordie and Nellie heard all these—even the plaintive wail of a child crying in a house a few doors farther up the "row," and the mother's attempts to soothe it into forgetfulness of its temporary pain or disappointment.

The little apartment seemed to have become suddenly cheerless. Nellie felt the silence most oppressive, for she was wondering how he was taking it all. Soon, however, he rose and reached for his cap. Looking at his wife with eyes that set all her fears at rest—for she saw pride in them, pride in her and the way she had acted—he said:—

"Thank ye, Nellie; ye are a' the woman I always thocht ye was, an' I'll see that nae dirty brute ever again gets the chance to insult ye," and he was out of the door before she could question him further.

Geordie went straight to where Walker lived and knocked at the door. A girl of fourteen came in answer to his knock, for Walker was a widower, his wife having died shortly after the birth of their only child.

"Is yer faither in?" enquired Geordie quietly, hardly able to control the raging anger in his heart.

"No, he's no' in," replied the girl. "Oh, is that you, Geordie?" she asked, recognizing him in the darkness. "My father said when he went oot that if ye cam' to the door, I was to tell ye he had nae places yet."

"That's a' richt," said Geordie, still very quietly. "Do ye ken onything aboot where he is this nicht?"

"No, unless he's up in Sanny Robertson's, or maybe in Peter Fleming's."

"Thank ye," said Geordie, turning away, "I'll go up an' see if he is there."

He knew that Peter Fleming was working that night, and had stopped on an extra shift to repair a road, by special instructions from Walker; so Geordie went direct to Fleming's house and knocked at the door. After an interval a woman's voice enquired, "Wha's that?" and Geordie thought there was anxiety in it.

"Open the door," said Geordie quietly. "What the hell are ye afert for?" and the woman, thinking it was her husband returned from work, immediately opened the door.

"You're shairly early," she said; then suddenly recognizing who the intruder was, she tried to shut the door.

"Na, na," said Geordie, now well in the doorway, "I want to see Black Jock."

"He's no' here," she lied readily enough, but with some agitation in her voice.

"You're a liar, Jean," replied Geordie, "that's him gaun oot at the room door," and Geordie withdrew hurriedly, determined that Black Jock should not escape him. He hurried to the end of the "row," and waited with all the passion of long years raging through his whole being. He stepped out as Walker advanced, and said: "Is that you, Walker?"

"Ay," came the answer, "what do ye want?" as he came to a halt.

"Just a meenit," said Geordie, placing himself in front of Walker, barring his way. "I want to warm yer dirty hide. It ought to have been done years ago, but I never kent till the nicht, and I'm gaun to dae it the noo," and the tones of his voice indicated that he meant what he said.

"Oh! What's wrang?" asked Walker in affected surprise. "I'll get ye a place," he went on hurriedly, "just as soon as I can—in fac' there's yin that'll be ready by the morn."

"I'm no gi'ein' a damn for yer place. It's you I'm efter the nicht. Come on, face up," and Sinclair squared himself for battle.

Thus challenged, Walker, who was like all bullies a coward at heart, tried to temporize, but Sinclair was in no mood for delay.

"Come on, pit them up, or I'll break yer jaw for you," he said threateningly.

"Man, Geordie, what ails ye the nicht?" asked Walker in hurried alarm, wondering wildly how he could stave off the chastisement which he knew from Geordie's voice he might expect. "Talk sensibly, man. Try an' ha'e some sense. What's the matter wi' ye?"

"Matter," echoed Geordie, "jist this. The wife has jist telt me a' aboot the nicht ye cam' chappin' to the door when I was lyin' hurt. She kent I'd break yer neck for it, and she was feart to tell me. So put up yer fists, ye black-hearted brute that ye are. I'm gaun to gi'e ye what we should hae gotten seven years syne, an' it'll maybe put ye frae preyin' on decent women. Come on."

"Awa', man, Geordie, an' behave yersel'," began Walker, trying to evade him.

"Tak' that, then, ye dirty brute!" and Geordie smashed his fist straight between Walker's eyes.

Roused at last, Walker showed fight and swung at Sinclair. He was the younger man by about two years, and had not had the hard work and bad conditions of the other, but Sinclair was a strong man, and was now roused to a great pitch, so he struck out with terrific force. Then the two closed and swayed about, struggling, cursing and punching each other with brutal might. Sinclair's extra weight and more powerful build soon began to tell, and he was able to send home one or two heavy blows on Black Jock's face and body. Panting and blowing, they separated, and as they did so, Sinclair caught his opponent a straight hard crash on the jaw that sent him rolling to the muddy road, and feeling as if a thousand fists had struck him all at once.

Walker lay for a short time, then gathering himself together, he rose to his feet and set off at a quick pace in the direction of his house, whilst Geordie, too, turned homewards, feeling that it was useless to follow him.

Mrs. Sinclair did not hear what had happened till a week later, when Geordie, being in a communicative mood, told her of the affair in simple, unaffected terms.

Shortly afterwards a great event happened in Lowwood, which made the deepest impression on Robert's mind. His father still being out of work, had sent a letter to Robert Smillie, who was then beginning to be heard of more and more in mining circles. In the letter Geordie explained, to the best of his ability, the local circumstances, and he mentioned his own case of persecution, and his agitation for the starting of a union. Smillie sent word in reply that he would come in two days, and Geordie enthusiastically set to work to organize a meeting, going round every house in the district, telling the folks that Smillie was coming, and exhorting them to turn out and hear him.

"I dinna think it'll do any guid," said old Tam Smith, when Geordie called upon him. "It's a' richt talkin' about a union, but the mair ye fecht the mair ye're oppressed. The bosses ha'e the siller, an' they can ay buy the brains to serve them."

Geordie made no reply, for he knew from experience that it was only too true.

"Just look at young Jamie Soutar," continued Tam. "He is yin o' the cleverest men i' the country. He wrocht wi' me as a laddie when he went into the pit, an' noo' he's travelin' manager for that big company doon the west country, an' I'm telt he's organizin' an' advocatin' the formin' o' what he calls a Coal Combine."

"That's a' richt, Tam. I admit it a', though I dinna jist ken what a Coal Combine means; but I ken that Bob Smillie is makin' great wark wi' the union he has formed. I ken he has gotten rises in wages for a' the men who ha'e joined, an' that he is advocatin' an eight hours day. If that can be done doon there, it can be done here; for there's naebody has ony mair need o' a eight hours day than miners."

"Oh, I'll turn oot a' richt at the meetin'," said Tam, who was always credited with seeing farther than most of his workmates, "an' I'll join the union, too, if it's formed; but ye'll see if ye live lang enough that the union'll no' be a' ye think it. The ither side will organize to bate ye every time." And with this encouraging prophecy, Geordie went on to the next house.

"No, I'm no' comin' to nae meetin'. I want naethin' to dae wi' yer unions. I can get on weel enough without them," curtly said Dan Sellars, the inmate. He was what Geordie somewhat expressively called a "belly-crawler," a talebearer, and one who drank and gambled along with Walker, Fleming, Robertson and a few others.

"Man, it'll no' do muckle guid," said another, "ye mind hoo' big Geordie Ritchie ran awa' wi' the money o' the last union we started? It'll gi'e a wheen bigmouths a guid job and an easy time. That's a' it will do."

"Oh, ay," answered Sinclair, "but that's no' to say that the union'll ay fail. Folks are no' a' Geordie Ritchies, an' they're no' a' bigmouths either. We're bound to succeed if we care to be solid thegither."

"I'll come to the meetin', Geordie, although I was sayin' that, but I'll no' promise to join yer union," was the answer, and Sinclair had to be content with that.

Thus went Geordie from house to house, meeting with much discouragement, and even downright opposition, but he was always good-humored, and so he seldom failed to extract a promise to attend the meeting.

The night of the meeting arrived, and the hall—an old, badly lit and ill-ventilated wooden erection—was packed to its utmost. There were eager faces, and dull, listless ones among the audience; there were eyes glad with expectancy, and eyes dulled with long years of privations and brutal labor; limbs young and supple and full of energy, and limbs stiff and sore, crooked and maimed.

Geordie Sinclair was chairman, and when he rose to open the meeting and introduce Smillie, he felt as if the whole world were looking on and listening.

"Weel, men," he began, halting and hesitating in his utterance, "for a lang time now there has been much cryin' for a union here. There has been a lot of persecution gaun' on, an' it has been lang felt that something should be done. We ha'e heard of how other men in other places ha'e managed to start a union, and how it has been a guid thing in risin' wages. Mr. Smillie has come here the nicht to tell us how the other districts ha'e made a start, and what thae other districts has gotten. If it can be done there, it can be done here. I ha'e wrocht aside Bob Smillie, an' I ken what kind of man he is. He has done great wark doon in the west country, an' he is weel fitted and able to be the spokesman for the miners o' Scotlan'. I'm no gaun' to say ony mair, but I can say that it gie's me great pleasure to ask Mr. Smillie to address ye."

A round of applause greeted Smillie as he rose to address them. Tall and manly, he dominated his audience from the very first sentence, rousing them to a great pitch of enthusiasm, as he proceeded to tell of all the many hardships which miners had to endure, of the "Block" system of persecution, and to point to the only means of successfully curing them by organizing into one solid body, so that they might become powerful enough to enforce their demands for a fuller, freer, and a happier life. Never in all his life did he speak with more passion than he did that night in Lowwood.

Little Robert was present in the hall—the only child there; and as Smillie spoke in passionate denunciation of the tyrannies and persecutions of the mine-owners and their officials, his little heart leapt in generous indignation. Many things which he had but dimly understood before, began to be plain to him, as he sat with eyes riveted upon Smillie's face, drinking in every word as the speaker plead with the men to unite and defend themselves. Then, as his father's wrongs were poured forth from the platform, and as Smillie appealed to them in powerful sentences to stand loyally by their comrade, the boy felt he could have followed Smillie anywhere, and that he could have slain every man who refused to answer that call. Away beyond the speaker the boy had already glimpsed something of the ideal which Smillie sketched, and his soul throbbed and ached to see how simple and how easy it was for life to be made comfortable and good and pleasant for all. Bob Smillie never won a truer heart than he did that night in winning this barefooted, ragged boy's.

Round after round of applause greeted the speaker when he had finished, and in response to his appeal to them to organize, a branch of the union was formed, with Geordie Sinclair as its first president. At the request of the meeting Smillie interviewed Black Jock next morning, and as a result Sinclair got started on the following day.

Smillie stayed overnight with Geordie. They were certainly somewhat cramped for room, though Geordie had just lately got another apartment "broken through," which gave them a room and kitchen.

The two men sat late into the night, discussing their hopes and plans, and the trade union movement generally.

"It's a great work, Bob, you ha'e set yersel', an' it'll mean thenklessness an' opposition frae the very men you want maist to help," said Sinclair as they talked.

"Ay, it will," was the reply, spoken in a half dreamy tone, as if the speaker saw into the future. "I ken what it'll mean, but it must be done. I have long had it in me to set myself this work, for no opposition ought to stand in the way of the uplifting of the workers. I ... It's the system, Geordie!" he cried, as if bringing his mind back to the present. "It is the system that is wrong. It is immoral and evil in its foundations, and it forces the employers to do the things they do. Competition compels them to do things they would not have to do if there were a cooperative system of industry. Our people have to suffer for it all — they pay the price in hunger, misery and suffering."

"Ay," said Geordie, "that's true, Bob. But what a lang time it'll tak' afore the workers will realize what you are oot for. They'll look on your work wi' suspicion, and a wheen o' them'll even oppose you."

"Ay," was the reply, "I know that. It will mean the slow building up of our own county first, bit by bit, organizing, now here, now there, and fighting the other class interests all the time. It will divide our energies and retard our work, and the greatest fight will be to get our own people to recognize what is wanted and how to get it. Then through the county we'll have to work to consolidate the whole of Scotland; from that to work in the English and Welsh miners, while at the same time seeking to permeate other branches of industrial workers with our ideas. And then, when we have got that length, and raised the mental vision of our people, and strengthened their moral outlook, we can appeal to the workers of other lands to join us in bringing about the time when we'll be able to regard each other, not as enemies, but as members of one great Humanity, working for each other's welfare as we work for our own."

"That's it, Bob," agreed Geordie, completely carried away with Smillie's enthusiasm. "That's it, Bob. If we can only get them to see hoo' simple and easy it a' is ... Oh, they maun be made to see it that way!" he burst out. "We'll work nicht an' day but in the end we'll get them to see it that way yet."

"Yes, but it won't be easy, Geordie," he replied. "Our people's lives have been stunted and warped so long, they've been held in bondage and poverty to such an extent, that it will take years—generations, maybe—before they come to realize it. But we must go on, undeterred by opposition, rousing them from their apathy, and continually holding before them the vision of the time we are working to establish. Ay, Geordie," —and a quieter note came into his voice, "I hope I shall be strong enough to go on, and never to give heed to the discouragements I shall undoubtedly meet with in the work; but I've made up my mind, and I'll see it through or dee."

The talk of the two men worked like magic upon the impressionable mind of young Robert, who sat listening. Long after all had retired for the night he lay awake, his little mind away in the future, living in the earthly paradise which had been conjured up before him by the warm, inspiring sentences of this miners' leader, and joyful in the contemplation of this paradise of happy humanity, he fell asleep. Could he have foreseen the terrible, heartbreaking ordeals through which Smillie often had to pass, still clinging with tenacity to the gleam that led him on, praying sometimes that strength would be given to keep him from turning back; of the strenuous battle he had, not only with those he fought against, but of the greater and more bitter fights he too often had with those of his own class whom he was trying to save; and of the fights even with himself, it would have raised Smillie still more in the estimation of this sensitive-hearted collier laddie.

CHAPTER VII
ON THE PIT-HEAD

"Hooray, mither, I've passed the examination, an' I can leave the school noo!" cried Robert one day, breaking in upon his mother, as she was busily preparing the dinner. She stopped peeling the potatoes to look up and smile, as she replied: "Passed the fifth standard, Robin?" she said, lovingly.

"Ay," said the boy proudly, his face beaming with smiles. "It was quite easy. Oh, if you had just seen the sums we got; they were easy as winking. I clinked them like onything."

"My, ye maun hae been real clever," said Mrs. Sinclair encouragingly.

"Sammy Grierson failed," broke in Robert again, too full of his success to contain himself. "He couldna' tell what was the capital of Switzerland! Then the inspector asked him what was the largest river in Europe, an' he said the Thames. He forgot that the Thames was just the biggest in England. I was sittin' next him an' had to answer baith times, an' the inspector said I was a credit to the school. My, it was great fun!" and he rattled on, full of importance at his success.

"Ay, but maybe Sammy was just nervous," said his mother, continuing her operations upon the potatoes, and trying to let him see that there might have been a cause for the failure of the other boy to answer correctly.

"Ach, but he's a dunce onyway," said the boy. "He canna spell an easy word like 'examination,' an' he had twenty-two mistakes in his dictation test," he went on, and she was quick to note the air of priggish importance in his utterance.

"Ay, an' you're left the school now," said Mrs. Sinclair, after a pause, during which her busy fingers handled the potatoes with great skill. "Your faither will be gey pleased when he comes hame the day," she said, giving the conversation a new turn.

"Ay, I'll get leavin' the school when I like, an' gaun to the pit when I like."

"Would ye no' raither gang to the school a while langer?" observed the mother after a pause, and looking at him with searching eyes.

"No," was the decisive reply. "I'd raither gang to work. I'm ready for leaving the school and forby, all the other laddies are gaun to the pit to work."

"But look at the things ye micht be if ye gaed to the school a while langer, Robin," she went on. "The life of a miner's no' a very great thing. There's naething but hard work, an' dangerous work at that, an' no' very muckle for it." And there was an anxious desire in her voice, as if trying to convince him.

"Ay, but I'd raither leave the school," he answered, though with less decision this time. "Besides, it'll mean more money for you," he concluded.

"Then, look how quick a miner turns auld, Rob. He's done at forty years auld," she said, as if she did not wish to heed what he said, "but meenisters an' schoolmaisters, an' folk o' that kin', leeve a gey lang while. Look at the easy time they hae to what a collier has. They dinna get up at five o'clock in the mornin' like your faither. They rise aboot eight, an' start work at nine. Meenisters only work yae day a week, an' only aboot two hoors at that. They hae clean claes to wear, a fine white collar every day, an' sae mony claes that they can put on a different rig-oot every day. Their work is no' hard, an' look at the pay they get; no' like your faither wi' his two or three shillin's a day. They hae the best o' it," she concluded, as she rested her elbows on her knees and again searched his face keenly to see if her arguments had had any effect upon him.

"Ay, but I'd raither work," reiterated the boy stubbornly.

"Then they hae plenty o' books," continued the temptress, loth to give up and keen to draw as rosy a picture as possible, "and a braw hoose, an' a piano in it. They get a lang holiday every year, and occasional days besides, an' their pay for it. But a collier gets nae pay when he's idle. It's the same auld grind awa' at hard work, among damp, an' gas, an' bad air, an' aye the chance o' being killed wi' falls of stone or something else. It's no' a nice life. It's gey ill paid, an' forby naebody ever respects them."

"Ay, mither; but do you no' mind what Bob Smillie said?" chipped in the boy readily, glad that he could quote such an authority to back his view. "It's because they dinna respect themselves. They just need to do things richt, an' things wadna' be sae bad as they are," and he felt as if he clinched his argument by quoting Smillie against her.

"Ay, Robin," she replied, "that's true; but for it a', you maun admit that the schoolmaister an' the meenister hae the best o' it." But she felt that her counter was not very effective.

"My faither says meenisters are nae guid to the world, but schoolmaisters are," said the boy, with a grudging admission for the teaching profession. "But I dinna care. I'd raither gang to work. I dinna want to gang ony langer to the school. I'm tired o' it, an' I want to leave it," and there was more decision in his voice this time than ever.

"A' richt, Robin," said Mrs. Sinclair resignedly, as she emptied the peeled potatoes into a pot and put them on the fire.

There were now seven of a family, and she knew that Robert was needed to increase the earnings, and that meant there was nothing but the pit for him.

"You maun hae been real clever, though, to pass," she said again, after a pause. "How many failed?"

"Four, mither," he cried, again waxing enthusiastic over the examination. "Mysie Maitland passed, too. She was first among the lasses, and I was first in the laddies."

"Eh, man, Bob, learnin' is a gran' thing to hae," she said wistfully, looking at him very tenderly.

"Ay, but I'm gaun to the pit," he said decisively, fearing that she was again going to enlarge upon the schoolmaster's life.

"Very weel," she said after a bit, "I suppose ye'll be lookin' for a job. Your faither was saying last nicht that ye're too young to gang into the pit. Ye maun be twelve years auld afore ye get doon the pit noo, ye ken. So I suppose it'll be the pithead for ye for a while."

She had often dreamed her dream, even though she knew it was an impossible one, that she would like to see her laddie go right on through the Secondary School in the county town to the University. She knew he had talents above the ordinary, and, besides, her soul rebelled at the thought of her boy having to endure the things that his father had to go through with. She was an intelligent woman, and though she had had little education, she saw things differently from most of the women of her class. She had character, and her influence was easily traced in her children, but more especially in Robert, who was always her favorite bairn. She was wise, too, and had fathomed some secrets of psychology which many women with a university training had never even glimpsed.

She often maintained that her children's minds were molded before she gave them birth, and that it depended upon the state of mind she was in herself during those nine months, as to what kind of soul her child would be born possessing. It may have been merely a whim on her part, but she held tenaciously to her belief, acted in accordance with it, and no one could dissuade her from it. Robert was her child of song, her sunny offspring, stung into revolt against tyranny of all kinds. His soul, strong and true as steel, she knew would stand whatever test was put upon it. Incorruptible and sincere, nothing could break him. Generous and forgiving, he could never be bought.

"I'll gang the nicht, mither, an' see if I can get a job. I micht get started the morn," he said breaking in upon her thought.

"A' richt, Robin," she replied with a sigh of resignation. "I suppose it'll hae to be done. It'll be yer first start in life, an' I hope ye'll aye be found doin' what's richt; for guid never comes o' ill thinkin' or ill doin'."

"If I get a job, mither, maybe I'll get one-an'-tippence a day like Dick Tamson. If I do it'll be a big help to you, mither. My! I'll soon mak' a poun' at that rate," and he laughed enthusiastically at the thought of it. A pound seemed to represent riches to his boyish mind. What might his mother not do with a pound? Ever so many things could be bought. And that was merely a start. His wages would soon increase with experience, and when he went down the pit, which would be soon, he'd earn more, and his mother would maybe be able to buy new clothes for all the family.

He wondered what it would be like to have a new suit of clothes — real new ones out of a shop. Hitherto he had only enjoyed "make downs," as they were called — new ones made out of some one's cast-off clothing. But a real new suit, such as he had seen the schoolmaster's boy sometimes wearing! That would be a great experience! And so, lost in contemplation of the things big wages might do, the day wore on, and he was happy in his dreams.

That same night Robert went to call on the "gaffer," Black Jock, and as he neared the door he met Mysie Maitland.

"Where are ye goin', Rab?" she enquired shyly.

"To look for a job," he replied proudly, feeling that now he was left school, and about to start work, he could be patronizing to a girl. "Where are you gaun?" he asked, as Mysie joined him in the direction of Walker's house.

"I'm gaun to look for a job, too," she replied. "I'm no' gaun back to the school, an' my mither thinks I'll be as weel on the pit-head as at service. An' forby, I'll be able to help my mither at nichts when I come hame, an' I couldna' do that if I gaed to service," she finished by way of explanation. As Mysie was the oldest of a family of six, her parents would be glad to have even her small earnings, and so she, too, was looking for a job.

When Walker came to the door, Robert took the matter in hand, and became spokesman for both himself and Mysie.

"We've left the school the day, Mr. Walker, an' Mysie an' me want to ken if ye can gie us a job on the pitheid?" and Walker noted with amusement the manly swagger in the boy's voice and bearing.

"We dinna' usually start lasses as wee as Mysie," replied Walker, eyeing the children with an amused smile, "but we need twa or three laddies to the tables to help the women to pick stones."

Mysie's face showed her keen disappointment. She knew that it was not customary for girls to be employed as young as she was; and Robert noted her disappointed look as well.

"Could ye no' try Mysie, too?" he asked, breaking in anxiously. "She's a guid worker, an' she'll be able to pick as many stanes as the weemen. Willn't ye, Mysie?" And he turned to the girl for corroboration with assurance.

As Mysie nodded, Walker saw a hint of tears in the girl's eyes, and the quivering of the tiny mouth; and as there is a soft spot in all men's hearts, even he had sympathy, for he understood what refusal meant.

"Weel, I micht gie her a trial," he said, "but she'll hae to work awfu' hard," and he spoke as one conferring an especial concession upon the girl.

"Oh, she'll work hard enough," said Robert. "Mysie's a guid worker, an' you'll see ..."

"Oh, then," said Walker hurriedly breaking in upon Robert's outburst of agreement, "ye can both come oot the morn, and I'll try and put ye both up."

"How muckle pay will we get?" asked Robert, who was now feeling his importance, and felt that this was after all the main point to be considered.

"Well, we gie laddies one an' a penny," replied Walker, still smiling amusedly at the boy's eagerness, "an' lasses are aye paid less than callants. But it's all big lasses we hae, an' they get one an' tippence. I'll gie Mysie a shillin' to begin wi'," and he turned away as if that settled the matter, and was about to close the door.

"But if she picks as many stanes as a laddie, will ye gie her the same pay as me?" interrupted Robert, not wishing the interview to end without a definite promise of payment.

"She's gey wee," replied Walker, "an' she canna' expect as much as a laddie," and he looked at Mysie, as if measuring her with a critical eye to assess her value.

"But if she does as muckle work, would ye gie her the same money?" eagerly questioned the boy, and Mysie felt that there was no one surely so brave as Robert, nor so good, and she looked at him with gratitude in her eyes.

"Very weel," said Walker, not desiring to prolong the interview. "Come oot the morn, an' I'll gie ye both one an' a penny."

"Six an' sixpence a week," said Mysie, as they tramped home. "My, that's a lot o' money, Rab, isn't it?"

"Ay, it's a guid lot, Mysie," he replied, "but we'll hae to work awfu' hard, or we'll no' get it. Guid nicht!" And so the children parted, feeling that the world was about to be good to them, and all their thought of care was bounded by six and sixpence a week.

Mysie was glad to tell the result of the whole interview to her parents. She was full of it, and could talk of nothing else as she worked about the house that night. Her mother had been in delicate health for a long time, and so Mysie had most of the housework to do. Matthew Maitland and his wife, Jenny, were pleased at the result, and gave Robert due credit for his part—a credit that Mysie was delighted to hear from them.

The next morning the two children went to work, when children of their years ought to have been still in bed dreaming their little dreams.

The great wheels at the pithead seemed terrible in their never-ending revolutions, as they flew round to bring up the loads of coal. The big yawning chasm, with the swinging steel rope, running away down into the great black hole, was awesome to look at, as the rope wriggled and swayed with its sinister movements; and the roar and whir of wheels, when the tables started, bewildered them. These crashed and roared and crunched and groaned; they would squeal and shriek as if in pain, then they would moan a little, as if gathering strength to break out in indignant protest; and finally, roar out in rebellious anger, giving Robert the idea of an imprisoned monster of gigantic strength which had been harnessed whilst it slept, but had wakened at last to find itself impotent against its Lilliputian captor— man.

An old man instructed them in their duties.

"You'll staun here," he panted, indicating a little platform about two feet broad, and running along the full length of the "scree." "You'll watch for every bit stane that comes doon, an' dinna' let any past. Pick them oot as soon as you see them, an' fling them owre there, an' Dickie Tamson'll fill them into the hutch, an' get them taken to the dirt bing."

"A' richt," said Robert, as he looked at the narrow platform, with its weak, inadequate railing, which could hardly prevent anyone from falling down on to the wagon track, some fifteen or twenty feet below on one side, or on to the moving "scree" on the other.

"Weel, mind an' no' let any stanes gang past, for there are aye complaints comin' in aboot dirty coals. If ye dinna work an' keep oot the stanes, you'll get the sack," and he said this as if he meant to convey to them that he was the sole authority on the matter.

He was an old man, and Robert, as he looked at him, wondered if he had ever laughed. "Auld Girnie" they called him, because of his habit of always finding fault with everything and everybody, for no one could please him. His mouth seemed to be one long slit extending across his face, showing one or two stumps sticking in the otherwise toothless gums, and giving him the appearance of always "grinning."

The women workers' appearance jarred upon Robert. So far women to him had always been beings of a higher order, because he had always thought of them as being like his mother. But here they were rough and untidy, dressed like goblins in dirty torn clothes, with an old dirty sack hanging from the waist for an overall. Instinctively Robert felt that this was no place for women. One of them, who worked on the opposite side of the scree from Robert—a big, strong, heavily-built young woman of perhaps twenty-five—in moving forward tore her petticoat, which caught in the machinery, and made a rent right up above her knee.

"Ach, to hell wi' it," she cried in exasperation, as she turned up the torn petticoat, displaying a leg all covered with coal grime, which seemed never to have been washed.

"Is that no' awfu'? Damn my soul, I'll hae to gang hame the nicht in my sark tail," and she laughed loudly at her sally.

"I'll put a pin in it, it'll do till I gang hame," she added, and she started to pin the torn edges together. But all day the bare leg shone through the torn petticoat, and rough jokes were made by the men who worked near by— jokes which she seemed to enjoy, for she would hold up the torn garment and laugh with the others.

The women and boys never seemed to heed the things that filled Robert and Mysie with so much amazement. The two children bent over the swinging tables as the coal passed before them. They eagerly grabbed at the stones, flinging them to the side with a zeal that greatly amused the older hands.

"Ye'll no' keep up that pace lang," said one woman. "Ye'll soon tire, so ye'd better take it easy."

"Let them alone," broke in the old man, who had a penny a day more for acting as a sort of gaffer. "Get on wi' yer own work, an' never mind them."

"Gang you to hell, auld wheezie bellows," replied one woman coarsely, adding a rough jest at his breathlessness, whilst the others laughed loudly, adding, each one, another sally to torment the old man.

But after a time Robert felt his back begin to ache, and a strange dizzy feeling came into his head, as a result of his bent position and the swinging and crashing of the tables. He straightened himself and felt as if he were going to break in two. He glanced at Mysie, wondering how she felt, and he thought she looked white and ill.

"Take a wee rest, Mysie," he said. "Are ye no' awfu' dizzy?"

Mysie heard, but "six and sixpence a week" was still ringing in her head. Indeed, the monotonous swing of the tables ground out the refrain in their harsh clamor, as they swung backwards and forwards. "Six and sixpence a week," with every leap forwards; "six and sixpence a week" as they receded. "Six and sixpence" with every shake and roar, and with each pulsing throb of the engine; and "six and sixpence a week" her little hands, already cut and bleeding, kept time with regular beat, as she lifted the stones and flung them aside. She was part of the refrain—a note in the fortissimo of industry. The engines roared and crashed and hissed to it. They beat the air regularly as the pistons rose and fell back and forth, thump, thud, hiss, groan, up and down, out and in: "Six and sixpence a week!"

Mysie tried to straighten herself, as Robert had advised, and immediately a pain shot through her back which seemed to snap it in two. The whole place seemed to be rushing round in a mad whirl, the roof of the shed coming down, and the floor rushing up, when with a stagger Mysie fell full length upon a "bing" of stones, bruising her cheek, and cutting her little hands worse than ever. This was what usually happened to all beginners at "pickin' sklits."

One of the women raised Mysie up, gave her a drink from a flask containing cold tea, and sat her aside to rest a short time.

"Just sit there a wee, my dochter," she said with rough kindness, "an' you'll soon be a' richt. They mostly a' feel that way when they first start on the scree."

Mysie was feeling sick, and already the thought was shaping in her mind that she would never be able to continue. She had only worked an hour as yet, but it seemed to her a whole day.

"Six and sixpence a week" sang the tables as they swung; "six and sixpence a week" whirred the engines; "six and sixpence a week" crashed the screes; and her head began to throb with the roar of it all. "Six and sixpence a week" as the coal tumbled down the chutes into the wagons; "six and sixpence" crunched the wheels, until it seemed as if everything about a pit were done to the tune of "six and sixpence a week."

It was thundered about her from one corner, it squealed at her from another, roared at her from behind, groaned at her in front; it wheezed from the roof, and the very shed in which they stood swayed and shivered to its monotonous song. "Six and sixpence a week" was working into every fiber of her being. She had been born to it, was living it, and it seemed that the very wheels of eternity were grinding out her destiny to its roar and its crash, and its terrible regular throb and swing.

She grew still more sick, and vomited; so one of the women took her by the hand and led her down the narrow rickety wooden stair out across the dirt "bing" into the pure air. In a quarter of an hour she brought her back almost well, except for the pain in her head.

"Where the hell hae ye been, Mag?" wheezed the old gaffer, addressing the woman with irritated authority.

"Awa' an' boil yer can, auld belly-crawler," was the elegant response, as she bent to her work, taking as little notice of him as if he were a piece of coal.

"Ye're awa' faur owre much," he returned. This was an allusion to clandestine meetings which were sometimes arranged between some of the men in authority—"penny gaffers," as they were called—and some of the girls who took their fancy.

After all, gaffers had certain powers of advancement, and could increase wages to those who found favor in their eyes, to the extent of a penny or twopence per day, and justified it by representing that these girls were value for it, because they were better workers. Again, matters were always easier to these girls of easy virtue, for they got better jobs, and could even flout the authority of lesser gaffers, if their relations with the higher ones were as indicated.

Mag replied with a coarse jest, and the others laughed roughly, and Mysie and Robert, not understanding, wondered why the old man got angry.

Thus the day wore on, men and women cursed while familiarities took place which were barely hidden from the children. Talk was coarse and obscenely suggestive, and the whole atmosphere was brutalizing. Long, however, before the day was ended, Robert and Mysie were feeling as if every bone in their little bodies would break.

"Just take anither wee rest, Mysie," said Robert. "I'll keep pickin' as hard as I can, an' ye'll no' be sae muckle missed."

"Oh, I'll hae to keep on, too," she replied, almost despairingly, with a hint of tears in her voice. "Ye mind I promised to work hard, an' ye said I was a guid worker, too. If I dinna' keep on I micht only get a shillin' a day."

"But I'll pick as much as the twa o' us can do," pursued Robert, with persuasive voice. "I'll gang harder, until ye can get a wee rest."

So Mysie, in sheer exhaustion, stopped for a little, and the dizzy feeling was soon gone again. Yet the horrible pain in the back troubled them all day, and the dizziness returned frequently, but the others assured them that they'd soon get used to it. Their hands were cut, bruised and dirty, and poor little Mysie felt often that she would like to cry, but "six and sixpence a week" kept time in her heart to all her troubles, and seemed to drive her onward with relentless force.

With rough kindness the women encouraged the two children, and did much to make their lot easier. But it was a trying day—a hard, heartbreaking day, a day of tears and pains and discouragement, a horrible Gethsemane of sweat and agony, whose memory not even "six and sixpence a week" would ever eradicate from their minds, though it made the day bearable.

The great wheels groaned and swished like the imprisoned monster of Robert's imaginings, and at last came to a halt at the end of the shift; but in the pattern which they had that day woven into the web of industry, there were two bright threads—threads of great beauty and high worth—threads which the very gods seemed proud of seeing there, twisted and twined, and lending color of richest hue to the whole design—threads of glorious fiber and rare quality, which sparkled and shone like the neck of a pigeon in the sunshine. These threads in the web of industry, which had shone that day for the first time, were the lives of two little children.

CHAPTER VIII
THE MANTLE OF MANHOOD

Months passed, and Robert still worked on the pithead. Much of the novelty had passed, and he was accustomed to the noise and clamor, though he never lost the feeling that he was working with, or, indeed, was part of, some giant monster, imprisoned and harnessed, it is true, but capable of titanic labors and fall of unexpectedness. It was ever-present, implacable and sinister, yet so long as its fetters held, easily controlled.

The warm weather had come, and the lure of the moors called to him at his work. Away out over there—somewhere—there were strange wonders awaiting him. He watched the trains, long, fast, and so inevitable-looking, rushing across the moor about a mile and a half from where he worked, and often, he thought that perhaps some day one of those flying monsters would bear him away from Lowwood across the moors into the Big City. What was a city like? And the sea? How big would it be? It was a staggering thought to imagine a stretch of water that ended on the sky-line—no land to be seen on the other side! What a wonderful world it must be!

But a touch of bitterness was creeping into his character, and for this his mother's teaching was responsible. Nellie was always jealous of the welfare of the working class, and was ever vigilant as to its interests. She did not know how matters could be rectified, but she did know that she and her like suffered unnecessarily.

"There's no reason," she would say, "for decent folk bein' in poverty. Look at the conditions that puir folk live in!"

"Hoot ay! Nellie, but we canna' help it," a neighbor would reply. "It's no' for us to be better."

"What way is it no'?" she would demand indignantly. "Do you think we couldna' be better folk if we had no poverty?"

"Ay, but the like o' us ken no better, an' it wadna' do if we had mair. We micht waste it," and the tone of resignation always maddened her to greater wrath.

"There's mair wasted on fancy fal-lals among the gentry than wad keep many a braw family goin'. Look at the hooses we live in; the gentry wadna' keep their dogs in them. The auld Earl has better stables for his horses than the hooses puir folk live in!"

"That's maybe a' richt, Nellie, but you maun mind that we're no' gentry. We havena' been brocht up to anything else. Somebody has got to work, an' we canna' help it," and the fatalistic resignation but added fuel to her anger.

"Ay, we could help it fine, if we'd only try it. It's no' richt that folk should hae to slave a' their days, an' be always in hardships, while ither folk who work nane hae the best o' everything. I want a decent hoose to live in; I want to see my man hae some leisure, an' my weans hae a chance in life for something better than just work and trouble," and her voice quivering with anger at the wrongs inflicted upon her, she would rattle away on her favorite topic.

"There you go again. You are aye herp, herpin' at the big folk, or aboot the union. I wonder you never turn tired, woman," the reply would come, for sometimes these women were unable to understand her at all.

"I'll never turn tired o' that," she would reply. "If only the men wad keep thegither an' no' be divided, they'd soon let the big folk see wha' was the maist importance to the country. Do you think onybody ever made a lot o' money by their ain work? My man an' your man hae wrocht hard a' their days. They've never wasted ony o' their hard-earned money, an' yet they hae naething."

"No, because it takes it a' to keep us," would be the reply, as if that were a conclusive answer, difficult to counter.

"Well, how do ye think other folk mak' a fortune? Do ye think they work harder than your man does? No! It's because our men work so hard that other folk get it aff their labor. Do they live a better life than your man or mine? They waste mair in yae day, whiles, than wad keep your family or mine for a whole year. Is it because they are honester than us? No. You ken fine your man or yoursel' wadna' hae the name o' stealin'. But they steal every day o' their lives, only they ca' it business. That's the difference. It's business wi' them, but it wad be dishonest on oor pairt. Awa', woman! It's disgraceful to think aboot. Naebody should eat wha disna work, an' I dinna care wha hears me say it," and the flashing eyes and the indignant voice gave token of her righteous wrath.

"That's a' richt, Nellie, but it has aye been, an' I doot it'll aye be. We just canna help it," would come the reply.

"I tell you it's everybody's duty to work for better times. We've no richt to allow the things that gang on. There's nae guid in poverty and disease an' ill-health, an' we should a' try to change it; and we could if only you'd get some sense into your held, an' no' stand and speak as if you felt that God meant it."

"Ay, Nellie, that's a' richt, but it's the Lord's will, an' we maun put up wi' it."

At this juncture Mrs. Sinclair's patience would become exhausted, and she would flare up, while the neighbor would suddenly break off the discussion and go off home.

Her children were taught that it was a disgrace not to resent a wrong, and Robert, though only a boy, was always sturdily standing up against the things he considered wrong at the pit-head.

Robert dreamed and built his future castles. There was great work ahead to do. He never mentioned his longings and visions to anyone, yet Mysie's sweet, shy face was creeping into them always, and already he was conscious of something in her that thrilled him. He was awkward, and his speech did not come readily, in her presence. Whole days he dreamed, only waking up to find it was "knocking-off" time. There was an hour's break in the middle of the day, and then he wandered out on the moor. Its silence soothed him, and he would lie and dream among the rough yellow grass and the hard tough heather, bathing his soul in the brooding quietness of it all.

He was now twelve years of age, and longing to get at work down the pit. It was for him the advent of manhood, and represented the beginning of his real work.

One night in the late summer, after the pit had knocked off and the "day-shift" was returning home, he and Mysie were walking as usual behind the women. He had meant to tell her the great news all day, but somehow she was so different now, and besides a man should always keep something to himself as long as possible. It showed strength, he thought.

"I'm goin' doon the pit the morn, Mysie," he said, now that he had come to the point of telling her, and speaking as casually as he could.

"Oh, are you?" said Mysie, and stopped, disappointingly, and remained silent.

"Ay. I'm twelve now, you ken, an' I can get into the pit," feeling a bit nettled that she was silent in the face of such a happening.

"Oh!" and again Mysie stopped.

"My faither has got a place a week syne that'll fit John an' him an' me. The three o' us are a' goin' to work thegither. If he could have gotten yin sooner, I'd hae been doon a month syne. But he's aye been waitin' to get a place that wad suit us a'," he said, volunteering this information to see if it would loosen her tongue to express the regret he wanted her to speak.

But again Mysie did not answer. She only hung her head and did not look up with any interest in his news.

"It's aboot time I was in the pit now, ye ken. You used to get doon the pit at ten. My faither was in it when he was nine, but you're no' allowed to gang doon now till you are twelve year auld. I'm going to draw aff my faither and John," and he was feeling more and more exasperated at her continued silence.

Yet still Mysie did not speak, and merely nodded to this further enlightenment.

"I've never telt onybody except yoursel'," he said, hurt at her seeming want of interest, and feeling that what he was going to say was less manly than he intended it to be. Indeed he was aware that it was decidedly childish of him to say it, but, like many wiser and older, he could not keep his dignity, and took pleasure in hurting her; for there is a pleasure sometimes in hurting a loved one, because they are loved, and will not speak the things one wants them to say, which if said might add to one's vanity and sense of importance. "So ye'll just be by yoursel' the morn, unless they put Dicky Tamson owre aside you," he added viciously.

"I dinna want Dicky Tamson aside me," she said with some heat, and a hint of anxiety in her voice, which pleased him a little. "He's an impudent thing," and again she relapsed into silence, just when he thought his pleasure was going to be complete.

"Oh, they'll maybe put Aggie Lowrieson on your side o' the table," he volunteered, glad that at last she had shown some feeling.

"They can keep Aggie Lowrieson too," she said shortly. "I dinna' want her. I'll get on fine mysel'," and she said no more.

He talked of his new venture all the way home, and he felt more and more hurt because she did not reply as eagerly and volubly as he wished.

"It'll be great goin' doon the pit," he said, again feeling that he was going to be priggish. "Pickin' stanes is a' guid enough for a laddie for a wee while, an' for women, but you're the better to gang into the pit when you're the age. You get mair money for it. Of course, it's hard work, but I'll be earnin' as much as twa shillin's a day in the pit, and that'll be twelve shillin's a week."

But Mysie could not be drawn to look at his rosy prospects, and still kept silent, so that the last few hundred yards were covered in silence. At the end of the row where they always parted, he could not resist adding a thrust to his usual "good-night."

"Guid nicht then, Mysie. I thocht may be ye'd be vexed, seem' that Dickie Tamson can torment you as muckle as he likes now." And so he went home feeling that Mysie didn't care much.

But Mysie had a sore heart that night. She knew only too well that Dick Tamson would torment her, and would be egged on by the other women to kiss and tease her, and they would laugh at it all. Robert had always been her champion, and kept Dick, who was a mischievous boy, at a distance. She was sorry that Robert was going down the pit, and it seemed to her that she'd rather go to service now. The harsh clamor and the dirty disagreeable work were bearable before, but it would not be the same with Robert away. She knew that she would miss him very much. She thought long of it when she lay down in her bed that night. He had no right to think that she was not vexed, and she cried quietly beneath the blankets.

"Here's Mysie greetin'," cried her little brother, who lay beside her. "Mither, Mysie's greetin'."

"What's wrang wi' her?" called the mother anxiously from the other bed.

"I dinna' ken," answered the boy, "she'll no' tell me."

"What is't that's wrang with you, Mysie?" again called the mother more sharply.

"I've a sore tooth," she answered, glad to get any excuse, and lying with promptitude.

"Well, hap the blankets owre your head," the mother advised, "and it'll soon be better. Dinna' greet, like a woman."

But Mysie still continued to cry softly, choking back the sobs, and keeping her face to the wall, so as not to disturb the other sleeper beside her—cried for a long hour, until exhaustion overcame her, and at last she fell asleep, her last thought being that Robert had no right to misjudge her so.

Robert, on the other hand, as is the prerogative of the man, soon forgot all about his disappointment at Mysie's seeming want of interest in his affairs, and was busy with his preparations for the next day.

He had a lamp to buy, for Lowwood was an open-light pit, and was soon busy on the instructions of his father learning the art of "putting in a wick" to the exact thickness, testing his tea flask, and doing all the little things that count in preparing for the first descent into a coal mine. He was very much excited over it all, and babbled all the evening, asking questions regarding the work he would be called upon to do, and generally boring his father with his talk.

But his father understood it all, and was patient with him, answering his enquiries and advising him on many things, until latterly he pleaded for a "wink o' peace," and told the boy "for any sake" to be quiet.

Geordie Sinclair knew that this enthusiasm would soon evaporate. Only too well he knew the stages of disappointment which the boy would experience, and for this reason he was kindly with him.

He was now looking forward with better prospects. Robert was the second boy now started, and already matters were somewhat easier; but he shuddered to think of the lot of the man who was battling away unaided, with four or five children to support, and depending on a meager three and sixpence or four shillings of a daily wage to keep the house together. For himself the prospect was now better, and in looking back he realized what a terrible time it had been—especially for his wife; for hers was the more difficult task in laying out the scanty wages he earned.

It never had seemed to strike him with such force before, even when matters were at their worst, what it had meant to her; and as he looked at her, sitting knitting at the opposite side of the fire, he was filled with compassion for her, and a new beauty seemed to be upon her lined face, and in the firm set of her mouth.

Thus he sat reviewing all the terrible struggle, when she had slaved to keep him and the children, during the time he was injured, and a pang shot through, as the conviction came to him, that perhaps he had not been as helpful as he might have been to her, when a little praise even might have made it easier for her.

Impulsively he rose to his feet and crossed to where she sat, taking her in his arms and kissing her.

"Losh, Geordie, what's wrong with you!" she enquired, looking up with a pleased sparkle in her eyes, for he was usually very undemonstrative.

"Oh, just this, Nellie," he said with embarrassment in every feature of his face, "I've been thinking over things, and I feel that I havena' given you encouragement as I should have done, for all that you have done for me and the bairns."

"You fair took my breath away," said Nellie with a pleased little laugh; then, as she looked at his glowing face, something came into her throat, and the tears started.

"There now, lassie," he said, again gathering her into his arms, and kissing her tenderly, "it's all past now, my lass, and you'll get it easier from this time forth. God knows, Nellie, you are worth all that I can ever do for you to help," and the happy tears fell from her eyes, as she patted his rough, hairy cheek, and fondled him again, as she had done in their courting days.

"I'll wash the floor for you, lass," he said impulsively, almost beside himself with happiness, as he realized that this little act of his had made them both so happy. "You've been in the washing tub all day, and I ken you'll be scrubbin' on the floor first thing in the morning, as soon as we are away to the pit. But I'll do it for you the nicht. The bairns are all in bed, and I'll no' be long. You sit an' tak' a rest," and he was off for the pail and a scrubbing brush, and was back at the fireside pouring water from the kettle before his wife realized it.

"Oh, never mind, Geordie," she said remonstratingly, "I'll do it myself in the morning. You've had your own work to do in the pit, an' you need all the rest you can get."

"No," he said decisively. "You sit doon, lass. I'll no' be lang. Just you sing a bit sang to me, just as you used to sing, Nellie, an' I'll wash out the floor," and he was soon on his knees, scrubbing away as if it were a daily occurrence with him. And Nellie, pleased and happy beyond expression, sat in the big chair by the fireside and sang his favorite ballad, "Kirkconnel Lea."

> Oh, that I were where Helen lies,
> For nicht and day on me she cries,
> Oh, that I were where Helen lies
> On fair Kirkconnel Lea.
>
> Oh, Helen fair, beyond compare,
> I'll mak' a garland o' your hair
> Shall bind my heart for evermair
> Until the day I dee.

And Nellie Sinclair never in all her life sang that song so well as she did that night; and she never sang it again. Robert, who was lying in the room, heard her glorious voice, and marveled at the complete mastery she showed over the plaintive old tune. It was as if her very soul reveled in it, as the notes rose and fell; and it stirred the boy into tremendous emotional excitement, as the tragedy was unfolded in the beautiful words and the sadness of the old tune.

It was a memorable night of quiet happiness for all, and there was so much of tragedy lying behind it unseen and unknown. But so often are the sweetest moments of life followed by its sadness and its sorrow.

CHAPTER IX
THE ACCIDENT

Next morning at five o'clock Robert leapt from his bed, full of importance at the prospect of going down the pit. Stripping off his sleeping shirt, he chattered as he donned the pit clothes. The blue plaid working-shirt which his mother had bought for him felt rough to his tender skin, but unpleasant as it was, he donned it with a sense of bigness. Then the rough moleskin trousers were put on and fastened with a belt round the waist, and a pair of leg-strings at the knees. The bundles of clothes, separately arranged the night before, had got mixed somewhat in Robert's eagerness to dress, with the result that when his brother John rose, with eyes half shut, and reached for his stockings, he found those of Robert instead lying upon his bundle.

"Gie's my socks," he ordered grumpily, flinging Robert's socks into the far corner of the kitchen. "You've on the wrong drawers too. Can ye no' look what you're doin'?" and the drawers followed the socks, while Robert looked at his mother with eyes of wonderment.

"Tak' aff his socks, Rob," she said, "he's a thrawn, ill-natured cat, that, in the mornin'."

"Well, he should look what he's doin' an' no' put on other folk's claes," and immediately the others burst out laughing, for this advocate of "watchin' what he was doin'" had in his half sleepy condition failed to see that he had lifted his jacket and had rammed his leg down the sleeve in his hurry and anger.

"Noo, that'll do," said Geordie, as John flung the jacket at Robert, because he laughed. "That'll do noo, or I'll come alang yer jaw," and thus admonished John was at once silent.

Robert soon had his toilet completed, however, even to the old cap on his head, upon which sat the little oil-lamp, which he handled and cleaned and wiped with his fingers to keep it bright and shiny, whilst all the time he kept chattering.

"For ony sake, laddie, hand your tongue," said Geordie at last, as he drew in his chair to the table to start upon the frugal breakfast of bread and butter and tea. "Your tongue's never lain since you got up."

Robert, thereupon, sat down in silence at the table, though there were a hundred different things he wanted to ask about the pit. He could not understand why everyone felt and looked so sleepy, nor divine the cause of the irritable look upon each face, which in the dim light of the paraffin lamp gave a forbidding atmosphere to the home at this time of the day.

At last, however, the meal was over, and when Geordie had lit his pit lamp and stuck his pipe in his mouth, all three started off with a curt "Good morning" to Mrs. Sinclair, who looked after her boys with a smile which chased away the previous irritability from her face.

Arrived at the pit-head, they found a number of miners there squatting on their "hunkers," waiting the time for descending the shaft. As each newcomer came forward, the man who arrived immediately before him called out: "I'm last." By this means — "crying the benns," — as it was called — the order of descent was regulated on the principle of "First come, first served." Much chaffing was leveled at little Robert by some of the younger men regarding his work and the things which would have to be done by and to him that day.

At last came the all important moment, and Robert, his father and two men stepped on to the cage. After the signal was given, it seemed to the boy as if heaven and earth were passing away in the sudden sheer drop, as the cage plunged down into the yawning hole, out of which came evil smells and shadows cast from the flickering lamps upon the heads of the miners. The rattling of the cage sent a shiver of fear through Robert, and with that first sudden plunge he felt as if his heart were going to leap out of his mouth. But by the time he reached the "bottom," he had consoled and encouraged himself with the thought that these things were all in the first day's experience of all miners.

That morning Robert Sinclair was initiated into the art of "drawing" by his brother John. The road was fairly level, to push the loaded "tubs," thus leaving his father to be helped with the pick at the coal "face." After an hour or two, Robert, though getting fairly well acquainted with the work, was feeling tired. The strange damp smell, which had greeted his nostrils when the cage began to descend with him that morning, was still strong, though not so overpowering as it had been at first. The subtle shifting shadows cast from his little lamp were becoming familiar, and his nervousness was not now so pronounced, though he was still easily startled if anything unusual took place. The sound of the first shot in the pit nearly frightened him out of his wits, and he listened nervously to every dull report with a strange uneasiness. About one o'clock his father called to him.

"Dinna tak' that hutch oot the noo, Robert. Just let it staun', an' sit doon an' tak' yir piece. Ye'll be hungry, an' John an' me will be out the noo if we had this shot stemmed."

"A' richt," cheerfully replied the boy, withdrawing down to the end of the road, where his clothes hung upon a tree, and taking his bread from one of his pockets, he sat down tired and hungry to await his father and John.

Geordie's "place" was being worked over the old workings of another mine which had exhausted most of the coal of a lower seam many years previously, except for the "stoops" or pillars, which had been left in. This was supposed to be the barrier beyond which Rundell's lease did not go. It would be too dangerous to work the upper seam with the ground hollow underneath, so the "places" had all been stopped as they came up, with the exception of Geordie Sinclair's. Sinclair was puzzled at this, and he often wondered why his place had not been stopped with the others. He was more uneasy, too, when he began to find large cracks or fissures in the metals, and spoke of this to Andrew Marshall a few nights before; but he did not like to seem to make too much of it, and the matter was passed over, till the day before, when Walker visited the place for a few minutes, when Geordie accosted him.

"What way is my place going on?" he asked, and was told that it was a corner in the barrier, which extended for one hundred yards and must go on for that distance, and that there was really no danger, as the ground below was solid.

So, busily working away, and finding still more rents in the floor and roof, Sinclair thought it must just be as he had seen it in other places of a like kind, the weight of the upper metals which were breaking over the solid ground by reason of the hollow beneath between the stoops, though in this case it did not amount to much as yet.

The coal was easy to get; he had one boy "forrit to the pick," with Robert as "drawer," and his prospects seemed good, he thought, as he was busily preparing a shot, ramming in the powder, and "stemming" up the hole. He was busy ramming the powder in the prepared hole, while the elder boy prepared clay, with which to stem or seal it up after the powder had been pressed back, leaving only the fuse protruding.

"Here's a tree cracking," said the boy, drawing his father's attention to a breaking prop; but as this is a common occurrence in all mines where there is extra weight after development, Geordie thought nothing of it at the time, intending merely, before he lighted his shot, to put in a fresh prop.

"Bring in another prop, sonny," he said to the boy, "and I'll put it in when I have stemmed this hole," and the boy turned to obey his order.

But suddenly a low crackling sound, caused by the breaking of more props, was heard, then a roar and a crash as of thunder, followed by a long rumbling noise, which left not a moment for the two trapped human beings to stir even a limb or utter a cry. The immensity of the fall created a wind, which put out little Robert's lamp; the great rumbling noise filled him with a dreadful fear, and he sprang involuntarily to his feet.

"Faither! Faither!" he called, terror in his voice and anxiety in his little heart, but there was no reassuring answer. He felt his breathing getting difficult; the air was thick with dust and heavy with the smell of rotting wood and damp decaying matter.

"Faither! Faither!" he called again louder in his agony, darting forward, thinking to go to their assistance, and knocking his head against a boulder.

"John! Faither! I'm feart," and he began to cry. Afraid to move, unable to see, he staggered from one side to another, bruising his face and arms against the jagged sides, the blood already streaming from his bruises, and his heart frantic with fear.

"Oh, faither! faither! Where are ye?" and he began to crawl up the incline, in desperate fear, while still the rumbling and crashing went on in long rolling thunder. "Oh! oh!" he moaned, now almost mad with terror. "Faither! John! Where are ye! Oh! oh!" and he fell back stunned by striking his head against a low part of the roof.

Again he scrambled to his feet, certain now that some disaster had happened, since there was no response to his appeals, and again he was knocked to the ground by striking his head against the side of the roadway. But always he rose again, frantically dashing from side to side, as a caged lark, when first caught, dashes itself against the bars of its prison; until finally, stunned beyond recovery, he lay in a semi-conscious condition, helpless and inert, his bruises smarting but unfelt, and the blood oozing from his nose and mouth.

Andrew Marshall, working about fifty yards away, heard the roar and the crash, and the boy's cries, and at once ran to Geordie's place. In his haste and anxiety he nearly stumbled over the prostrate boy, who lay unconscious in the roadway.

"Good God! What has happened?" he exclaimed, anxiously bending over the boy and raising him up, then dashing some cold tea from Robert's flask upon him, and forcing some between his lips. Then, when the boy showed signs of recovery, he plied him with anxious questions.

"Where's yir faither? What's wrang?" But the boy only clung to him in wild terror, and nothing connected could be got from him.

Andrew lighted the boy's lamp and tore up the brae, leaving Robert shrieking in nervous fright.

"Great Christ! It has fa'en in!" he cried, when he had got as far as he could go. "Geordie! Geordie! Are ye in there?" and as no answer came, he began tearing at the great blocks of stone, flinging them like pebbles in his desperation, until another warning rumble drove him back. Immediately he realized how helpless he was alone, so he went back to the boy and hurried him down the brae and out to where some other men were at work. A few hasty words, and Robert was passed on, and Andrew went back with the men, only to find how hopeless it all was; for occasionally huge falls continued to come away, and it seemed useless to attempt anything till more help was procured.

Andrew hurried off to the bottom and overtook Robert, sending back others to help, and he ascended the shaft and was off to break the news to Mrs. Sinclair; after which he returned to the pit, determined to get out all that remained of Geordie and the boy John.

CHAPTER X
HEROES OF THE UNDERWORLD

Matters were now much easier and more comfortable for Geordie Sinclair and his wife. They had long since added another apartment to their house, and the "room" was the special pride of Nellie, who was gradually "getting a bit thing for it" just as her means permitted. They had two beds in each apartment, and the room was furnished. Mrs. Sinclair had long set her mind upon a "chest of drawers," and now that that particular piece of furniture stood proudly in her room, much of her day was given to polishing it and the half-dozen stuffed bottomed chairs, which were the envy of every housewife in the village. A large oval mirror stood upon the top of the drawers, and was draped with a piece of cheap curtain cloth, bleached to the whiteness of new fallen snow.

This mirror was a much-prized possession, for no other like it had ever been known in the village. The floor was covered with oilcloth, and a sheepskin rug lay upon the hearthstone, while white starched curtains draped the window. The getting of the waxcloth had been a wonderful event, and dozens of women had come from all over the village to stand in gaping admiration of its beauty. This was always where Mrs. Sinclair felt a thrill of great pride.

"Ye see," she would explain, "it's awfu' easy to wash, and a bit wipe owre wi' soap an' watter is a' it needs."

"My, how weel aff ye are!" one woman would exclaim, "I'm telt that ye maunna use a scrubbin' brush on't, or the pattern will rub off."

"Oh, ay," Nellie would laugh with a hint of superior wisdom in it. "Ye'll soon waste it gin ye took a scrubber to it. An' ye maunna use owre hot water to it either," she would add.

"Oh my!" would come in genuine surprise. "Do you tell me that. Eh, but you're the weel-aff woman now, to hae a room like that, an' rale waxcloth on the floor!"

"I thocht it was a fine, cheerie bit thing," Nellie would say. "It mak's the hoose ever so much mair heartsome."

"So it is," would come the reply. "It's a fine, but cheerie thing. You're a rale weel-aff woman, I can tell ye," and the woman would go home to dream of one day having a room like Mrs. Sinclair's, and to tell her neighbors of the great "grandeur" that the Sinclair's possessed, whilst Nellie would set to, and rub and polish those drawers and that mirror, and the stuff-bottomed chairs till they shone like the sun upon a moorland tarn, and she herself felt like dropping from sheer exhaustion.

She even took to telling the neighbors sometimes, when they came on those visits that "working folk should a' hae coal-houses, for coal kept ablow the beds makes an awfu' mess o' the ticks."

"Oh, weel," would be the reply, made with the usual sigh of resignation, "I hae had a house a gey lang while now, an' I dinna think I've ever wanted ony sic newfangled things as that."

"That's what's wrang," Mrs. Sinclair would reply. "We dinna want them. If we did, we'd soon get them. What way would the gentry hae a' thae things, an' us hae nane?"

"That's a' richt, Nellie," would be the reply. "We wadna ken what to do wi' what the gentry has got. They're rich an' can afford it, an' forby they need them an' we don't. I think I'm fine as I am."

"Fine as ye are!" with bitter scorn in her tones. "Ye'll never be fine wi' a mind like that."

"Wheesht, woman Nellie! You're no feart. Dinna talk like that. We micht a' be strucken doon dead!"

This usually ended the discussion, for Scots people generally—and the workers especially—are always on very intimate terms with the Deity, and know the pains and penalties of too intimate allusions to His power.

Yet, with all her discontent, Mrs. Sinclair found life very much easier than it had been, for now that she had some of the boys started to work, she had made her house "respectable," and added many little comforts, besides having a "bit pound or twa lyin' in the store." So she looked ahead with more hope and a more serene heart. Her children were well-fed and clothed, and the old days of hunger and struggling were over, she thought. Geordie was now taking a day off in the middle of the week to rest, as there was no need for him to slave and toil every day as he had done in the past. After all it would only be a very few years till he would no longer be able to work at all.

Rosy looked the future then, as Mrs. Sinclair, on the day on which young Robert went down the pit, showed off her room "grandeur" to an admiring neighbor.

"My, what braw paper ye hae, Nellie. Wha put it on for ye? Was it yirsel'?" asked the visitor with breath bated in admiration.

"Ay, it was that. I just got the chance o' the bargain, an' I thocht I'd tak' it," she replied, with subdued pride.

"Oh, my! it's awful braw, an' sae weel matched too! I never saw anything sae well done. You're rale weel-off, do ye ken."

"My God! What's wrang?" cried Nellie suddenly, gazing from the window with blanched cheeks.

"I doot there's been an accident. I heard the bell gang for men three tows a' rinnin', an' I see a lot o' men comin' up the brae. I doot the pit's lowsed."

Both of them hurried to the door, and found that already a crowd of women had flocked to the end of the row, and were standing waiting anxiously on the men, in order to learn what had happened. They did not talk, but gazed down the hill, each heart anxious to know if the unfortunate one belonged to her. The sickening fear which grips the heart of every miner's wife, when she sees that procession from the pit before the proper quitting hour, lay heavy upon each one. The white drawn faces, the set firm lips, and the deep troubled breathing told how much the women were moved.

Wives and mothers, sweethearts and sisters, oh, what a hell of torture they suffered in those few tense moments whilst waiting for the news, which, though to a great extent it may relieve many, must break at least one heart. No man, having once seen this, ever wants to witness it again. Concentrated hell and torture with every moment, stabbing and pulling at each heart and then—then the sad, mournful face of Andrew Marshall as he steps forward slowly past Mag Robertson, past Jean Fleming, past Jenny Maitland, past them all, and at last putting a kindly hand on the shoulder of Nellie Sinclair, he says, with a catch in his voice that would break a heart of granite: "Come awa' hame, Nellie. Come awa' hame. Ye'll need to bear up."

Then it is whispered round: "It's Geordie Sinclair killed wi' a fa'." And hope has died, and dreams have fled, and the world will never again look bonnie and fresh and sweet and full of happiness, nor the blood dance so joyously, nor the eyes ever again sparkle with the same soft loving glance.

No more happy evenings, such as the night before had been, when the glamor and romance of courtship days had come back, and they had found a new beauty of love and the glory of life, in the easier circumstances and rosy hopes ahead.

Misery and suffering, and the long keen pain, the sad cheerless prospect, and over all the empty life and the broken heart.

Lowwood was plunged into gloom when the news of the accident was known, and every heart went out in sympathy to Nellie Sinclair and her young family. It was indeed a terrible blow to lose at one and the same time her husband and her eldest boy.

It was two days later, and the bodies had not yet been recovered. Men toiled night and day, working as only miners fighting for life can work, risking life among the continually falling débris to recover all that remained of their comrades.

"It couldna ha'e been worse," said Jenny Maitland sorrowfully to her next door neighbor. "It's an awfu' blow."

"Ay," rejoined her neighbor, applying the corner of her apron to her eyes. "It mak's it worse them no' bein' gotten yet. I think I'd gae wrang in the mind if that happened to our yin," and then, completely overcome, she sat down on the doorstep and sobbed in real sorrow.

"I suppose it's an awfu' big fall. He had been workin' on the top o' some auld workin's, an' I suppose they wadna ken, an' it fell in. It maun hae been an awfu' trial for wee Rob, poor wee man. His first day in the pit, an' his father an' brither killed afore his een!"

"Hoo has Nellie taken it, Jenny?" enquired the neighbor, after a little, when her sobs had subsided.

"Ye'd break yir heart if ye could see her," replied Jenny sorrowfully. "I gaed owre when oor yin gaed out wi' the pieces—he cam' hame at fower o'clock to get mair pieces, for they're goin' to work on to ten the nicht—an' I never saw onything sae sad-lookin' as her face. She has never cried the least thing yet. Never a tear has come frae her, but she'd be better if she could greet."

"Do ye tell me that! Puir Nellie! It's an awfu' hand fu' she is left wi', too," commented the neighbor.

"Ay, she jist looks at ye sae sad-like wi' her big black een; never a word nor a tear, but just stares, an' she's that thin an' white lookin'. I look for her breakin' doon a'thegither, an' when she does I wadna like to see her. The bits o' weans gang aboot the hoose wonderin' at her, and she looks to them too, but ye'd think she'd nae interest in onything. She jist looks out o' the window an' doon the brae to the pit. It's awesome to look at her."

"Oh, puir body!" and again the kindly neighbor was overcome, and Jenny joined her tears too in silent sympathy.

"The minister was owre last nicht," said Jenny after a little, "but I dinna think she ever spoke to him. He cam' in just when I was comin' oot, an' I dinna like to leave her. He talked away a wee while an' then put up a prayer; but there was nae consolation in't for onybody. I think the sicht o' her face maun hae been too muckle for him. He didna stay very lang, and gaed awa' saying he'd come back again. Nellie has everything ready—the bed a' made, wi' clean sheets an' blankets on them—an' there she stan's always at that window, lookin' doon the brae. It would break yer heart to see her, Leezie, she's that vexed lookin'." So they wept and sorrowed together.

Down in the pit, Andrew Marshall, Matthew Maitland, Peter Pegg, and a number of others toiled like giants possessed. Their naked bodies streamed with sweat and glistened in the light of their lamps. Timber was placed in position, and driven tight with desperation in every blow from their hammers; blocks of rock were tossed aside, and smashed into fragments, ere being filled into the tubs which were ever waiting ready to convey the débris to the pit-head. Few words were spoken, except when a warning shout was given, when some loose rubble poured down from the great gaping cavern in the roof, and then men jumped and sprang to safety with the agility of desperation, to wait till the rumbling had ceased, only to leap back again into the yawning hell, tearing at the stones, and trying to work their way into the place where they knew Geordie and the boy were lying. It seemed impossible that human efforts would ever be able to clear that mountain away.

"Wait a minute, callans," said Andrew, almost dropping with exhaustion, and drawing his hands across his eyes to wipe the sweat from them, whilst he "hunkered" down, his back against a broken tree which stood jutting out from the building, supporting a broken "baton" (cross-tree), which bent down in the center, making the roadway low and unsafe. "Let us tak a minute's thocht, and see if we can get a way o' chokin' up that stuff fear fallin' doon. We'll never get it redd up goin' like this."

So they sat down, tired but still desperate, to listen to each one suggesting a way of stopping the débris from continuing to fall. Baffled and at their wits' end, they could think of nothing.

At last in came a number of other men to relieve them—men equally anxious and desperate as they, burning with the desire to get to grips with this calamity which had come upon two of their comrades.

"I'm no' goin' hame," said Andrew decisively, "till I see Geordie out." He was almost dropping with exhaustion, but he could not think of leaving his dead friend in there. So at last it was agreed that he should stay, and at least give the benefit of his advice. The others, more tired than ever they had been before in all their experience of the mines, where hard work is the rule, trudged wearily home, to be met by the waiting groups of women and children, who at all times stood at the corners of the village eagerly asking for news, "If they'd been gotten yet."

After a few minutes' deliberation a plan was decided on by Andrew and his comrades of trying to choke up the hole in the roof with timber, and the work went on desperately, silently, heroically. Time and again their efforts were baffled by new falls, but always the same persistent eager spirit drove them back to their toil. So they worked, risking and daring things of which no man who never saw a like calamity has any conception, and which would have appalled themselves at any other time.

"Look out, boys," called Tam Donaldson, springing back to the road as the warning noise again began, and great masses of rock came hurtling down, filling the place with dust and noise.

A cry of pain and horror broke upon them as they ran, and brought them back while the crumbling mass was still falling.

"Great God! It's wee Jamie Allan," roared one man above the din. "He's catched by the leg! Here, boys, hurry up! Try an' get this block broken afore ony mair comes doon. God Almichty! Are we a' goin' to be buried thegither? This bit, boys! Quick!" And they tore at the great masses of stone, the sweat streaming from every pore of their bodies, cursing their impotence as they smashed with big hammers the rock which lay upon Jamie's leg.

"Mind yersel's, laddies!" warned Jamie, as again the trickling noise began, heralding another fall. "Leave me, for God's sake, an' get back!" But not one heeded. Desperate and strong with the strength of giants, they toiled on, the sight of suffering so manifest in Jamie's eyes, as he strove not to cry out, spurring them onward.

"Ye'll never lift that bit, Tam," said Jamie, as four of them tore at the block which lay upon his leg. "It's faur too big. Take an ax an' hack the leg off. I doot it'll be wasted anyway. Oh, dear! Oh, dear!" And unable longer to endure the pain, he roared aloud in agony, and tore at the stone himself with his fingers, like an imprisoned beast in a trap.

"Here, boys, quick!" cried Andrew, getting his long pinch in below the stone, upon a fine leverage. "Put yir weight on this, Tam, an' Jock an' Sanny'll try an' pull Jamie out. Hurry up, for she's working for anither collapse. A'thegither!" and so they tugged and tore, and strained and pulled, while the roars of the imprisoned man were deafening.

"A'thegither again, laddies!" encouraged Andrew. "This time!" and with a tremendous effort the stone gave way, and Jamie was pulled clear, his leg a crushed mass of pulpy blood and shattered bones. They dragged him back clear of any further falls, and improvised a stretcher on which to carry home his now unconscious body.

"That was a hell o' a narrow shave," quietly observed Tam Donaldson, as they panted together, and tried to collect themselves. "His leg's wasted, I doot, an' will need to come off." When they had their stretcher ready, the wounded man was tenderly placed upon it, carefully covered up with the jackets of the others; whilst half-a-dozen of them carried him to the pit bottom, and finally bore him home, where the doctor was ready waiting to attend to him.

Andrew and a few others worked away, and at last managed to get the running sore in the roof choked up with long bars of timber, and even though it continued to rumble away above them, the heavy blocks of wood held, and so allowed them to work away in comparative safety.

Peter Pegg and Matthew Maitland returned at six o'clock next morning, bringing with them another band of workers to relieve those who had worked all night, but still Andrew Marshall would not leave the scene of the disaster. He worked and rested by turns, advising and guiding the younger men, who never spared themselves. They performed mighty epics of work down there in the darkness amid the rumbling, falling roof. It was a great task they were set, but they never shirked the consequences. They never turned back. Risks were taken and accepted without a thought; tasks were eagerly jumped to, and the whole job accepted as if it were just what ordinarily they were asked to do.

Crash went the hammers; thump went the great blocks of material into the tubs, and the men quietly got away the tubs as they were filled. Night and day the great work went on, never ceasing, persistent, relentless. If one man dropped out a minute to breathe and rest when exhausted, another sprang into his place, and toiled and strove like an engine.

There was something great and inspiring even to look on at those mighty efforts—something exhilarating and elevating in the play of muscles like great long shooting serpents under the glistening skins of the men. Arms shot out, tugged and tore, jerked and wrenched, then doubled up and the muscles became knots, bulging out as if they would break through the skin, as the great blocks were lifted; and then the blocks were cast into the tub, the knots untied themselves, and slipped elastically back into their places, and the serpents were momentarily at rest until the body bent again to another block. Out and in they flew, supple and silent, quick as lightning playing in the heavens; they zig-zagged and shot this way and that, tying and untying themselves, darting out and doubling back, advancing and retiring in rhythmic action, graceful and easy, powerful and inevitable.

Bending and rising, the swaying bodies gleamed and glistened with greasy dust and sweat, catching the gleams from the lamps and reflecting them in every streaming pore. Straining and tearing, the muscles, at every slightest wish, seemed to exude energy and health, glowing strength and power.

It was all so natural and apparently easy—an epic in moleskin and human flesh, with only the little glimmer of oil-lamps, which darted from side to side in a mad mazurka of toil, crossing and recrossing, swinging and halting, the flames flattening out with every heave of their owners' bodies, then abruptly being brought to the steady again. Looked at from the road-foot, it was like a carnival of fireflies engaged in trying how quickly they could dart from side to side, and cross each other's path, without coming into collision.

Who shall sing in lyrical language the exhilaration of such splendid men's work? Who shall catch that glow of strength and health, and work it into deathless song? The ring of the hammers on the stone, the dull regular thud upon the timber, the crash of breaking rock, and the strong, warm-blooded, generous-hearted men; the passionate glowing bodies, and above all, the great big heroic souls, fighting, working, striving in a hell of hunger and death, toiling till one felt they were gods instead of humans—gods of succor and power, gods of helpfulness and strength.

So the work went on hour after hour, and now their efforts were beginning to tell. No more came the rumbling, treacherous falls; but perceptibly, irresistibly was the passage gradually cleared, and the way opened up, until it seemed as if these men were literally eating their way into that rock-filled passage.

"Can ye tell me where Black Jock is a' this time?" enquired Andrew, as Peter and Matthew and he sat back the road, resting while the others worked. "Rundell has been here twa or three times, for hours at a time, but I hae never seen Walker yet."

"I hae never seen him either, an' I was hearin' that he was badly," returned Peter, and his big eye seemed to turn as if it were looking for and expecting some one to slip up behind him.

"Ay," broke in Matthew, "badly! I wadna say, but it micht be that he's badly; but maybe he's not."

"Do ye ken, boys," said Andrew quietly, taking his pipe out of his mouth, and speaking with slow deliberation, "I'm beginnin' to think Black Jock is guilty o' Geordie's death. Geordie, as we a' ken, had ay something against Walker. There was something he kent aboot the black brute that lately kept him gey quiet; for, if ye noticed, whenever Geordie went to him about anybody's complaint, the men aye won. I ken Walker hated him, an' I'm inclined to think that he has deliberately put Geordie into this place, kennin' that the lower seam had been worked out lang, lang syne. His plans wad tell him as muckle about the workin's, and I ken, at least, he's never been in Geordie's place since it was started, an' there's nae ither places drivin' up sae far as this. They're a' stoppit afore they come this length; an' forby, frae what Rundell has let drap the day, he never kent that the coal was being worked as far up as this. By — —! Peter, gin I could prove what I suspect, I'd murder the dirty brute this nicht! I would that!"

"Would Nellie no' ken, think ye, what it was that Geordie had against Black Jock that kept him sae quiet?" enquired Peter.

"I couldna' say," answered Andrew, "but some day when I get the chance I'll maybe ask her, an' if it is as I think, then there'll be rows."

"Let me ken, Andrew," broke in Matthew. "Let me ken if ever ye discover onything; an' ye can count on me sharin' the penalties o' hell along wi' ye for the murder o' the big black brute."

"I heard," said Peter, "that he was boozin' wi' Mag Robertson and Sanny. But we'll no' be long in kennin', for ill-doin' canna hide."

After three frantic days of fighting against calamity, during which Andrew never left the fight except for that brief journey to tell Nellie the news, at last they came upon the crushed mass of bloody pulp and rags, smashed together so that the one could not be told from the other—father and son, a heap of broken bones and flesh and blood.... And no pen can describe accurately the scene.

The light had gone out from one woman's heart, the hope had been crushed from her life. The rainbow which had promised so much vanished. The lust and urge had gone out of eager life. Never again would the world seem fair and beautiful. Instead, all the weary fight and desperate battle with poverty and privation over again; the dull misery and the drab gray existence, and always the pain—the heavy, dragging pain of a broken life. With a woman's "Oh! my God!" the world for one heart stood still, and the blind fate of things triumphed, crushing a woman's soul in the process.

CHAPTER XI
THE STRIKE

A week had passed, and Geordie Sinclair and his boy, or at least all that could be gathered up of them, had been laid to rest.

Nellie was very ill, and was now in bed. The reaction had been too much for her. But, as Jenny Maitland had said: "She's never cried yet, an' it would hae been better gin she had. She jist looked at ye wi' her big black e'en sae vexed-like and faraway lookin', an' never spoke hardly. When they carried out the coffins, she sprang up gin she wad follow them, but was putten back to bed again. It was heart-vexin' to look at her."

Robert suffered, too. The sympathy of everyone went out to him. At night when he went to bed the whole scene was reënacted before him in all its horror. Those tense moments of tragedy had so powerfully impressed his boyish mind that he could never forget them.

At the end of the week Andrew Marshall visited them to talk over matters. A collection had been made at the pay-office by the men employed at the pit, and a beautiful wreath purchased and placed upon the grave. A substantial balance had been handed over to Mrs. Sinclair, and this defrayed the expenses of the funeral. After Andrew had spoken of various things, he broke on to the object of his errand that night.

"I hae been thinkin', Nellie," he began nervously, "that I could tak' Rob in wi' me. Ye see, I ha'e no callans o' my ain, and I ha'e aye to get yin to draw off me. So, gin ye're agreeable, I could tak' Rob, an' I'll be guid to him. He can come an' be my neighbor, an' as he'll hae to get work in ony case, he micht as weel work wi' me as wi' ony ither body. Forby I'll maybe be able to pay him mair than plenty ithers could pay him, an' that is efter a' the point to be maist considered. What do ye think?"

But Mrs. Sinclair could not think; she merely indicated to him that he might please himself and make his own arrangements with the boy, which Andrew did, and Robert went to work with him the following week. He was a mass of nerves and was horribly afraid—indeed, this fear never left him for years—but, young as he was, he recognized his responsibility, to his mother and the rest of the family. He was now its head, and had to shoulder the burden of providing for it, and so his will drove him to work in the pit, when his soul revolted at the very thought of it. Always the horror of the tragedy was with him, down to its smallest detail; and sometimes, even at work, when his mind wandered for a moment from his immediate task, he would start up in terror, almost crying out again as he had done on the day of the accident.

Andrew kept his word and was good to the boy now in his care. Indeed, he took, as some said, more care of the boy than if Robert had been his own, for he tried to save him from every little detail that might remind him of the accident.

"That's yours, Robin," he said, when pay-day came, as he handed to the boy the half of the pay earned.

"Na, I canna' tak' that, Andrew," replied Robert, looking up into the broad, kindly, honest face of the man. "My mither wouldna' let me."

"Would she no'?" replied Andrew. "But you are the heid o' the hoose, Robin, sae just tak' it hame, an' lay it down on the dresser-head. We are doin' gey weel the noo, an' forby, ye're workin' for it. Noo run awa' hame wi't, an' dinna say ocht to yir mither, but just put it doon on the dresser-head." And so the partnership began which was to last for many years.

About this time there happened one of those tremendous upheavals, long remembered in the industrial world, the great Scottish Miners' Strike of 1894. The trade union movement was growing and fighting, and every tendency pointed to the fact that a clash of forces was inevitable. The previous year had seen the English miners beaten after a protracted struggle. They had come out for an increase in wages, and whilst it was recognized that they had been beaten and forced to go back to work suffering wholesale reductions, yet a newer perspective was beginning to appear to the miners of Scotland.

"We'll never be able to beat the maisters," said Tam Donaldson, when the cloud first appeared upon the industrial horizon. "The English strike gied us a lesson we shouldna forget."

"How's that?" enquired Peter Pegg, as he sat down on his hunkers one night at the end of the row, while they discussed the prospects of the coming fight.

"Weel, ye saw how the Englishmen fought unitedly, an' yet they were beaten, an' had to gang back on a reduction. We'll very likely be the same, for the maisters are a' weel organized. What we should do is to ha'e England an' Scotland coming out together, an' let the pits stan' then till the grass was growin' owre the whorles. That would be my way o' it, and I think it would soon bring the country to see what was in the wind."

"That's richt, Tam. It would soon bring the hale country to its senses; for nae matter what oor fight is, we are aye in the wrang wi' some folk; so the shock o' the hale country comin' out would mak' them tak' notice, an' would work the cure."

So they talked of newer plans, while Smillie toiled like a giant to educate and organize the miners. He had taken hold of them as crude material, and was slowly shaping them into something like unity. A few more years and he would win; but the forces against him knew it, too, and so followed the great fight which lasted for seventeen weeks.

Singularly enough, while there was undoubtedly much privation, there was not very much real misery, as the strike had started early in a warm, dry summer.

Communal kitchens were at once established throughout the country. Everybody did his best, and the womenfolk especially toiled early and late. A committee was appointed in each village to gather in materials. Beef at a reasonable price was supplied by a local butcher. A horse and cart were borrowed, which went round the district gathering a cabbage or two here; a few carrots or turnips there, parsley at another, and so on, returning at night invariably laden with vegetables for the next day's dinner. Sometimes a farmer would give a sheep, and the local cooperative society provided the bread at half the cost of production. Those farmers who were hostile gave nothing, but it would have paid them better had they concealed their hostility, for sometimes, even in a single night, large portions of a field of potatoes would disappear as by magic.

Robert worked in this fight like a man. He helped to cut down trees and saw them into logs, to cook the food at the soup kitchen. Everything and anything he tried, running errands, and even going with the van to solicit material for the following day's meals.

All were cheerful, and no one seemed to take the fight bitterly. Sports were organized. Quoiting tournaments were got up, football matches arranged, games at rounders and hand-ball—every conceivable game was indulged in, with sometimes a few coppers as prizes but more often a few ounces of tobacco or tea or a packet of sugar. Dances in the evenings were started at the corner of the row to the strains of a melodeon, and were carried on to the early hours of the morning. It was from these gatherings that the young lads generally raided the fields and hen runs of the hostile farmers, returning with eggs, butter, potatoes, and even cheese—everything on which they could lay their hands.

At one of these gatherings Robert related his experience with "auld Hairyfithill." Robert had been round with the van that day, and calling at Wilson's, or Hairyfithill Farm, to ask if they had any cabbage to give, he heard the old man calling to the servant lass: "Mag! Mag! Where are ye? Rin an' bring in the hens' meat; there's thae colliers coming."

Nothing daunted, Robert had gone into the kitchen to ask if they had anything to give the strikers.

"Get awa' back to yer work, ye lazy loons, ye!" was the reply from old Mr. Wilson. "Gie ye something for your soup kitchen! Na, na! Ye can gang an' work, an' pay for your meat. Gang awa' oot owre, and leave the town, an' dinna come back again." And so they had drawn blank at Hairyfithill.

"It wad serve him richt, if every tattie in his fields was ta'en awa'," said Matthew Maitland, after the story had been told and laughed over.

"It wad that," agreed a score of voices; but nothing was done nor anything further said, so the dancing proceeded.

About two o'clock in the morning while the dancing was still going on and a fire had been kindled at the corner in which some of the strikers were roasting potatoes and onions a great commotion was suddenly caused, when Dickie Tamson and two other boys drove in among them old Hairyfithill's sow which he was fattening for the market. Some proposed that the pig be killed at once.

"Oh no, dinna kill it," said Matthew Maitland, with real alarm in his voice. "Ye'd get into a row for that. Ye'd better tak' it back, or there may be fun."

"Kill the damn'd thing," said Tam Donaldson callously, "an' it'll maybe a lesson to the auld sot. Him an' his hens' meat! I'd let him ken that it's no' hens' meat the collier eats—at least no' so lang as he can get pork."

"That's jist what I think, too, Tam," put in another voice. "I'd mak' sure work that the collier ate pork for yince. Come on, boys, an' mum's the word," and he proceeded to drive the pig further along the village, followed by a few enthusiastic backers. They drove it into Granny Fleming's hen-house in the middle of the square, put out the hens, who protested loudly against this rude and incomprehensible interruption of their slumbers, and then they proceeded to slaughter the pig.

It was a horrible orgy, and the pig made a valiant protest, but encountered by hammers and picks, knives and such-like weapons, the poor animal was soon vanquished, and the men proceeded to cut up its carcass. It was a long and trying ordeal for men who had no experience of the work; yet they made up in enthusiasm what they lacked in science, and by five o'clock the pig was cut up and distributed through a score of homes. Every trace of the slaughter was removed, and the refuse buried in the village midden, and pork was the principal article on the breakfast table that morning in Lowwood.

"I hear that auld Hairyfithill has offered five pound reward for information about his pig," said Tam Donaldson a few mornings later.

"Ay, an' it's a gran' price for onybody wha kens aboot it," said auld Jamie Lauder. "Pork maun hae risen in price this last twa-three days, for I'm telt it was gaun cheap enough then."

"That is true," said Tam, "but it was a damn'd shame to tak' the auld man's pig awa', whaever did it. But I hear them saying that the polisman is gaun to the farm the nicht to watch, so that the tatties 'll no' be stolen," he went on, as some of the younger men joined them, "an' I suppose that the puir polisman hasna' a bit o' coal left in his coal-house. It's no' richt, ye ken, laddies, that a polisman, who is the representative o' law and order in this place, should sit without a fire. He has a wife an' weans to worry aboot, an' they need a fire to mak' meat. Maybe if he had a fire an' plenty o' coal it wad mak' him comfortable, an' then he'd no' be sae ready to leave the hoose at nicht an' lie in a tattie pit to watch thievin' colliers. If a man hasna' peace in his mind it'll mak' him nasty, an' we canna' allow sic a thing as a nasty polisman in this district!"

"That's richt, Tam," said one of the younger men. "It would be a shame to see a woman an' twa-three weans sittin' withoot a fire an' a great big bing o' coal lyin' doon there at the pit. We maun try an' keep the polisman comfortable."

That night the policeman without in any way trying to conceal his purpose walked down through the village and across the strip of moor and took up his position at the end of Hairyfithill's potato field. At once a group of young men led by Tam Donaldson set off with bags under their arms after it was dark for the pit at the other end of the village and were soon engaged in carrying coal as if their lives depended on it.

"Noo, lads, the first bag gangs to the polisman, mind," said Tam, shouldering his load and walking off.

"A' richt, Tam. If we a' gang wi' the first bag to him that'll be nine bags, then we can get two or three bags for hame. Dinna hurry; we ha'e a' nicht to carry, an' we can get in a fine lot afore daylicht breaks."

"That's richt," said Tam, "but mind an' no' tire yersels too much, for ye've a nicht at the tatties the morn. The polis'll be at the bing the morn's nicht efter this carry-on, an' when he is busy watchin' for coal thieves, we maun see that we get in a denner or twa o' tatties. I heard him sayin' he could not be everywhere at yince, an' couldna' both watch coal thieves an' tattie stealin' at yin an' the same time."

All this time matters went very smoothly. The men were very firm, having great trust in Smillie. After about six weeks, however, from various causes a suspicious atmosphere began to be created. Hints had been appearing from time to time in the newspapers that matters were not altogether as the miners thought they were. Then vague rumors got afloat in many districts and spread with great rapidity, and these began to undermine the confidence of the strikers.

"What think ye o' the fecht noo, Tam?" enquired Matthew Maitland one night as they sat among the others at the "Lazy Corner," as the village forum was called.

"I dinna ken what to think o' it," replied Tam glumly. "Do ye think there's any truth in that story aboot Smillie havin' sell't us?"

"It wad be hard to ken," replied Matthew Maitland, taking his pipe out of his mouth and spitting savagely upon the ground. "But I heard it for a fact, and that a guid wheen o' men doon the country hae gaen back to their work through it. An' yet, mind ye, Smillie seemed to me to be a straight-forret man an' yin that was sincere. Still, ye can never tell; an' twa-three hunner pound's a big temptation to a man."

"Ay," said Tam dryly, "we hae been diddled sae often wi' bigmoothed men on the make, that it mak's a body ay suspicious when yin hears thae stories. I heard Wiston, the coal-maister, had gien him five hunner pounds on the quiet."

"I heard that too," replied Matthew, "but, like you, I'm loth to think it o' Smillie. I'd believe it quicker aboot yon ither chiel, Charlie Rogerson. He comes oot to speak to us ay dressed in a black dress-suit, wi' white cuffs doon to his finger nebs, his gold ring, his lum hat, an' a' his fal-de-lals."

"Weel, I dinna believe a word o' this story aboot Bob," said Robert quietly, who had "hunkered" down beside the two men who sat so earnestly discussing matters while the others went on with their games and dancing.

"Do ye no', Rob?" said Tam.

"No, I do not," was the firm reply, "for nae matter what happens in a fight, it's ay the opeenion o' some folk that the men ha'e been sell't."

Robert, though young, took a keen interest in the fight. While other lads of his age looked upon it as a fine holiday, the heavy responsibilities he had to face gave him a different outlook, and so the men seemed to recognize that he was different from the other boys, and more sober in his view-point.

"This story is set aboot for the purpose o' breakin' oup the men," he continued. "We hear o' Smillie haein hale rows o' cottages bought, an' a lot ither rubbish, but I wouldna believe it. It's a' to get the men to gang back to their work; an' if they do that, it'll no' only break the strike, but it'll break up the union, an' that's what's wanted mair than anything else. I've heard Smillie an' my faither talkin' aboot a' thae things lang syne, an' Smillie says that's what the stories are set aboot for. We should ha'e sense enough no' to heed them, for I dinna think Smillie has sell't us at a'."

There was a fine, firm ring in the boy's voice as he spoke which moved the two older men, and made them feel a little ashamed that they had been so ready to doubt.

"Ah, weel, Rob," said Tam, "maybe you are richt, but a lot o' men ha'e gaen back to their work already, an' it'll break up the strike if it spreads. But we'll ha'e to get some tatties in the nicht; the polisman's goin' to be watchin' auld Burnfoot's hen-hoose, sae it'll be a grand chance for some tatties," and the talk drifted on to another subject.

About the eighth week of the strike the news went round the village that Sanny Robertson and Peter Fleming were "oot at the pit."

"I wad smash every bone in their dirty bodies if I had my way o' it. I would," said Matthew Maitland, with emphasis. Matthew was always emphatic in all he said, though seldom so in what he did.

"But we'll ha'e to watch hoo we act," said Andrew Marshall more cautiously. "It's agin the law, ye ken, to use force."

"I wadna' gi'e a damn," said Peter Pegg, his big eye making frantic efforts to wink. "I wad see that they blacklegged nae mair."

"Sae wad I," promptly exclaimed half a dozen of the younger men.

"We maun see that they don't do it ony mair."

"Ay, an' I hope we'll mak' sure work that they sleep in for twa-three mornin's."

"I'll tell ye what," said old Lauder, "let us get a few weemin' and weans thegither, an' we'll gang doon to the pit an' wait on them comin' up frae their shift. The bairns can get tin cans an' a stane for a drumstick, an' we'll ha'e a loonie band. We can sing twa or three o' thae blackleg sangs o' Tam Donaldson's, an' play them hame."

"That's the plan, Jamie," replied Tam, who had suddenly seen himself immortalized through his parodies of certain popular songs. "Let us get as mony women an' callans as possible, and we can mak' a damn'd guid turnout. We'll sing like linties, an' drum like thunder, an' the blacklegs'll feel as if they were goin' through Purgatory to the tune o':"

> Tattie Wullie, Tattie Wullie,
> Tattie Wullie Shaw,
> Where's the sense o' workin', Wullie? —
> Faith, ye're lookin' braw.

or

> Peter Fleming, Peter Fleming,
> Peter, man, I say,
> Ye've been workin', ye've been workin',
> Ye've been workin' the day.
>
> Peter Fleming, Peter Fleming,
> If ye work ony mair,
> Peter Fleming, Peter Fleming,
> Your heart will be sair.

With little difficulty a band of men, women and children was organized and proceeded to the pit to await the coming up of the culprits. Hour after hour they waited patiently, determined not to miss them, and the time was spent in light jesting and singing ribald songs.

"I wadna' like if my faither was a blackleg," observed Mysie Maitland to the girl next her.

"No, nor me, either!" quickly agreed the other. "It wad be awfu' to hear folk cryin' 'Blackleg' after yir faither, wadna' it, Mysie?"

"Ay," was the reply. "I wadna' like it."

"They should a' be hunted oot o' the place," put in Robert, who was standing near. "They are just sellin' the rest o' the men, an' helpin' to break up the strike. So ye mind, Mysie, hoo Tam Graham's lass aye clashed on the rest o' us on the pit-head? She's just like her faither, ay ready to do onything agin the rest, if it would gi'e her a wee bit favor."

"Ay, fine I mind o' it, Rob," Mysie replied eagerly. "Do ye mind the day she was goin' to tell aboot you takin' hame the bit auld stick for firewood? When I telt her if she did, I'd tell on her stealin' the tallow frae the engine-house an' the paraffin ile ay when she got the chance. She didna say she'd tell then."

"Ay, Mysie. Maybe I'd ha'e gotten the sack if she had telt. But she was aye a clashbag. But here they come!" he shouted animatedly, as the bell signaled for the cage to rise, and presently the wheels began to revolve, as the cage ascended.

"May the tow break, an' land the dirty scums in hell," prayed one man.

"Ay, an' may the coals they howkit the day roast them forever," added another. Though they prayed thus, yet once again they found that the "prayer of the wicked availeth naught." Buckets of water, however, and even bits of stone and scrap iron were surreptitiously flung down the shaft; and when the blacklegs did appear, they were nearly frightened out of their senses. It would have gone hard with them as they left the cage, but someone whispered, "Here's the polis!" and so the crowd had to be content with beating their tin cans; and keeping time to the songs improvised by Tam Donaldson, they escorted the blacklegs to their homes.

Next morning a large number of the strikers gathered at the Lazy Corner, enjoying themselves greatly.

"They tell me," said Tam Donaldson, "that our fren's ha'e slept in this morning."

A laugh greeted this sally, which seemed to indicate that most of them knew about the sleeping-in and the reason for it.

"Ay, they'd be tired oot efter their hard day's work yesterday," replied another.

"Ay, an' they dinna seem to be up yet," said a third, "for I see the doors are still shut, an' the bairns are no' awa' to the school. They maun ha'e been awfu' tired to ha'e slept sae lang."

"Let's gang doon and gi'e them a bit sang to help to keep their dreams pleasant," suggested Tam Donaldson, as they moved off down the row and stopped before Jock Graham's door. Tam, clearing his throat, led of:

Hey, Johnnie Graham, are ye wauken yet,
Or is yer fire no' ken'lt yet?
If you're no wauken we will wait,
An' tak' ye to the pit in the mornin'.

Black Jock sent a message in the dark,
Sayin': Johnny Graham, come to your wark,
For tho' ye've been locked in for a lark,
Ye maun come to the pit in the mornin'.

You an' Fleeming, an' Robertson tae,
Had better a' gang doon the brae,

An' you'll get your pay for ilka day
That ye gang to your work in the mornin'.

Then, leading off on to another, Tam, with great gusto, swung into a song that carried the others along uproariously:

O' a' the airts the win' can blaw,
It canna blaw me free,
For I am high an' dry in bed,
When workin' I should be;
But ropes are stronger faur than is
Desire for work wi' me,
An' sae I lie, baith high an' dry—
I'll hae to bide a wee.

I canna say on whatna day
I'll gang again to work,
For sticks an' stanes may break my banes,
As sure's my name's McGurk.
Gie me the best place in the pit,
Then happy I shall be,
Just wi' yae wife to licht oor life,
Big dirty Jock an' me!

After a round or two of applause and some shouts from the children, Tam broke out in a new air:

This is no' my ain lassie,
Kin' though the lassie be,
There's a man ca'd Black Jock Walker,
Shares this bonnie lass wi' me.
She's sweet, she's kin', her ways are fine,
An' whiles she gies her love to me.
She's ta'en my name, but, oh, the shame,
That Walker shares the lass wi' me.

This is no' my ain lassie,
She is changefu' as the sea,
Whiles I get a' her sweet kisses,
Whiles Black Jock shares them wi' me.
She's fat and fair, she's het and rare,
She's no' that trig, but ay she's free,

It pays us baith, as sure as daith,
That Walker shares the lass wi' me.

This sent the crowd wild with delight, and cries of "Good auld Tam!" were raised. "Damn'd guid, Tam! Ye're as guid as Burns." All of which made Tam feel that at last his genius was being recognized. The explanation of the joke was to be found in the fact, as one song had hinted, that the strikers had securely fastened the doors of all the blacklegs' houses with ropes, and jammed the windows with sticks, so that the inmates could not get out. Even the children could not get out to go to school. It was late in the afternoon before the police heard of it, and came and cut the ropes, and so relieved the imprisoned inmates.

This happened for a morning or two, and then the practice stopped, for the police watched the doors throughout the whole night. This preoccupation of the police was taken advantage of to raid again old Hairyfithill's potato field, and also to pay a visit to the bing for coal, and a very profitable time was thus spent by the strikers, even though the blacklegs were at their work in a few days.

What was happening in Lowwood was typical of almost all other mining villages throughout the country. Everywhere high spirits and cheerfulness prevailed among the men. As for the leaders, the situation proved too big for some of them to cope with it, the responsibility was too great; and so they failed at the critical moment. The demand of an increase of a shilling a day, for which the men had struck, had been conceded by some of the owners, whilst others had offered sixpence. Some of the leaders were in favor of accepting these concessions, and allowing the men at the collieries concerned to resume work, and so be able to contribute considerably to help keep out those whose demands had not been met. Others of the leaders refused to agree to this, and insisted that as all had struck together, they should fight together to the end, until the increase was conceded to all. This difference of opinion was readily perceived and welcomed by the coalmasters, and stiffened their resolution, for they saw that disagreement and divisions would soon weaken the morale of the men, and such proved to be the case.

No one can imagine what Smillie suffered at this time, as he saw his splendid effort going to pieces; but being a big man, he knew that it was impossible to turn back. His plans might for the moment miscarry; but that was merely a necessary, yet passing, phase in the great evolution of Industrialism, and his ideals must yet triumph.

As the result of the differences among the leaders, the strike collapsed at the end of seventeen weeks. The men were forced to return to work on the old terms. In some cases a reduction was imposed, making their condition worse than at the start. The masters sought to drive home their victory in order to break the union. In many parts of the country they succeeded, while in others the spirit of the men resisted it. Generally it ended in compromise; but, so far as the Union was concerned, it was a broken organization; branches went down, and it was many years afterwards before it was again reestablished in some of the districts.

Though at the time it might have seemed all loss, yet it had its advantages, and especially demonstrated the fact that there was a fine discipline and the necessary unity among the rank and file. The next great work was to find out how that unity could be guided and that discipline perfected—how to find a common ideal for the men. This was Robert Smillie's task, and who shall say, looking at the rank and file to-day, that he has failed?

CHAPTER XII
THE RIVALS

Eight years passed, and Robert grew into young manhood. One of his younger brothers had joined him and Andrew Marshall in the partnership. It had been a long, stiff struggle, and his mother knew all the hardness and cruelty of it. In after years Robert loved his mother more for the fight she put up, though it never seemed to him that he himself had done anything extraordinary. He was always thoughtful, and planned to save her worry. On "pay-nights," once a fortnight, when other boys of his age were getting a sixpence, or perhaps even a shilling, as pocket-money, so that they could spend a few coppers on the things that delight a boy's heart, Robert resolutely refused to take a penny. For years he continued thus, always solacing himself with the thought that it was a "shilling's worth less of worry" his mother would have.

Yet, riches were his in that the enchantment of literature held him captive, and his imagination gained for him treasures incomparably greater than the solid wealth prized by worldly minds. His father had possessed about a dozen good books, among others such familiar Scottish household favorites as "Wilson's Tales of the Borders," "Mansie Waugh," by "Delta," "Scots Worthies," Allan Ramsay's "Gentle Shepherd," Scott's "Rob Roy" and "Old Mortality," and the well-thumbed and dog-eared copy of Robert Burns' Poems.

"Gae awa', man Robin," his mother would say sometimes to him, as he sat devouring Wilson's "Tales" or weeping over the tragic end of Wallace's wife Marion as recounted in Jean Porter's entrancing "Scottish Chiefs."

"Gang awa' oot an' tak' a walk. Ither laddies are a' oot playin' at something, an' forby it's no' healthy to sit too long aye readin'."

"Ach. I canna' be bothered," he would answer. "I'd raither read."

"What is't you're readin' noo?" she would enquire. "Oh, it's the 'Scottish Chiefs,' an' I'm jist at the bit aboot Wallace's wife being murdered by Hazelrig. My! It's awfu' vexin'."

"Ay, it's a fine book, Robin. Ye might read that bit oot to me."

"A' richt," and he would start to read while Nellie sat down to listen. Soon both were engrossed in the sad story, so powerfully told, and the tears would be running from the mother's eyes as her fancy pictured the sorrows of Wallace, while Robert's voice would break, and a sob come into his throat, as he proceeded. When finally the passage was reached where the brutal blow was struck, the book would have to be put down, while mother and son both cried as if the grief depicted were their own.

"It's an awfu' gran' book, Rob," she would say after a time, while she strove to subdue the sobs in her breast. "Puir Wallace! It maun ha'e been an awfu' blow to him, when he heard that Marion was killed. But you maun read on a bit far'er, for I'm no' gaun tae work ony mair till I see that dirty beast Hazelrig get his deserts. He has wrocht for it, sae jist gang on noo till you feenish the bit aboot him gettin' killed wi' Wallace. He deserves it for killin' a woman."

Thus Robert would have to go on, until the incident in question had been reached in the story, and as it unfolded itself his voice would grow firmer and stronger as he became infected with the narrative, while his mother's eyes would glow, and her body be tense with interest, and an expectant expression would creep over her face, betraying her excitement. In the interview between Wallace and Hazelrig in the house in the Wellgate in Lanark, when Wallace dramatically draws his sword in answer to the supplication for mercy, and says: "Ay, the same mercy as you showed my Marion," Robert's voice would thunder forth the words with terrible sternness, while Nellie would gasp and catch her breath in a quick little sob of excitement, as the feeling of satisfied justice filled her heart. And when the blow fell that laid the English governor low, she would burst out: "Serves him richt, the dirty tyrant. He's got what he deserved, an' it serves him right!"

On another occasion Robert would suddenly burst out laughing, when reading Delta's chronicle of the adventures of Mansie Waugh, the Scottish "Handy Andy."

"What are you laughing at, Robin?" Nellie would enquire, a smile breaking over her face also.

"Oh, it's Mansie Waugh, mither. Oh, but it's a gran' bit. Listen to this," and he would begin to read the passage, where Mansie, simple soul that he was, was described as going into the byre in the morning to learn if the cow had calved during the night, and finding, on opening the door, the donkey of a traveling tinker, he turned and ran into the house, crying: "Mither! Mither! The coo has calved, an' it's a cuddy!"

Whenever he reached this part of the story, his mother would go off into a fit of uncontrollable laughter which left her helpless and crumpled up in a heap upon the nearest chair. Her laugh was very infectious; it began with a low, mirthful ripple, well down in the throat, and rose in rapid leaps of musical joy till it had traveled a whole octave of bubbling happy sounds, when it culminated in a peal of double forte shakes and trills, that made it a joy to hear, and finally it died out in an "Oh, dear me! What a callan Mansie was!"

As Robert approached manhood, he took more and more to the moors, wandering alone among the haunts of the whaup and other moor birds, wrestling with problems to which older heads never gave a thought, trying to understand life and to build from his heart and experience something that would be satisfying. Silent, thoughtful, "strange" to the neighbors, a problem to everyone, but a bigger one to himself, life staggered him and appalled his soul.

Earnestly he worked and tested his thought against the thought of others, sturdily refusing everything which did not ring true and meet his standard. Old religious conceptions, the orthodoxy of his kith and kin, were fast tested in the crucible of his mind and flung aside as worthless. The idea of Hell and the old Morrisonian notion of the Hereafter appeared crude and barbarous. His father's fate and the condition of the family left to welter in poverty, the cruelty of life as it presented itself to the great mass of the working class, could not be reconciled with the Church's teaching of an all-loving and omniscient Father.

With the audacity of youth, he felt that he could easily have constructed a better universe. He felt that Hell could have no terrors for people condemned to such hardship and suffering as he saw around him. Life was colorless for them; stinted of pleasure and beauty, with merely the joys of the "gill-stoup" on a Saturday night at the local "store" to look forward to, there was in it no real satisfaction either for the body or the mind. Would he, indeed, have to wait till after death before knowing anything of real happiness or comfort? His mind refused to accept this doctrine so frequently expounded to working class congregations by ministers, who were themselves comparatively well endowed with "treasures upon earth."

Life was good, life was glorious if only it could be made as he dreamed it. This fair earth need be no vale of tears. There were the blue skies, the white tapestry of cloudland ever varying; there was the wind upon his face and the sweet rain; there was the purl of mountain brook, the graceful sweep of the river, the smile of the flowers, the songs of the birds; the golden splendor of the day and the silver radiance of the night.

But above and beyond all there was an ever-increasing love of his fellows, there were noble women like his mother to reverence, and there were sweet children to cherish. Surely life was good, and never was meant to be the mean, sordid thing that too often was the lot of people like himself. Heaven could and should be realized here and now. At twenty, he finished by accepting Humanity as it is, to be understood and loved, to be served, and, if necessary, to die for it.

Though thus naturally reserved and meditative, yet he was not unloved. There was no more popular lad in the village. Everyone in a tight corner came to him for help and advice. He was private secretary to half the village and father confessor to the other half. He served everyone, and in return all loved him more or less. In the course of time he came to occupy the place his father had held before him as president of the local branch of the Union, which had been recently revived. His duties as a Union official forced him more and more into mixing with others, and into taking a larger interest in the affairs of the locality.

Gradually with the activities of public life his moodiness gave place to a healthy cheerfulness, and his enthusiasm soon led him into taking part in nearly every form of sport which gave life more zest. His interest being roused, he was wholehearted in his application, whether as a member of the executive of any local sports association, or as a participant in the game itself. He was elected to the committee responsible for organizing the Lowwood Annual Games, but resigned because having taken up racing as his pet pastime for the time being, he wanted to compete in some of the items.

At last the "Sports" day arrived. The pits were idle, for this was one of the recognized holidays. Everyone looked forward eagerly to this day, and prepared for it, each in his or her own way. For weeks before it the children practiced racing, and trained themselves in jumping, football, quoiting and such sports. Young men stole away to secret places in the moor to train and harden themselves, timing their performances and concentrating on the strenuous day ahead when they would compete with one another in fair tests of speed, strength, skill and endurance.

One event was always a special attraction, even to professional racers all over the country. This was known as the "Red Hose Race," about which many legends were told. The most popular of these was to the effect that the stockings were knitted each year by the Laird's wife, and if no one entered for the race, the Laird must run it himself, or forfeit his extensive estate to the Crown. In addition to the Red Hose, there was a substantial money prize. To win the race was looked upon as the greatest achievement of the year, for it was one of the oldest sporting events and had been run for so many years that its origin seemed lost in the mists of antiquity. Robert made up his mind to win the Red Hose in this particular year. Mrs. Graydon, of Graydon House, had intimated that she herself would be present and would hand over the stockings to the proud winner in person, but it was not by any means on this account that Robert was so keen to win. It was the older lure that brought every year athletes of fame to run in the historic race.

"So you are going to run in the Red Hose," said a voice behind Robert while the people were all gathering to watch the preliminary races of the boys and girls. Robert turned from the group of young men who had been discussing the event with him, and met the smiling face of Peter Rundell, dressed in immaculate style and looking as fresh and fine a specimen of young manhood as anyone could wish to see.

"Yes," he said with a smile, "and I intend to win it."

"Do you?" returned Peter light-heartedly. "I have also entered for it, though I had no intention of doing so when I came over; but Mr. Walker, who, as you know, is on the committee, pressed me to go in, and so I consented."

"Oh!" said Robert, in surprise, "I thought after last year's success you were not going to run again." Then, in a bantering tone, and with a smile upon his lips, "I suppose we'll be rivals in this, then; but I gi'e you fair warning that I'm gaun to lift the Red Hose if I get a decent chance at all."

"Well, I have set my mind on winning it, too," replied Peter. "I'd like to lift it, just to be able to say in after years that I had done so."

"That's just hoo I feel aboot the matter too," lightly answered Robert. "I'd like jist to be able to say that I had won the Red Hose. I feel in good form for it, so you'd better be on your mettle."

"Well, I shall give you the race of your life for it," said Peter, entering into the same light spirited boasting. "I hear Mair and Todd and Semple are also entered, but with a decent handicap I won't mind these, even with their international reputation."

"All right," said Robert. "I suppose I shall have the greater pleasure in romping home before you all. Are the handicaps out yet?"

"Yes, I saw the list just before I spoke to you. Semple and Mair are scratch, with Todd at five yards. You start at twenty-five, and I get off at the limit forty.'

"Oh!" said Robert, a note of surprise in his voice. "Walker has surely forgotten who are the runners! Why, last year you won nearly all the confined events, and you were second in the Red Hose with twenty-five yards. He means you to romp home this year!" and there was heat in Robert's voice as he finished.

"Well, I daresay it is a decent handicap," said Peter, "and even though Semple is among the crowd, I should manage, I think, to pull it off with anything like luck."

"I should think so," said Robert. "Walker has just made you a present of the race. But I suppose it can't be helped, though it isn't fair. Anyhow, I'll give you a chase for it."

"All right. Half an hour and we shall be on," and Peter went on round the field, exchanging greetings with most of the villagers.

He was finishing his education at a Technical College in Edinburgh, and at present was home on holidays. He was a well set up young man, and though popular with most people, yet he brought with him an air of another world among the villagers, which made them feel uncomfortable. They recognized that his life was very different from their own, and while they talked to him when he spoke to them, and were agreeable enough to him, they felt awed and could not break down the natural reserve they always had towards people of another station of life. He was perhaps a little too thoughtless and impulsive, though generous-hearted enough. He drifted into things, rather than shaped them to his own ideas, and was often not sufficiently careful of the positions in which he found himself as a consequence of thoughtless acts.

The week before he had caught and kissed Mysie Maitland, who was now serving at Rundell House, merely because he was taken with her pretty face. From that Peter already believed himself in love with her, because she had not resented his action. He had even walked over with her from the village, when she had been home visiting her parents one night, and had felt more and more the witchery of her pretty face and the lure of her fine little figure.

Up to this time Mysie had always believed herself in love with Robert— Robert who was always so strange from the rest of young men. He had always been her hero, her protector; but there was something about him for which she could not account and which she could not have defined. Such was her admiration that she believed it was in his power to do anything he cared to attempt; it was just possible that it was this strange sense of unknown power which fascinated her. They had never been lovers in the accepted sense of the word. They had never "walked out" as young people in their social station usually do, but yet had always felt that they were meant for one another.

Only once had Robert kissed her, and that moment ever lived with her a glowing memory. She had been home and was returning through a moorland pass, when she came across him lying upon the rough heather, his thoughts doubtless full of her, for he had seen her in the village, and knew she must return that way.

"Oh, Rob!" she cried, her face flushing with excitement as she saw him. "Ye nearly frichted me oot o' my wits the noo."

"Did I, Mysie?" he answered, springing to his feet. "I didna mean to dae that. Ye'll be getting back, I suppose."

"Ay," she returned simply, and a silence fell upon them, in which both seemed to lose the power of speaking.

Robert looked at her as she stood there, her full, curved breasts rising and falling with the excitement of the unexpected meeting, the long lashes of her eyes sweeping her flushed cheeks, as she stood with downcast eyes before him. The last rays of the setting sun falling upon her brown hair touched it with a rare strange beauty. Her red lips like dew-drenched roses—luscious, pure, alluring, were parted a little in a half smile. But it was the fascinating movement of the breast, full, round and sensuous, that stirred and made an overpowering appeal to every pulse within him. It seemed so soft, so tender, so wonderfully alluring. At the moment he could not understand himself or her. There was a strange, surging impetus raging through him that he felt absolutely powerless to subdue, and he swayed a little as he stood.

"Oh, Mysie!" he cried, leaping forward and clasping her in his strong, young arms, and crushing her against him, holding her there, gasping, powerless but happy.

"You are mine, Mysie. Mine!" and he kissed her budded lips in an ecstasy of passion and warm-blooded feeling, while a thousand fevers seemed to course through him as he felt the contact of her body and her warm, eager lips on his. Blinded and delirious, he kissed her again and again in an impassioned burst of fervor, passion scorching his blood and filling his whole heart with the enjoyment of possession. She closed her eyes, and her head touched his shoulder, while the faint scent of her hair and its soft caressing touch upon his cheek maddened him to a fury of love.

"Say you are mine, Mysie! Say you are mine!" he cried, and his voice was strange and hoarse and dry with the desire within him. He felt her body yielding as it relaxed in his arms, as if in answer to some unspoken demand, and in a moment he realized himself and started back, hot shame surging over his face and conquering the passion in his blood. In that strange mad moment he had felt capable of anything—powerful, overmastering, relentless in his desires; and now—weak, shame-stricken and helpless. Ere he could say anything, Mysie had come to herself with a shock, and started away over the moor as if possessed by something that was mysterious and terrible.

That had happened a year ago, and though Robert sought to learn when she was in the village, and often watched her from a safe place where he was not seen, delighting his eyes with the sight of her figure, and feeling again the same hot shame come over him, as he had known that day on the moor, yet he had never met her near enough to speak to her, but had worshiped her at a distance and grown to love and desire her more and more with every day that passed.

He dreamed dreams around her, but was afraid to encounter her again. This strange mad love burned in his blood, until at times he was almost sick with desire and love. Every moor-bird called her name; every flower held the shyness of her face; the clouds of peaceful sunsets showed the glory of her hair, and the quiet, steadfast stars possessed the wonder of her eyes. The madness of the passionate moment of possession on the moor was at once his most treasured memory and his intensest shame.

As for Mysie, since she had not heard any more from Robert nor even seen him for almost a year, she felt quite flattered by the attentions of Peter Rundell. It was not that she was in love with either of the young men. Her nature was of the kind that is in love with love itself, and was not perhaps capable of a great love, such as had frightened her, when Robert, taken off his guard, had let her glimpse a strong, overmastering passion and a soul capable of great things. Already she dreamed of a grand house of which she would be mistress as Peter's wife, as she stood in the silence of her own room, pirouetting and smirking, and drawing pictures of herself in fine garments and stately carriage, playing the Lady Bountiful of the district.

CHAPTER XIII
THE RED HOSE RACE

"All competitors for the Red Hose, get ready!" called the bell-man, who announced the events at the sports, and immediately all was stir and bustle and excitement.

"Wha's gaun to win the day, Andrew?" enquired Matthew Maitland, as they stood waiting for the runners to emerge from the dressing tent.

"I dinna ken," answered Andrew Marshall. "That's a damn'd unfair handicap anyway. My neighbor is no' meant to lift it seemingly. Look at the start they've gi'en him, an' young Rundell starts at the limit."

"Ay!" said Matthew. "It's no' fair. It's some o' Black Jock's doings. He's meanin' young Rundell to wun it."

"Ay, it looks like it; but it's fashious kennin' what may happen. Rab's a braw runner," and Andrew spoke as one who knew, for he was the only person who had seen Robert train.

"Weel, it's harder for him to be a rinner than for young Rundell, a man wha never wrocht a day's work in a' his life, while Rab's had to slave hard and sair a' his days.... Though Rundell can rin too," he added, with ungrudged admiration.

"Ay, he ran weel last year, but they tell me he'd like to get the Red Hose to his credit, though for my pairt they'd been far better to ha'e presented it to him, than to gi'e him it that way. Man, he's a dirty brute o' a man, Black Jock!" and there was disgust in his voice. "Jist look at Mag Robertson there, flittering aboot quite shameless, and gecking and smirking at him, an' naebody daur say a word to her. She's a fair scunner!"

"If she belonged to me, I'd let her ken a different way o't."

"Ay, Andra," was the reply. "But ye maun mind that Mag mak's mair money than Sanny does. Jist look at her, the glaikit tinkler that she is. Black Jock's no' ill to please when that pleases him."

Mag Robertson, the subject of their talk, was quite oblivious, apparently, of the many remarks that were being passed about her, and she continued to follow Walker, who as a committee member, was busily arranging matters for the race.

"She's gie weel smeekit, Andra!" observed Matthew in a whisper, as Mag passed close by. "Did ye fin the smell o" her breath?"

"Ay!" replied Andrew. "She can haud a guid lot before ye see it on her. She's—" but a shout from the crowd cut his further revelations short.

"Here they come!" cried Matthew excitedly, as the tent opened, and young Rundell came out with confident bearing, leading the other half-dozen athletes to the starting place. "Let's gae roon' to the wunnin' post so as to see the feenish."

The competitors lined up, each on his separate mark, ready for the signal to start. Rundell, in a bright-colored costume of fine texture, showed well beside the other racer who started along with him at forty yards. Peter was slimly built, but there were energy and activity in his every movement; his legs especially, being finely developed, showed no superfluous flesh; his chest alone indicated any weakness, but withal he looked a likely winner.

Robert, on the other hand, while not carrying a great amount of flesh, was well built. The chest was broad and deep, the shoulders square and the head held well up, his nose being finely adapted for good respiration. The legs, by reason of heavy work in early life, were a little bent at the brawn, but were as hard as nails; they showed wonderfully developed muscles, and gave the impression of strength rather than speed.

They presented a fine picture of eager, determined young manhood, clean and healthy, and full of life and mettle. Each face betrayed how the mind was concentrated on, the work ahead, every thought directed with great intensity towards the goal, as they bent their bodies in preparation for the start.

The pistol cracked and rang out upon the midday air with startling suddenness, and immediately they were off on a fine start to the accompaniment of the cheering of the crowd which lined the whole track in a great circle. The first round ended with the runners much as they had started, the interval between each being fairly equally maintained. Semple, however, dropped out, not caring to overstrain himself as he had some heavy racing next day at another gathering, where a much higher money prize was the allurement.

Round the others went, the excitement growing among the crowd, who kept shouting encouraging remarks to the racers as they passed.

"Keep it up, Robin!" cried Andrew Marshall. "Keep it up, my lad. Ye're daein' fine."

"Come away, Rundell, the race is yer ain," shouted an enthusiastic supporter of Peter.

"Nae wonner!" answered Matthew Maitland, heatedly. "They've gi'en him the race in a present. Look at the handikep!"

"An' what aboot it?" enquired the other, not knowing what to answer.

"Plenty aboot it," replied Matthew. "If it hadna' been he was Peter Rundell, he wadna' ha'e gotten sic a start. Black Jock means him to get the race, an' it's no' fair. I wadna' ha'e the damn'd thing in that way, an' if he does win it he'll hae nae honor in it."

"But Rab's runnin' weel," Matthew continued, as he followed the runners with eager eyes, and stuck the head of his pipe in his mouth in his excitement, burning his lips in the process. "Dammit, I've burned my mooth," he ejaculated, spluttering, spitting and wiping his mouth. "But the laddie can rin. He's a fair dandie o' a rinner."

"He couldna' rin to catch the cauld," broke in Rundell's admirer, glad to get in a word. "Look at him. Dammit, ye could wheel a barrow oot through his legs. He jist rummles alang like a chained tame earthquake."

"What's that?" asked Matthew, somewhat nettled at this manner of describing Robert's slightly bent legs. "He canna rin, ye say! Weel, if he couldna' rin better than Peter Rundell, he should never try it. Look at Rundell!" he went on scathingly, "doubled up like a fancy canary, and a hump on his back like a greyhound licking a pot. Rinnin'! He's mair like an exhibition o' a rin-a-way toy rainbow. He's aboot as souple as a stookie Christ on a Christmas tree!" And Matthew glared at the other, as if he would devour him at a gulp.

"Look at him noo," he cried, as Robert began to overtake the young miner who had started equal with Rundell. "He's passed young Paterson noo, an' ye'll soon see him get on level terms wi' Rundell. Go on, Rob!" he yelled in delight, as Robert shot past. "Go on, my lad, you're daein' fine!"

Excitement was rousing the crowd to a great pitch, and yells and shouts of encouragement went up, and cheers rang out as the favored one went past the various groups of supporters.

All during the race as the competitors circled the course, excitement grew, until the last round was reached, when every one seemed to go mad. Only three remained to compete now for the prize, the others having given up.

But the shouts and cheers of the crowd seemed strangely far away to the racers, as each rounded the last corner for the final stretch of about one hundred yards. They were both spent, but will power kept them at it. They were not breathing, they were tearing their lungs out in great gulping efforts, and their hearts as well. Tense, determined, inevitability seemed to rest upon them.

Louder roared the crowd, hoarser and deeper the cheers, closer and closer the multitude surged to the winning post, yelling, shouting, crying and gesticulating incoherently as the two men sprinted along with great leaping strides, panting and almost breaking down under the terrible strain of the mile race.

Nearer and nearer they came, still running level, with hardly an inch to tell the difference; but in a pace like this Robert's greater strength and hard training were bound to tell. Fifty yards to go, and they came on like streaks of color, fleeting images of some fevered brain, and one girl's smile each knew was waiting there at the far end.

The prize for which both were now striving was that for which men at all times strive, which keeps the world young and sends the zest of creation wandering through the blood — a pair of dancing eyes, lit by the happy smile of love; for Mysie Maitland had smiled to them, each claiming the smile for himself, just before the race started.

And now the last ounce of energy was called up, but the mine-owner's son failed to respond. Dazed and stupid, his mind in a mad whirl, his legs almost doubling under him, he found his powers weaken and his strength desert him, and he staggered just as Robert was about to shoot past him; but in staggering he planted his spiked shoe right upon Robert's foot, and both men went down completely exhausted, Rundell unable to rise for want of strength and Sinclair powerless because of his lacerated foot.

"Guid God! He's spiked him!" roared Andrew in a terrible rage. "The dirty lump that he is — spiked him just when he was gaun to win, too!"

A howl of execration went up from Sinclair's supporters as he lay and writhed in agony, while Rundell lay still except for the heaving of his chest. For one tense moment they lay and the crowd was silent, whilst each man's heart was almost thumping itself out of place in his body, stretched upon the rough cinder track.

Then a low murmur broke from the crowd as they saw young Paterson coming round the track, almost staggering under the strain, but keenly intent on finishing now that his two formidable opponents were lying helpless. He had kept running during the last round merely to take the third prize. Now here was his chance of the coveted Red Hose, and he sprinted and tore along as fast as he was able, calling up every particle of effort he could muster, and intent on getting past before the two men could gather strength to rise.

"Come on, Rob!" roared Andrew Marshall, "get up an' feenish, my wee cock! Paterson's comin' along, an' he'll win. Get up an' try an' feenish it!"

Stirred by the warning, Robert tried to rise. He raised himself to his knees, but the pain in his injured foot was too great, and he fell forward on his face unconscious, and the race ended with Paterson as winner. It was an ironical situation, and soon the crowd were over the ropes, and the two opponents were carried to the dressing tent, where restoratives were applied under which they soon came round.

It was a poor ending to such a fine exhibition. A terrible anger smoldered in Robert's breast against the mine-owner's son for his unconscious action, an action which Robert, blinded by anger at losing, was now firmly convinced was deliberate, and he felt he would just like to smash Rundell's face for it.

Robert went home to have his injured foot attended to. He was too disgusted to feel any more interest in the games that day, and so he remained in the house, nursing his foot for the rest of the day, which passed as such days usually do. Everyone talked about his misfortune and regretted in a casual way the accident which had deprived him of the coveted honor.

It was in late June, and that night Peter Rundell, as he was returning from the games after every event had been decided, overtook Mysie on her way to Rundell House, after having spent the evening at her parents' home.

"It's a lovely evening, Mysie," he said, as he walked along by her side. "What did you think of the games to-day?"

"Oh, no' bad," replied Mysie, not knowing what else to say. "It was a gran' day, an' kept up fine," she continued, alluding to the weather.

"Yes. Didn't I make a horrible mess of things in the Red Hose?" he asked. Then, without waiting, he went on: "I was sorry for Sinclair. He's a fine chap, and ought to have won. It was purely an accident, and I couldn't help myself. I was beaten and done for, and it was hard lines for him to be knocked out in the way he was, just as he was on the point of winning, too."

"Oh, but ye couldna' help it," Mysie returned. "It was an accident."

"Yes; and I would rather Sinclair had got in, though. It was a good race, and Sinclair ought to have got the prize. It was rotten luck. I'm sorry, and I hope the poor beggar does not blame me. We seem always to be fated to be rivals," he continued, his voice dropping into reminiscent tones. "Do you remember how we used to fight at school? I've liked Sinclair always since for the way he stood up for the things he thought were right. I believe you were the cause of our hardest battle, and that also was an accident."

"Yes," replied Mysie, her face flushing slightly as she remembered the incident, and how Peter had been chosen, when her heart told her to choose Robert.

"Oh, well," said Peter, "I suppose we can't help these things. Fate wills it. Let's forget all about such unpleasant things. It's a lovely night. We might go round by the wood. It's not so late yet," and putting Mysie's arm in his, he turned off into the little pathway that skirted the wood, and she, caught by the glamor of the gloaming, as well as flattered by his attentions, acquiesced.

Plaintive and eerie the moor-birds protested against this invasion of their haunts. The moon came slowly up over the eastern end of the moor, flinging a silver radiance abroad, and softening the shadows cast by the hills. A strange, dank smell rose from the mossy ground—the scent of rotting heather and withered grass, mixed with the beautiful perfume from beds of wild thyme.

A low call came from a brooding curlew, a faint sigh from a plover, and the wild rasping cry of a lapwing greeted them overhead. Yet there was a silence, a silence broken for a moment by the cries of the birds, but a silence thick and heavy. Between the calls of the birds Mysie could almost hear her heart's quickened beat. Blood found an eager response, and the magic of the moonlight and the beauty of the night soon wrought upon the excited minds of the pair. Mysie looked in Peter's eyes more desirable than ever. The moonlight on her face, the soft light within her eyes, her shy, downcast look, and the touch of her arm on his charmed him.

"There are some things, Mysie, more desirable than the winning of the Red Hose," he said after a time, looking sideways at her, and placing his hand upon hers, which had been resting upon his arm. "Don't you think so?"

"I dinna ken," she answered simply, a strange little quiver running through her as she spoke.

"Isn't this better than anything else, just to be happy with everything so peaceful? Just you and I together, happy in each other's company."

"Ay," she answered again, a faint little catch in her voice, her heart a-tremble, and her eyes moist and shining. Then silence again, while they slowly strayed through the heather towards the little wooded copse, and Mysie felt that every thump of her heart must be heard at the farthest ends of the earth. Chased by the winds of passion raging within him, discretion was fast departing from Peter, leaving him more and more a prey to impulse and the unwearying persistence of the fever of love that was consuming him.

"Listen, Mysie, I read a song yesterday. It's the sort of thing I'd have written about you:

"In the passionate heart of the rose,
Which from life its deep ardor is feeing.
And lifts its proud head to disclose
Its immaculate beauty and being.
I can see your fine soul in repose,
With an eye lit with love and all-seeing,
In the passionate heart of the rose,
All athrob with its beauty of being."

He quoted, and Mysie's pulse leapt with every word, as the low soothing wooing of his voice came in soft tones like a gentle breeze among clumps of briars.

"Isn't it a beautiful song, Mysie?" he said. "The man who wrote that must have been thinking of someone very like you," and as he said this, he gave her hand a tender squeeze. Mysie thrilled to his touch and her heart leapt and fluttered like a bird in a snare, her breath coming in short little gasps, which were at once a pain and a joy.

"Dinna say that," she said, a note of alarm in her voice as she tried to withdraw her hand.

But he only held it closer, and bent his lips over it, his manner gentle but firm.

"Ay, it is true, Mysie; but I am so stupid I can't do anything of that kind. I'm merely an ordinary sort of chap."

Mysie did not answer, and once again silence fell between them, broken only occasionally by the cry of the birds or the bleating of a sheep.

"I believe I'm in love with you, Mysie," he said at last. "You've grown very beautiful. Could you care for me, Mysie?" he asked, looking at her in the soft moonlight, a smile on his lips, his voice keeping its seductive wooing tone, and his eyes kindling.

Mysie's experience of life had been gleaned from the love stories of earls and lords marrying governesses and ladies' maids after a swift and very eventful courtship. Already she saw herself Peter's wife, her carriage coming at her order, everyone serving her and she the queen of all the district. Illiterate but romantic, she was swept off her feet at the first touch of passion, and the flattery of being recognized!

She did not answer. She did not know what to say; and Peter stole his arm about her waist, so tempting, so sweet to touch, and they passed beneath the shadow of the trees as they entered the little wooded copse. The moonlight filtered down through the trees, working silvery patterns upon the pathway. The silence, heavy and scented, was broken only by the far-away wheepling of a wakeful whaup and the grumbling of the burn near by, which bickered and hurried to be out in the open again on its way to the river.

Mysie heard the sounds, felt the fragrance of young briars and hawthorn mingled with the smell of last year's decaying leaves which carpeted the pathway. She noted the beauty of the foliage against the moon, heard the swift scurry of a frightened rabbit and the faint snort of a hedge-hog on the prowl for food.

"What have you to say to me, Mysie?" Peter persisted, his hot breath against her cheek, his blood coursing through his veins in red-hot passion. "Could you care for me, Mysie? I want you to be mine!"

"I dinna ken what to say," she at last answered, distress in her voice, yet pleased to be wooed by this young man. "Wad it no' be wrang to ha'e onything to dae wi' me? I'm only your mither's servant." She felt it was her duty to put it this way.

"No, you are my sweetheart," he cried, discretion all gone now in his eager furtherance of his pleading. "I want you—only you, Mysie," and he caught her in his arms in a strong burst of desire for her. "Mine, Mysie, mine!" he cried, his lips upon hers and hers responding now, his hot eyes greedily devouring her as he held her there in his strong young arms. "Say, Mysie, that you are mine, that I am yours, body and soul belonging to each other," and so he raved on in eager burning language, which was the sweetest music in Mysie's ears.

His arms about her, he made her sit down, she still unresisting and flattered by his words, he fondling and kissing her, his hands caressing her face, her ears, her hair, her neck, his head sometimes resting upon her breast.

Maddened and scorched by the passion raging within him, lured by the magic of the night, and impelled by the invitation of the sweet dewy lips that seemed to cry for kisses, he strained her to his breast.

He praised her eyes, her hair, her voice, whilst he poured kisses upon her, his fire kindling her whole being into response.

Then a thick cloud came over the face of the moon, darkening the dell, blotting out the silvery patterns on the ground, chasing the light shadows into dark corners; and a far-off protest of a whaup shouting to the hills was heard in a shriller and more anxious note that had something of alarm in it; the burn seemed to bicker more loudly in its anxiety to hurry on out into the open moor; and the scents and perfumes of the wood sank into pale ghosts of far-off memories.

When passion, red-eyed and fierce for conquest, had driven innocence from the throne of virtue the guardian angels wept; and all their tears, however bitter, could not obliterate the stains which marked the progress of destruction.

At the end of the copse, when Mysie and Peter emerged, they neither spoke nor laughed. There was shame in their downcast faces, and their feet dragged heavily. His arm no longer encircled her waist, he did not now praise her eyes, her hair, her figure. Lonely each felt, afraid to look up, as if something walked between them. And far away the whaup wheepled in protest, the burn still grumbled, and the perfumes, and the sounds of the glen and all its beauty were as if they had never existed, and the thick cloud grew blacker over the face of the moon.

CHAPTER XIV
THE AWAKENING

Night after night for a week afterwards, Mysie lay awake till far on into the morning. She seemed to be face to face with life's realities at last. The silly, shallow love stories held no fascination for her. The love affairs of "Jean the Mill Girl" could not rouse her interest. Often she cried for hours, till exhaustion brought sleep, troubled and unrefreshing.

She grew silent and avoided company. She sang no more at her work, and she avoided Peter, and kept out of his way. She often compared Robert with him now, and loved to let her mind linger on that one mad moment of delirious joy a year ago, when he had crushed her to his breast, and cried to her to be his. Thus womanhood dawned for her, and its great responsibilities frightened her.

Robert, on the other hand, spent a week nursing his injured foot, but apart from the week's idle time, he suffered very little. He felt sore at losing the race, but was able now to look upon it as an unfortunate accident. But that smile which he had seen on the face of Mysie made him strangely happy, and it helped him to get over his disappointment. He was impatient to be out upon the moor again. He would wait for Mysie some night, he concluded, and tell her calmly that he wanted her to marry him.

His mother's prospects were fairly good now. The youngest boy would soon be working; besides, two other brothers were at work, while Jennie, his eldest sister, was in service, and Annie, the younger one, was helping in the house. He waited, night after night, after his injured foot was better—lingering on the moor by the path which Mysie must travel. He lay among the heather and read books, or dreamed of a rosy future, with her the center of his dreams; but no Mysie came along, and he began to grow anxious.

He wanted to make enquiries about her, but feared to arouse suspicion of having too keen an interest in her. By various ways he sought information, but never heard anything definite.

"I see Matthew Maitland's ither lassie has started on the pit-head," he said to his mother, as one night they sat by the fire before retiring.

"Ay," answered Mrs. Sinclair. "Matthew has the worst o' it by noo. Wi' his twa bits o' laddies workin', an' Mysie in service, an' Mary gaun to the pit-head, it should mak' his burden a wee easier."

"I dinna like the idea o' lasses gaun to work on the pithead," he said simply. "I aye mind of the time that Mysie an' me wrocht on it. It's no' a very nice place for lasses or women."

"No," his mother said. "I dinna like it either. Nae guid ever comes o' lasses gaun there. They lose a' sense o' modesty an' decency, after a while, an' are no' like women at a' when they grow aulder. Besides, it mak's them awfu' coorse."

"I wad hardly say that aboot them a'," he ventured cautiously. "Mysie's no' coorse, an' she worked on the pithead."

"No, Mysie's no' coorse," admitted his mother; "but Mysie didna work very lang on the pit-head. An' forby, we dinna ken but what Mysie micht hae been better if she had never been near it, or worse if she had stayed langer. Just look at Susan Morton, an' that Mag Lindsay. What are they but shameless lumps who dinna ken what modesty is?" and there was a spark of the old scorn in her voice as she finished.

"Oh, but I wadna gang as faur as you, mither," he said, "wi' your condemnations. I ken that baith Susan Morton an' Mag Lindsay are guid-hearted women. They may be coorse in their talk, an' a' that sort o' thing; but they are as kind-hearted as onybody else, an' kinder than some."

"Oh; I hae nae doot," she answered relentingly. "I didna mean that at a'; but the pit-head doesna make them ony better, an' it's no' wark for them at a'."

"I mind," said Robert reminiscently, "when Mysie an' me started on the pit-head, Mag Lindsay was awfu' guid to Mysie; an' I've kent her often sharin' her piece wi' wee Dicky Tamson, whiles when he had nane, if his mother happened to be on the fuddle for a day or twa. There's no a kinderhearted woman in Lowwood, mither, than Mag Lindsay. She'd swear at Dicky a' the time she was stappin' her piece into him. It was jist her wye, an' I think she couldna help it."

"Oh, ay, Mag's bark is waur then her bite. I ken that," was the reply. "An' wi' a' her fauts a body canna help likin' her."

"Speakin' of Mysie," said Robert with caution, "I hinna seen her owre for a while surely. Wull there be onything wrang?" and then, to hide the agitation he felt, "she used to come owre hame aboot twice a week, an' I hinna seen her for a while."

The Underworld | 111

"Oh, there canna be onything wrang," replied Nellie, "or we wad hae heard tell o' it. But t' is time we were awa' to oor beds, or we'll no' be able to rise in time the morn," and rising as she spoke, she began to make preparations for retiring, and he withdrew to his room also.

Still, day after day, he hung about the moorland path, but no Mysie, so far as he knew, ever came past. She had visited her parents only once since the games and her mother was struck by her subdued and thoughtful demeanor. But nothing was said at the time.

Robert grew impatient, and began to roam nearer to Rundell House, in the hope of seeing her. Always his thoughts were full of Mysie and the raging passion in his blood for her gave him no rest. He loved to trace her name linked with his own, and then to obliterate it again, in case anyone would see it. All day his thoughts were of her; and her sweet, shy smile that day of the games was nursed in memory till it grew to be a solace to his heart and its hunger.

He saw likenesses to her in everything, and even the call of the moor-birds awakened some memory of an incident of childhood, when Mysie and he had, with other children, played together on the moors. Even the very words which she had spoken, or the way she had acted, or how she had looked, in cheap cotton frock and pinafore, were recalled by a familiar cry, or by the sudden discovery of a bog-flower in bloom.

It was a glorious afternoon in late July. The hum of insect life seemed to flood the whole moor; the scent of mown hay and wild thyme, and late hawthorn blossom from the trees on the edge of the moor, was heavy in the air, and the sun was very hot, and still high in the heavens. The hills that bordered the moor drowsed and brooded, like ancient gods, clothed in a lordly radiance that was slowly consuming them as they meditated upon their coming oblivion.

The heather gave promise, in the tiny purple buds that sprouted from the strong, rough stems, of the blaze of purple glory that would carpet the moors with magic in the coming days of autumn. Yet there was a vague hint, in the too deep silence, and in the great clouds that were slowly drifting along the sky, of pent-up force merely awaiting the time to be set free to gallop across the moor in anger and destruction. The clouds, too, were deeply red, with orange touches here and there, trailing into dark inky ragged edges.

Far away, at the foot of the hills a crofter's cow lowed lazily, calling forth a summons to be taken in and relieved of its burden of milk. The sheep came nearer to the "bughts," and the lambs burrowed for nourishment, with tails wagging, as they drew their sustenance, prodding and punching the patient mothers in the operation of feeding. Robert, noting all, with leisured enjoyment strolled lazily into the little copse, and lay down beneath the cool, grateful shelter of the trees.

Drugged by the sweetness and the solitude, he fell asleep, and the sun was low on the horizon when he awoke, the whole copse ringing with the evening songs of merle and mavis, and other less musical birds, and, as he looked down the glade, he saw, out on the moorland path, coming straight for the grove, the form of Mysie—the form of which he had dreamed, and for which he had longed so much.

The hot blood mounted to his face and raced through his frame, while his heart thumped at the thought that now, in the quietness of the dell, he would meet her and speak to her. He would speak calmly, and not frighten her, as he had done on that former occasion; and he braced himself to meet her.

Impatiently he waited, and then, as he saw her about to enter the grove, he rose as unconcernedly as he could, trying hard to assume the air of one who had met her by accident, and stepped on to the path when Mysie was within ten yards or so of him.

The color left her face, and her limbs felt weak beneath her, as she recognized him, and he was quick to note the change in her whole appearance.

She was paler, he thought, and thinner, and the bloom of a few weeks ago was gone. Her eyes were listless, and the soft, shy look had been replaced by an averted shame-stricken one. She was plainly flurried by the meeting, and looking about trying to find if there were not, even yet, a way of evading it.

"It's a fine nicht, Mysie," he began, stammering and halting before her, "though I think it is gaun to work to rain."

"Ay," she responded hurriedly, her agitation growing, as she was forced to halt before him.

"I've come oot on the muir a wheen o' nichts noo, to try an' meet you," he began, getting into the business right away, "an' I had begun to think you had stopped comin' owre."

But Mysie answered never a word. Her face grew paler, and her agitation became more evident.

"Mysie," he began, now fully braced for the important matter in view, "I want you to marry me. I want you to be my wife. You've kenned me a' my life. We gaed to the school together, and we gaed to work together, an' I hae aye looked on you as my lass. I canna keep it ony langer noo. I hae wanted to tell you a lang time aboot it, an' to ask you to be my wife. My place at hame is easier noo. My mother has the rest o' the family comin' on to take my place, and her battle is gey weel owre, an' I can see prospects o' settin' up a hoose o' my ain, if you'll agree to share it with me. I haven't muckle to offer you, but I think you'll ken by this time that I'll be guid to you. Mysie, I want you. Will you come?"

For answer, Mysie burst into tears, her shoulders heaving with the sobs of her grief, her breast surging and falling, while her little hands covered her eyes, as she stood with bent head, a pitiable little figure.

"What is it, Mysie?" he enquired, his hands at once going tenderly over her bent head, and caressing it as he spoke, "What is it, Mysie? Tell me. Hae I vexed you by speakin' like that? Dinna greet, Mysie," he went on soothingly, his voice soft and tender, and vibrant with sympathy and love. "Dinna greet. But tell me what's wrang. I'm sorry if it's me that has done it, Mysie. Maybe I hae frightened you; but, there now, dinna greet. I didna mean ony harm!" and he stroked and caressed her hair softly with his hands, or patted her shoulders at every word, as a mother does with a fretful child.

"There noo, Mysie, dinna greet," he said again, the soft, soothing note of vexation in his voice growing more tender and husky with emotion. "Look up, Mysie, for I dinna like to see you greetin'. It maun be something gey bad, surely, to mak' you greet like this," and his hands seemed to stab her with every tender touch, and his soft words but added more pain to her grief.

But still Mysie never answered. Her tears instead flowed faster, and her sobs grew heavier, until finally she moaned like a stricken animal in pain.

"Mysie! Mysie! my dochter, what is it?" unable to control himself longer. "Surely you can tell me what ails you? What is it, Mysie? Look up, my dear! Look up an' tell me what ails you!"

"Oh, dear! Oh, dear!" moaned Mysie, the floodgates of her grief now wide, and her soul in torture.

"Mysie," he cried, taking her head between his hands and raising it up, "what is it that's wrang with you? Is it me that is the cause o' you being vexed?"

"Oh, no, no," she moaned, trying to avert her face. "Oh, dinna, Rob!" she pleaded, and the old familiar name smote him and thrilled him as of old.

"Tell me what is the matter," he said, a stronger note in his voice, the old masterful spirit asserting itself again. "What is wrang wi' you? I can't understand it, an' I wish to try an' help you."

But still she sobbed and there was no answer.

"Look here," he said. "Tell me plainly if I have been the cause of this."

"No; oh, no," she sobbed, again hiding her eyes with her hands.

"Very weel, then," he went on. "Will you no' tell me what is wrong? I canna understand it unless you tell me. Are you in ony trouble o' ony kind? Speak, Mysie." Then, his voice becoming more pleading in its tones, "Wad you be feart to be my wife, Mysie? I aye thocht you cared for me. I hae loved you a' my days. You maun ken that, I think. Speak up, Mysie, an' tell me if you care for me. I want you, an' I maun ken what you think o' it. Come, Mysie, tell me!"

"Oh, dinna ask me, Rob," she pleaded. "Dinna ask me!"

"What is the matter then?" he cried. "There's something wrong, an' you'll no' tell me. Very well, tell me what you mean to do. I hae asked you a fair question. Are you going to marry me? I want yes or no to that," and there was a touch of impatience creeping into his voice.

"Come on," he urged, after a short silence, broken only by Mysie's sobs, "gie me an answer. Or, if you wad raither wait a wee while, till this trouble has blawn by that is bothering you, I'm quite agreeable to wait."

"It'll never blaw by, Rob," she sobbed. "Oh, dinna ask me ony mair. I canna be your wife noo, an' I jist want to be left alane!"

The pain and despair in her voice alarmed him. It was so keen and poignant, and went to his heart like a knife.

"Oh!" he gasped in surprise, as he strove to call his pride to his assistance. It was so unlike what he had anticipated that it amazed him to have such a disappointing reply. Then, recovering somewhat:—"Very well!" with great deliberation, while his voice sounded unnaturally strained. Then the effort failing, and his pride breaking down: "Oh, Mysie, Mysie," he burst out in poignant agony again relapsing into the pleading wooing tones that were so difficult to withstand, "How I hae loved you! I thocht you cared for me. I hae built mysel' up in you, an' I'll never, never be able to forget you! Oh, think what it is! You hae been life itsel' to me, Mysie, an' I canna think that you dinna care! Oh, Mysie!"

He turned away, his heart sore and his soul wounded, and strode from the copse out on to the moor, a thousand thoughts driving him on, a thousand regrets pursuing, and a load of pain in his heart that was bearing his spirit down.

"Oh, dear God!" moaned Mysie, kneeling down, her legs unable to support her longer, "Oh, dear God, my heart'll break!" and a wild burst of sobbing shook her frame, and her grief overpowering flowed through the tears—a picture of utter despair and terrible hopelessness.

Robert tore away from the dell, his whole calculation of things upset. To think that Mysie could not love him had never entered his head. What was wrong with her? What was the nature of her terrible grief?

He kicked savagely at a thistle which grew upon the edge of the pathway, his pride wounded, but now in possession of the citadel of his heart; and on he strode, still driven by the terrible passion raging within him; resolving already, as many have done under like circumstances, that his life was finished. Hope had gone, dreams were unreal and vanishing as the mist that crawled along the bog-pools at night.

At the crest of the little hill, just where it sloped down to the village, he stood and looked back.

Good God! Was he seeing aright! The figure of a man, who in the gray gloaming looked well-dressed, was approaching Mysie, and she was slowly moving to meet him. A few steps more, and the man had the girl, he thought, in his arms, and was kissing her where they stood.

Was he dreaming? What was the meaning of all this? "Oh, Christ!" he groaned. "What does it all mean?" and he rubbed his eyes and looked again, then sat down, all his pride and anger raging within him as he watched, kindling the jungle instinct within him into a raging fire, to fight for his mate—his by right of class and association. He doubled back, as the two figures turned in the direction of the copse—the resolve in his mind to go back and forcibly tear Mysie from this unknown stranger. He would fight for her. She was his, and he was prepared to assert his right of possession before all the world.

In a mad fury he started forward, a raging anger in his heart, striding along in quick, determined, relentless steps, his blood jumping and his energy roused, and all the madness of a strong nature coursing through him; but after a few yards he hesitated, stopped, and then turned back.

After all, Mysie must have made an appointment with this man. She evidently wanted him, and that was her reason for asking to be left alone.

"Oh, God!" he groaned again, sitting down. "This is hellish!" and he began to turn over the whole business in his mind once more.

Long he sat, and the darkness fell over the moor, matching the darkness that brooded over his heart and mind. He heard the moor-birds crying in restlessness, and saw the clouds piling themselves up, and come creeping darkly over the higher ground, bringing a threat of rain in their wake. The moan in the wind became louder, presaging a storm; but still he sat or lay upon the rough, withered grass, fighting out his battle, meeting the demons of despair and gloom, and the legions of pain and misery, in greater armies than ever he had met them before.

Again he groaned, as his ear caught the plaintive note of a widowed partridge, which sat behind him upon a grassy knoll of turf, crying out on the night air, an ache in every cry, the grief and sorrow of his wounded, breaking heart.

It seemed to Robert that there was a strange sort of kinship between him and the bird—a kinship and understanding which touched a chord of ready feeling in his heart. The ominous hoot of an owl in the wood startled him, and he rose to his feet. He could not sit still. Idleness would drive him mad. He strode off on to the moor, away from the track, his whole being burning in torture, and his mind a mass of unconnected fancies and pains.

Over the bogs and through the marshes, the madness of despair within him, he heeded not the deep ditches and the bog-pools. They were the pits of darkness, the sty-pools, which his soul must either cross, or in which he must perish. He tore up the hills into the mists and the rising storm, the thick clouds, full of rain, enveloping him, and matching the terrible fury of his breast.

On, ever on, in the darkness and the mire, through clumps of whin and stray bushes of wild briar. On, always on, driven and lashed into action by the resistless desire to get away from himself. He knew not the direction he had taken. He had lost his bearings on the moor; the darkness had completely hidden the landmarks, and even had he been conscious of his actions, he could not have told in which part of the moor he was.

"Oh, God!" he groaned again, almost falling over a bush of broom; and sitting down, he buried his face in his hands, and, forgetful of the wind and the rain, which now drove down in torrents, sat and brooded and thought, his mind seeking to understand the chaos of despair.

What was the meaning of life? What was beyond it after death? Would immortality, if such there were, be worth having? Men in countless, unthinkable millions, had lived, and loved, and lost, and passed on. Did immortality carry with it pain and suffering for them? If not, did it carry happiness and balm? To hell with religions and philosophies, he thought; they were all a parcel of fairy tales to drug men's minds and keep them tame; and he glared impotently at the pitiless heavens, as if he would defy gods, and devils, and men. He would be free—free in mind, in thought, and unhampered by unrealities!

No. Men had the shaping of their own lives. Pride would be his ally. He would lock up this episode in his heart, and at the end of time for him, there would be an end of the pain and the regret, when he was laid among the myriad millions of men of all the countless ages since man had being.

This was immortality; to be forever robed in the dreamless draperies of eternal oblivion, rather than have eternal life, with all its torments—mingling with the legions of the past, and with mother earth—the dust of success and happiness indistinguishable from the dust of failure and despair. Time alone would be his relief—the great physician that healed all wounds.

The wind blew stronger and the rain fell heavier, the one chasing, the other in raging gusts, and both tearing round and lashing the form of the man who sat motionless and unaware of all this fury. The wind god tried to shake him up by rushing and roaring at him; but still there was no response. Then, gathering re-inforcements, he came on in a mad charge, driving a cloud of rain in front of him as a sort of spear-head to break the defense of fearlessness and unconcern of this unhappy mortal. Yet the figure moved not.

Baffled and still more angry, the wind god retired behind the hills again to rest; then, driving a larger rain-cloud before him, with a roar and a crash he tore down the slope, raging and tearing in a wild tumult of anger, straight against the lonely figure which sat there never moving, his head sunk upon his breast.

Beaten and sullen, the god again retired to re-collect his strength. He moaned and growled as he retired, frightening the moor-birds and the hares, which lay closer to earth, their little hearts quivering with fear. Young birds were tucked safely under the parent wing, as terror strode across the moor, striking dread into every fluttering little heart and shivering body. Low growled the wind, as he ran around his broken forces, gathering again new forces in greater and greater multitudes.

Just then, with an oath, the figure rose and faced the storm, striding again up the slope, as if determined to carry the war into the camp of the enemy.

A low growl came rumbling from the hills, as the wind god rushed along, encouraging his legions, threatening, coaxing, pleading, commanding them to fight, and so to overcome this figure who now boldly faced his great army.

The advance guard of the storm broke upon him in wild desperation, rushing and thundering, howling and yelling, sputtering and hissing, spitting and hitting at him, and then the main body struck him full in the face, all the bulk and the force of it hurled upon him with terrible impetuous abandon, and Robert's foot striking a tuft at the moment, he went down, down into a bog-pool among the slush and moss, and decaying heather-roots, down before the mad rush of the wind-god's army, who roared and shouted in glee, with a voice that shook the hills and called upon the elements to laugh and rejoice.

And the widowed partridge out upon the moor, creeping closer to the lee side of his tuft of moss, cried out in his pain, not because of the fury of the blast, but because of the heart that was breaking under the little shivering body for the dead mate, who had meant so much of life and happiness to him—cried with an ache in every cry, and the heart of the man responded in his great, overpowering grief.

CHAPTER XV
PETER MAKES A DECISION

Peter Rundell often wondered what had become of Mysie. For a day or two after the evening of the day of the games, he had shunned the possibility of meeting her, because of the shame that filled his heart.

His face burned when his thoughts went back to the evening in the grove on the moor. He wondered how it had all happened. He had not meant anything wrong when he suggested the walk. He could not account for what had occurred, and so he pondered and his shame rankled.

Then an uneasy feeling took possession of him and he felt he would like to see Mysie.

A week slipped away and he tried to find a way of coming in contact with her, but no real chance ever presented itself.

A fortnight passed and he grew still more uneasy. He grew anxious and there was a hot fear pricking at his heart. Then at last, one day he caught a glimpse of her, and his heart was smitten with dread.

She was changed. Her appearance was altered. She was thinner, much thinner and very white and listless. The old air of gayety and bubbling spirits was gone. Her step seemed to drag, instead of the bright patter her feet used to make; and his anxiety increased and finally he decided that he must talk with her.

There was something wrong and he wanted to know what it was. He tried to make an excuse for seeing her alone but no chance presented itself, and another week went past and he grew desperate. Then luck almost threw her into his arms one day in the hall.

"Mysie," he whispered, "there is something I want to discuss with you. Meet me in the grove to-night about ten. I must see you. Will you come?"

She nodded and passed on, not daring to raise her eyes, her face flaming suddenly into shame, and the color leaving it again, gave her a deeper pallor; and so he had to be content with that.

All day he was fidgety and ill at ease, torn by a thousand dreads, and consumed by anxiety, waiting impatiently for the evening, and puzzling over what could be the matter. He felt that for one moment of mad indiscretion, when allowing himself to be cast adrift upon the sea of passion, the frail bark of his life had set out upon an adventure from which he could not now turn back. He was out upon the great ocean current of circumstances, where everything was unknown and uncharted, so far as he was concerned. What rocks lay in his track, he did not know; but his heart guessed, and sought in many ways of finding a course that would bring his voyage to an end in the haven of comfort and respectability. Respectability was his god, as he knew it was the god of his parents. Money might save him; but there was something repugnant in the thought of leaving the whole burden of disgrace upon Mysie. For, after all, the fault was wholly his, and it was his duty to face the consequences. Still if a way could be found of getting over it in an easy way it would be better. But he would leave that till the evening when he had learned from Mysie, whether his fears were correct or not, and then a way might be found out of the difficulty.

But the day seemed long in passing, and by the time the clock chimed nine he was in a fever of excitement, and pained and ill with dread.

Yet he was late when it came the hour, and Mysie was there first and had already met Robert before he reached the grove.

When Robert had gone away, and she sat crying upon the moor, she felt indeed as if the whole world was slipping from her and that her life was finished. Only ruin, black, unutterable, stared her in the face. Oh, if only Robert had spoken sooner, she thought. If only that terrible beautiful night with its moonlight witchery had not been lived as it had been! If only something had intervened to prevent what had happened! And she sobbed in her despair, knowing what was before her and learning all too late, that Robert was the man she loved and wanted.

Then when her passionate grief had spent itself, she rose as she saw Peter coming hurriedly to meet her.

"What is the matter, Mysie?" he asked with real concern in his voice, noting the tear-stained face and her over-wrought condition. "What is it, Mysie?"

But Mysie did not answer just then, and they both turned and passed into the grove, walking separately, as if afraid of each other's touch, and something repellent keeping them apart.

They sat down, carefully avoiding the place where they had sat on that other fateful occasion, nearly a month before, and a long silence elapsed before words were again spoken.

"Now, Mysie," said Peter at last breaking the silence, and bracing himself to hear unpleasant news, "I want to know what is wrong. What is the matter?" and he feared to hear her tell her trouble.

But again only tears—tears and sobs, terrible in their intensity as if the frail little body would break completely under the strain of her grief.

"Mysie," he said, and his voice had a note of tender anxiety in it, "what is it, dear? Tell me."

"You shouldn't need to ask," she replied between her sobs. "You shouldn't need to ask when you should ken."

Again a long silence, and Peter felt he had got a heavy blow. A sickening feeling of shame smote his heart at the knowledge hinted at—a knowledge he had feared to learn.

"Is it—is it—am I the cause of it, Mysie? Is—is it—?" and his voice was hoarse and dry and pained.

She nodded, and Peter knew beyond all doubt that he was the cause of the misery.

Again a long silence fell between them, in which both seemed to live an eternity of silence and pain. Then clearing his throat, Peter spoke.

"Mysie," he said, "there is only one thing to be done then," and there was decision in his voice and a desire which meant that he was going to rise to a height to which neither he nor Mysie ever expected he would rise. "We must get married."

She looked at him, with eyes still wet, but searching his face keenly.

"Ay. It's a' richt sayin' that now, efter the thing's done," she said bitterly.

"But it is the only thing, Mysie, that can be done," he replied quickly. "I can't think of anything else."

"You should hae thought aboot that afore. It's nae use now," she said bluntly.

"Why, Mysie," he asked in surprise. "Why is it no use? Wouldn't you like to marry me?"

"No," she replied firmly. "I would not! Do you think I have no thought o' mysel'? If nothing had happened, you would never hae thought aboot me for your wife. But now that you've done something you canna get oot o' you'd like to mak' me believe you want to help me bear the disgrace, while a' the time you don't want to. But it's no' my disgrace," and there was heat creeping into her voice. "It is yours, an' you should hae thocht aboot a' that afore," and her voice was very angry as she finished.

"You are wrong, Mysie," he replied mollifyingly. "I love, you and I told you that before it happened, and I also hinted that I wanted to marry you."

"Ay, but that was just at the time. Maybe if nothing had happened, an' I had never been in your company again, you'd soon hae forgotten."

"No, Mysie, you are wrong. I love you, and I've brought you to this, for which I am sorry, so we must be married," he said decisively.

"Why?" she asked, and her eyes met his honestly and fairly.

"Because it is the right thing to do," he replied quietly.

"Is that a'?" she asked.

"Is it not enough? What else is there to do?" Mysie was silent, and after a while Peter went on;—"It is a duty, dear, but I am going to face it, and shoulder the responsibility. It is the right thing to do, and it must be done."

"Ay, an' you are gaun to dae it, just as a bairn tak's medicine; because you are forced. I asked if that was a', and it seems to be. But what if I don't have onything mair to dae with you?"

"You would not do that, Mysie," he said hurriedly, and incredulously. It had never entered his mind that she would refuse to marry him, and he looked upon his offer as a great service which he was doing her. "Why, what could you do otherwise?" he asked looking blankly at her.

"I could work as I hae always done," she said sharply. "You surely think you are a catch. Man, efter what has happened I feel that I wudna care than I never saw you again. You hae little o' rale manliness in you. You thocht it was gran' to carry on wi' a workin' lassie, maybe," and there was bitter scorn in her voice, "an' now when you hae landed yourself into a mess you are grinning like a bear with the branks an' wantin' to dae what is richt as you call it," and Mysie was now really in a temper.

"Mysie, you must not speak like that," he broke in, in earnest tones. "You know I love you, and loving you as I do, I want to shield you as much—"

"Ay, but you want to shield yourself first," she said.

"No, dear, it is only of you I am thinking. I love you very much and want to do what is right. Even although this had not happened, I was going to ask you to be my wife. Will you marry me, Mysie?"

"What'll your folks say?" she asked bluntly. "You ken that I'm no' the wife you would have gotten nor the yin your folk would like you to get," she said, searching his face with a keen look. "I'm no' born in your class. I'm ignorant an' have not the fine manners your wife should have, an' I doot neither your faither nor your mither wad consent to such a thing."

"But I won't ask them," he replied. "I am a man for myself, and do not see why they should be asked to approve my actions in this."

"Ay, that's a' richt; but what aboot your ain feelings in the matter? Am I the lass you wad hae ta'en, Peter, if this hadna happened?" and there was a world of hungry appeal in her voice as she finished. It was as if she wanted to be assured that it was for herself alone that he really wanted to marry her.

"Why should you not?" he enquired.

"That's no' the question," she said, noting the evasion. "You ken as weel as I dae that it wad be an ill match for you. You've been brought up differently. You've had eddication, an' an easy life. You've been trained faur differently, an' you canna say that you'd no' tire o' me. I have not as muckle learning as wad make me spell my ain name, an' I could never fill the position o' your wife with the folk I'd have to mix with."

"That's all right, Mysie," he said, ready to counter her argument. "You have not been educated, that is true, but it is only a question of having you trained. If one woman can be educated and trained so can another. This is what I propose to do: I go back to Edinburgh in a fortnight to finish my last year. My father has put the colliery into a company, and he has a large part of the management on his shoulders. He expects when I come home next year to gradually retire. I shall be the controlling power then, and he will slip out of the business and end his days in leisure."

"Ay, but you are thinking a' the time aboot the disgrace," she said. "Your whole thought is about your position, an' you hae never a real thought aboot me." She was somewhat mollified; but there was still a hard note in her voice, and not a little distrust too. "Are you sure you are no' proposin' this just because o' the trouble? I don't want peety! I am pairtly to blame too," this with a softer note creeping into her voice, and making it more resigned. "If it's no' oot o' peety for me, I could bear it better. But I'll no' hae peety. I can look after mysel' an' face the whole thing, even though I ken it'll break my mither's heart."

"I know what it is for you, Mysie," he said. "I am trying to look at the whole thing from your point of view. That's why I have planned to give you some sort of a training, and make it as easy for you as possible. It is for your position I am worrying and when I come into my father's place I will be able to put all things right for you, and make you really happy."

"But you have not faced the main bit yet," she said as he ceased speaking. "Where do I come in? You hae got this to face now, an' it'll no' wait a' that time."

"Yes, I know," he replied, "I'm just coming to that. At first it won't perhaps look too nice to you, but remember, Mysie, I want to face the matter honestly and you'll have to help me. Very well," he went on. "As I said, I go back to Edinburgh in three weeks at most—I'll try and go in a fortnight, and you must go with me—not traveling together. We must keep all our affairs to ourselves, and not even your parents or mine must know. When I go away you'll come the day after. You can travel over the moor to Greyrigg station, take the 4:30 train from there and I can meet you at Edinburgh. I'll get a house next week when I go to arrange for my term. I shall tell no one. You can live in the house I get and I can continue perhaps in lodgings, and I shall come and visit you as often as I can."

He stopped for a little and then resumed:—"I shall buy books for you and come and teach you the things you'll need to learn, or I can get someone to do it, if you'd like that better. Then when you are thoroughly trained, I can bring you home to Rundell House and all will be well."

"An' what aboot—what aboot—" she paused, averting her face. "Are you no' forgettin' that it'll tak' a lang time for me to learn a' I'll need; for I'm gey ill to learn."

"No, Mysie," he replied reassuringly. "When you arrive in Edinburgh, we can go next day to be married before the Sheriff. It's all right, Mysie dear," he assured her as he saw the questioning look in her eyes. "Don't think I'm trying to trap you. I want to make what amends I can for what has happened. You'll be my wife just as surely as if the minister married us. If you are not content with that we can easily get married with a minister after we decide to come back here."

"But wad that be a true marriage?" she asked, scarcely able to credit what he told her. "Wad I get marriage lines?"

"Oh, yes. It would be legal, and you'd get marriage lines. Now what do you say?"

"I dinna like the thocht o' no' tellin' my mither. Will I hae to gang away, an' no' tell her?"

"Oh, you must not tell anyone," he replied quickly. "No one must know or all our plans will go crash, and we'll both be left to face the shame of the whole thing. So you must not tell."

"Mither will break her heart," she broke in again with a hint of a sob. "She'll wonder where I am, an' worry aboot me, wi' nae word o' me! Am I just to disappear oot o' everybody's kennin' altogether? Oh, dear! It'll break my mither's heart," and she cried again at the thought of the pain and anxiety which her parents would experience.

So they sat and talked, he trying to soothe and allay her anxiety and she, at first openly skeptical, and then by and by allowing herself to be persuaded.

All this time they had been too engrossed in their own affairs to notice how the wind had risen and that a storm was already breaking over the moor. Then suddenly realizing it, they started for home.

It was nearing midnight, and the clouds being thick and low made the mossy ground very dark. The rain was coming down heavily and everything pointed to a wild night.

"I'm sorry I did not bring a coat with me," said Peter, taking the windward side of Mysie, so as to break the storm for her. "I had no idea that it was going so rain when I came away," and they plowed their way through the long rough grass, plashing through the little pools they were unable to see, while the wind raged and tore across the moor in a high gale.

He had a key in his pocket and when they arrived at Rundell House he noiselessly opened the door, and they entered, slipping along like burglars.

When Mysie reached her room, she sat down to think matters over for herself, forgetful of the fact that she was wet. She sat a long time pondering in her slow untrained way over the arrangements which had been come to, her mind trying to get accustomed to the thought that she was going to be Peter's wife and to leave Lowwood.

But somehow the thought of being his wife did not appeal to her now, as it had done when she had pictured herself the lady of the district with her dreams of everything she desired, and fancying herself the envy of every woman who knew her.

The secrecy of the business she did not like; but she told herself it would all come right; that it was necessary under the circumstances and that afterwards when she had been taught and trained in the ways of his people she would come back and all would be well.

Then in the midst of all this looking into the future with its doubts and promises, came the thought of Robert, and her pulses thrilled and her blood quickened; but it had come too late.

Would she rather be at Rundell House as Peter's wife or sitting in a one-roomed apartment sewing pit clothes perhaps, or washing and scrubbing in the slavery in which the women folk of her class generally lived? Ah, yes, as Robert's wife that would have been happiness. But it was all too late now. She had turned aside—and she must pay the penalty of it all.

Long she sat, and cried, and at last realizing that she was cold and shivering, she took off her clothes and crawled off to bed, her last thought of Robert as he had left her, the pain in his eyes and the awful agony in his voice: "Oh, Mysie, how I hae loved you! An' I thocht you cared for me!" rang in her ears as she lay and tossed in sleepless misery.

In the morning she was in a high fever and unable to rise out of her bed. She had a headache and felt wretched and ill. In her exhausted state, weakened by worry and her resistance gone, the drenching, the chill and the long sitting in her lonely room had overmastered her completely.

She raved about Robert, crying to him in her fevered excitement, and he, all unconscious, was at that time at his work, tired also and exhausted by his terrible night upon the moor.

When he stumbled and fell into the mossy pool, his mind became more collected and, scrambling out, he stood to consider where he was, trying to find his bearings in the thick darkness.

The low whinnying of a horse near by gave him a clew and he started in the direction of the cry, concluding that it was some of the horses sheltering behind a dyke which ran across the moor from the end of the village.

He crawled and scrambled along, and after going about twenty yards he came to the dyke, at the other side of which stood the cowering horses.

"Whoa, Bob," he said soothingly, and one of them whinnied back in response as if glad to know that a human being was near. He moved nearer to them, and began to stroke their manes and clap their necks, to which they responded by rubbing their faces against him and cuddling an affectionate return for the sympathy in his voice.

"Puir Bob," he said, tenderly, as he patted the neck of the animal which rubbed its soft nose against his arm. It seemed so glad of the companionship and reached nearer as Robert put out his other hand to stroke sympathetically the nose of the other horse, as he also drew near.

"Puir Rosy," he said. "Was you feart for the wind and the rain? Poor lass! It's an awfu' nicht to be oot in!" and they rubbed themselves against him and whinnied with a low pleased gurgle, grateful for his kindness and company as he patted and stroked the soft velvet skins, and they rubbed themselves against him as if each were jealous lest his attentions be not equally divided.

He stood for a short time, thus fondling and patting them, then keeping to the dyke, he made his way along it and he thus came out right at the end of the village, and knowing his way now with confidence, he was soon at the door of his home. Cautiously opening it, afraid he would awaken the inmates, whom he concluded must all be asleep, he slipped in quietly, bolting the door behind him, and reached the fire.

"Dear me, Rob," said his mother. "Where in the name o' goodness hae you been the nicht! I sat up till after midnight aye expectin' you'd be in, sae I gaed awa' to my bed to lie wauken till you should come in. You are awfu' late."

He did not answer but stooped to take off his boots, and Mrs. Sinclair was soon out of bed and upon the floor.

"Michty me, laddie! You are wringin' wet! Where have you been? Rain and glaur to the e'en holes! Get thae wet claes off you at yince, an' I'll get dry shirts for you, an' then awa' till your bed!" she rattled on, running to the chest in the room and coming back with dry clothes in her arms. "My, I never kent you oot o' the hoose as late as this in a' your life! Have you been oot in a' that rain?"

"Ay," he answered, but venturing nothing more, as he went on changing.

"It's been an awfu' nicht o' wind and rain," she again observed, glancing at his dripping clothes, and conveying a hint that explanations were desirable.

"I canna understand at a' what way you hae bidden oot in a' that rain, Lod's sake? It's enough to gie you your daeth o' cauld. You are wet to the skin, an' there's no a dry steek on you? Hae you been oot in it a'?" and her curiosity she felt was too crudely put to be answered.

Robert knew that she was bent on having an explanation, and that if he gave her any encouragement at all she'd soon have the whole story out of him.

"Yes," he said curtly, "but I'm no' gaun to talk ony the nicht. I'm gaun to my bed for an oor before risin' time."

"You'll never gaun till your work the day," she said in warm concern. "You'll never be able. You'd better tak' a rest, my laddie. A day will no' mak' muckle difference noo. We're no sae ill aff, an' I wadna like to hae onything gaun wrang. Gang away till your bed, an' dinna bother aboot your work. A guid rest'll maybe keep you frae getting the cauld."

"I'm a' richt, mither," he replied as airily as he could. "Dinna worry; an' be sure an' wauken me for my work. I'm na gaun to bide in when there is naething wrang. You gang awa' to your bed," and she knowing that was the last word, did not speak further, and as he withdrew to his room, she went back to bed wondering more and more at the mystery of it all.

But he did not sleep. Torn by worry and in spite of his earlier resolution to think no more about it he lay and thought and wondered about Mysie, and the man he saw, joining her at the end of the grove; and when Nellie opened the door to call him that it was "rising time," Robert answered to the first cry, and his mother was more amazed than ever; for he generally took a good many cries, being a heavy sleeper. But being sensible she kept her wonder to herself, knowing if it were anything which she had a right to know he'd tell her in his own good time.

CHAPTER XVI
A STIR IN LOWWOOD

"My! Div you ken what has happened?" asked Mrs. Johnstone, bursting in upon Mrs. Sinclair one day about two weeks later. "My, it's awfu'!" she continued in breathless excitement, her head wagging and nodding with every word, as if to emphasize it, her eyes almost jumping out with excitement, and her whole appearance showing that she had got hold of a piece of information which was of the first importance. "My, it's awfu'," she repeated again lifting her hands up to a level with her breast, and then letting them fall again, "Mysie Maitland has ran away frae her place, an' naebidy kens where she has gane to. An' Mrs. Rundell, mind you, has been that guid to her too, givin' her her caps an' aprons, an' whiles buyin' her a bit dress length forby, an' she gi'ed her boots and slippers, an' a whole lot o' ither things to tak' hame for the bairns—things that were owre wee for the weans at Rundell Hoose but were quite guid to wear. My, it's awfu'! Isn't it?"

"Mysie Maitland!" exclaimed Mrs. Sinclair in astonishment. "When did this happen? Where has she gane? Are you sure you hinna made a mistake?" and Mrs. Sinclair was all excitement, hanging in breathless anxiety upon the tidings her neighbor brought.

"I hae made nae mistake, Nellie Sinclair," returned Leezie, "for it was her ain mother wha telt me the noo. I was at the store, an' when I was comin' hame I met Jenny hersel' gaun awa' tae Rundell Hoose. She was greetin' an' I couldna' get oot o' spierin' at her what was wrang, an' she telt me her ain self."

"You dinna mean tae tell me that Mysie Maitland has disappeared? In the name o' a' that's guid, what has happened to bring aboot sic news?"

"Aye, it's true, Nellie," replied Mrs. Johnstone, feeling very important now that she knew Mrs. Sinclair had not heard the news.

"When did this happen?" asked the latter, still incredulous. "Are you sure that's true? Dear me! I dinna ken what the world's comin' to at a'!"

"Ay, it's awfu'! But it's true. You never ken what thae quate kin' o' modest folk will dae. They look that bashfu' that butter wadna' melt in their mouths; an' a' the time they are just as like to gang wrang as ither folk."

"But wha said Mysie Maitland has gang wrang?" enquired Mrs. Sinclair, flaring up in Mysie's defense. "I wadna' believe it, though you went down on your bended knees to tell me. A modester, weel-doin' lassie never lived in this place!"

"Weel, I dinna ken whether she has gane wrang or not; but she has ran awa', an' it is gey suspeecious conduct that for ony lassie that is weel-doin'. She is jist like the rest of folk."

"It canna' be true," said Mrs. Sinclair, still unable to believe the news. "I canna' take it in."

"Ay, but it is true," persisted her neighbor with assurance. "For I tell you, it was her ain mother what telt me hersel'. It seems she has been missing since the day afore yesterday. She gaed awa' in the afternoon to see her mither, an' as she hadna been keepin' very weel for a day or two an' no comin' back that night, Mrs. Rundell jist thought that Jenny had keepit her at home for a holiday. But she didna turn up yesterday, an' thinkin' maybe that the lassie had turned worse, Mrs. Rundell sent owre word jist the noo, to ask how she was keepin'; an' Jenny was fair thunder-struck when the man came to the door to ask. Puir body! Jenny's awfu' puttin' aboot owre the matter. I hope," she added, with the first show of sympathy, "that naething has happened to the lassie. That wad be awfu'!"

"Dear keep us!" exclaimed Nellie. "I hope nothing has happened to her."

"God knows!" replied Mrs. Johnstone piously, for want of something else to say. "It's awfu'!"

"Do they ken naething at a' aboot her at Rundells'?" again enquired Mrs. Sinclair.

"No' a thing they ken, ony mair than you or me. She left her bits o' claes, jist as if she meant to come back. Her new frock was in her drawer jist as she had put it by efter tryin' it on. An' a braw frock it is. She has nothing except what she was wearin' at the time she gaed oot. Her guid boots jist yince on her feet are in her room, a' cleaned jist as she took them off the last time she had them on. I canna' believe it yet. My! it's awfu'! It'll be a sair, sair heart her faither'll hae when he hears about it. He had aye an' awfu' wark wi' Mysie, an' thought the world o' her. If he got Mysie richt he ay seemed to think that a' else was richt. I hope nae harm has come to her. I dinna ken what the world's comin' to at a', I'm sure? My, it's awfu', isn't it?" and Mrs. Johnstone went out to spread the news, leaving Mrs. Sinclair more mystified and astonished than ever she had been in her life.

Mysie missing! She could not understand it, and always she tried to crush back the suggestion which was plainly evident in Leezie's statement that Mysie had "gang wrang." It could not be that, for Mysie was never known to have dealings with anyone likely to betray her like that. It was a hopeless puzzle altogether, and she could not account for it.

It was nearing "lousing time" and Mrs. Sinclair was busy getting the dinner ready, and water boiled to wash the men coming in from the pit, and she wondered how Robert would take the news.

She knew, having guessed, as most mothers do guess, that Mysie held a sacred corner in Robert's heart; though noticing the silence during the last two weeks, and his renewed attention to books and study, she wondered if anything had come between Mysie and himself. Had he at last spoken to her and been discouraged? She could hardly harbor that thought, for she felt also that Mysie's heart enshrined but one man, and that was Robert. Yet what could be the meaning of all this mystery?

It was true Mysie and Robert had never walked out as young men and women of their class do; but she knew in their hearts each regarded the other with very warm affection, and thinking thus she worked about the house preparing things and running occasionally over to Maitland's house, to see that the dinner was cooking all right, and giving little attentions wherever they were needed, in Mrs. Maitland's absence.

She did not mention the news to Robert when he came in, but she watched him furtively as she worked about the house getting the water into the tub for him to wash, before placing the dinner on the table; but she guessed from his face that he must have already heard of it on his way home.

He was silent as he pulled off his rough blue flannel shirt and stooping over the well-filled tub of hot water, he began to lave the water over his arms, and the upper part of his body.

At last, Mrs. Sinclair could hold herself in no longer, and looking keenly at the half-naked young man as he straightened himself, having washed the coal-dust from his hands and arms, he began to rub his breast and as much of his back as he could reach, she said, "Did you hear aboot Mysie, Rob?"

"Ay," he returned simply, trying to hide his agitation and his blanching face. "I heard that she had disappeared frae her place, an' that nae news o' her could be got. Is it true, mither?"

"Ay, it's true, Rob," she replied. "But I hinna got ony richt waye o' it yet. Jenny's awa' owre to Rundell Hoose, an' we'll no' ken onything till she comes back. It's an awfu' business, an' will pit her faither an' mither a guid lot aboot. I wonder what'll hae ta'en her."

"It's hard to ken," he replied in a non-committal voice. "Hae you ony idea, mither, as to what has brought this aboot?"

"No, Rob, I canna' say; but folks' tongues will soon be busy, I hae nae doot, an' there will be a lot o' clip-clash, an' everybody kennin' nothing, will ken the right way o't, an' every yin will hae a different story to tell."

"Ay, I hae nae doot," he said, again stooping over the tub flinging some water over his head, and beginning to rub the soap into a fine lather upon his hair. "Everybody will ken the right wye o' it, and will claver and gossip, when they wad 'a be better to mind their ain affairs, an' let ither folk alane."

His mother did not speak for a little, but went on with her work. There was something on her mind about which she wanted to speak, and she bustled about and washed, and clattered the dishes; and every plate and spoon, as they were laid dripping from the basin of warm water, plainly indicated that something troubled her.

Finally, when the last steaming dish had been laid upon the table, and she had begun to wipe them dry, she cleared her throat, and in a somewhat strained sort of voice asked, "Dae you ken, Rob, onything aboot Mysie?"

"No, mither," he replied at once, as he ceased rubbing the white foaming lather on his hair, and again straightened himself up to look at her, as she spoke; his head looking as if a three inch fall of snow had settled upon it, giving the black dirty face and the clean eyes shining through the dust, a weird strange appearance. "What makes you ask that?"

"Oh, I dinna ken, Rob, but jist thought you micht hae kent something," she answered evasively.

"No, I dinna ken onything at all aboot her, mither," he said. "If I had kent onything, dae you think I'd hae kept quiet?"

"Oh, I dinna mean that, Rob," she replied with relief in her voice, "but I thought that you might hae heard something. That Leezie Johnstone was in here the day, an' you ken hoo she talks. She was makin' oot that Mysie had gane wrang, and had ran awa' tae hide it."

"Leezie Johnstone had little to do sayin' onything o' the kind," he said with some heat in his voice. "There never was a dirty coo in the byre but it liket a neighbor. I suppose she'll be thinkin' that a' lasses were like her. These kind of folk hae dam'd strange ideas aboot things. They get it into their heads it is wrang to do certain things when folk are no married, but the cloak of marriage flung aboot them mak's the same things richt. They hinna the brains o' a sewer rat in their noddles, the dam'd hypocrites that they are!"

"Dinna swear, Rob!" said Mrs. Sinclair, interrupting him. "Do you ken," she went on, her astonishment plainly evident in her face and voice, "that is the first time I ever heard you swear in a' my life!"

"Well, mither, I am sorry; but I couldna' help it. Folk like that get my temper up gey quick; because they get it into their heids that marriage makes them virtuous, even though they may be guilty o' greater excesses after than they were before marriage."

"Ay, that's true, Rob!" she agreed. "But it is a sad business a' thegether. I wonder what has come owre the bit lassie. God knows where she may be?"

But Robert was silent, and no matter how much she tried to get him to speak, he would not be drawn into conversation, but answered merely in short grunts; but she could see that he was very much disturbed at what had happened. After a few days the sensation seemed to pass from the minds of most of the villagers, who soon found something new to occupy them, in connection with their own affairs.

About this time much interest was being manifested in mining circles. The labor movement was beginning to shape itself into solidarity towards political as well as industrial activity. Robert Smillie and the late J. Keir Hardie, and many other tireless spirits, had succeeded in molding together the newly created labor party, infecting it with an idealism which had hitherto not been so apparent, and this work was making a deep impression upon the minds of the workers, especially among the younger men.

The Miners' Union had been linked up into national organizations; and a consolidating influence was at work molding the workers generally, and the miners particularly, imbuing them with a newer hope, a greater enthusiasm and a wider vision.

About a fortnight after the news of Mysie's disappearance, Keir Hardie paid a visit to Lowwood, and a large crowd gathered to hear him in the village hall. Smillie also was advertised to speak, and great interest was manifested, and much criticism passed by the miners.

"I don't give in wi' this dam'd political business," said Tam Donaldson, who was frankly critical. "I've aye stood up for Smillie, but I dinna' like being dragged intae this Socialist movement. A dam'd fine nest o' robbers an' work-shy vermin. Trade Union officials should attend tae Trade Union affairs. That's what we pay them for. But it looks to me as if they were a' that dam'd busy trying to get intae Parliament, thet they hinna time to look after oor affairs."

"I'm kind o' suspeecious aboot it mysel', Tam," said Robert quietly, as they made their way to the hall that night. "I'm no' sure jist yet as to what this Socialism is, it looks frae the papers to be a rotten kind o' thing an' I'm no' on wi' it. But I'll wait an' hear what Hardie an' Smillie say aboot it, afore a' make up my mind."

"To hell wi' them an' their Socialism," said Tam with some heat. "I want a shillin' or twa on my day. It's a' yin damn to me hoo mony wives they gie me. I canna' keep the yin I hae. What the hell wad a workin' man dae wi' three wives? An' they tell me they're goin' to abolish religion too. Not that I'm a religious man mysel', but I'm damn'd if I'd let them interfere wi' it. If I want religion I've a guid richt to hae it; an' forby, if they abolish religion, hoo wad folk do wi' the funerals? I can see hoo they'll do wi' marriages, for there's to be nane. You've to get your wife changed every two-three years, an' the weans brought up by the State as they call it. But the puirhouse is a dam'd cauld step-mother, an' I'd be up against that."

Thus discussing the subject, they reached the hall to find it packed, everyone being keen to see and hear this man, who was making such an uproar in the country with his advocacy of Socialism.

Robert was chairman, and had labored hard to prepare a few remarks with which to open the meeting. He wanted to be non-committal, and his reading and self-teaching had been of immense service to him. His mother's influence in the molding of his character, unconsciously to himself, had made his mind just the sort of soil for the quick rooting of the seed to be sown that night.

It was certainly a great occasion. Robert thought as he looked at this man, that he had never seen anyone who so typefied the spirit of independence in his bearing. His figure was straight, the eyes fearless, yet kindly and gentle; but the proud erect head, the straight stiff back which seemed to say "I bend to no one" impressed Robert more than anything else in all his make up.

Yet there was nothing aggressive about him with it all; but on the contrary, an atmosphere of kindliness exuded from him, creating a wonderful effect upon those with whom he came in contact. The wild stories of this turbulent agitator, which everyone seemed to hear, and be acquainted with, made the audience hostile to begin with. It was not a demonstrable hostility; but one felt it was there, ready to break out, and overwhelm this stormy petrel of the political world.

Yet they patiently waited for Hardie to begin, tolerating Smillie, and even applauding his ringing denunciations of the wrongs they suffered, but critically waiting on his attempts to switch them on to Socialism. Then came Hardie, halting and stammering a little as he began his address. The audience thinking this was due to his searching for a way to delude them, became more suspicious and critical, and ready to stop him, if he tried any tricks upon them; but broad-minded enough and fair enough to give him a hearing, until he trespassed upon them too much.

So it was in this atmosphere that Socialism first was heard in Lowwood; but soon the speaker became less halting as he warmed to his subject, until not only was he fluent, but eloquent, and powerful, winning his audience in spite of themselves.

They sat and listened, and were soon under his sway, watching his every gesture and thawing under his spell, as they watched the fine head thrown back with its inimitable poise, the back straight and stiff, the eyes aglow with the light of the seer, and the hands gracefully rising and falling to emphasize some point.

What a change soon came over them! Gradually as the speaker developed his subject the faces changed, and they were soon responsive to his every demand upon them. The clear ringing voice, insistent, strong, yet catching a cadence of gentleness and winsomeness that moved them to approval of everything he said.

There was deep humanity about him, that was strangely in contrast with the monster he had been to their fancy before they saw and heard him. This was not the politics of the vulgar kind, of which the newspapers had told; on the contrary, every man in the hall felt this was the politics to which every reasonable man subscribed. It was the politics of the fireside, of sweetness and light, of justice and truth, of humanity and God.

In burning words he denounced the wrongs under which the people suffered, winning them by his warm-blooded championship of their cause, appealing to them to forsake the other parties, form an independent party for themselves; and sketching in glowing words the picture of the world as it might be, if only a saner and more human view were taken by those who ruled.

It made an indelible impression on Robert's mind. The way was so simple, so clear, so sure, that if only men like Hardie could go round every town and village in the land, he believed that a Utopia might be brought into being in a very few years; that even the rich people, the usurpers, would agree that this state of affairs might be brought about, and that they'd gladly give up all they had of power over the lives of others, to work cooperatively for the good of all; and already he was deciding in youth's way, he would give his life, every moment of it, to help Hardie and Smillie, and all those other great spirits to win the world to this state of affairs. Body and soul he would devote to it, and so help to make the world a brighter and happier place for all human beings.

His was the temperament that having found an ideal would storm the gates of Heaven to realize it; or wade through hell, suffering all its penalties to gaze upon the face of that he sought.

So the meeting ended in great enthusiasm, and the audience was amazed and pleased to find that this man Hardie was not the vulgar-minded, loud-mouthed ignorant agitator of which the press had told them; but was just one of themselves, burning with a sense of their wrongs, with ability to express their thoughts in their own words, and with an uncompromising hatred of the system which bred these wrongs in their lives.

Tam Donaldson and Robert compared notes after the meeting was over in the following conversation:

"What do you think o' it, Tam?"

"Christ! but it was great," was the reply.

"What aboot the three wives noo, Tam?"

"Oh, for ony sake, dinna rub it in, Rob. I feel that small that I could hide myself in the hole of my back tooth. Man, do you ken, I jist felt as if we were a' back in the Bible times again, wi' auld Isaiah thundering oot his charges and tellin' the oppressors o' the people what he thought of them. The white heid o' Hardie maun hae been gey like Isaiah's. Or sometimes it was like John the Baptist, comin' to tell us o' the new world that was ready to dawn for the folk! Man, it was hellish guid, and frae this day I'm a Socialist. I've always been fightin' the oppressors o' the workers, an' only wish I had a tongue like Hardie, so that I could gang roon' the hale country tellin' folk the rale God's truth aboot things. Guid God! Rob, it was better than goin' to the kirk!"

"Ay, it was gran', Tam. I'm goin' to read up this Socialism; for it seems to me to be worth it."

"So will I. I hae got twa or three bits o' books that I bought, an' I'll swallow them as quick as I can. Lod! It seems as if a new world had opened up a' thegether the night. I'm that dam'd happy, I could rin roon' an' tell everybody aboot it! But I suppose we maun gang awa' hame to bed; for we'll hae to gang to oor work the morn, though it's dam'd cauld comfort to think o' gaun oot to the pit, when we could hae better conditions to work in if only folk had the sense to do right."

Thus they parted, full of the subject which had stirred them so much that night.

Robert went home, full of vision of an emancipated world, his whole heart kindled and aglow with the desire to be a spokesman like Hardie on behalf of the workers, and thoroughly determined to devote the rest of his life to it.

"There's nae word o' Mysie yet," said Nellie, when he came in, and her words seemed to shock him with their unexpectedness.

"Is there no'?" he replied, trying hard to bring his mind back to the realities. "What kind o' word did Jenny get frae the polis?"

"Oh, they ken naething aboot her," said Nellie. "A' that is kenned is jist what we heard already. The polis hae been searchin' noo for a fortnight an' nae trace o' her can be got. Mr. Rundell has pit it in the papers; but I hae my doots aboot ever seeing her again. Mysie wasna' the lassie that wad keep her folk in suspense. She wad ken fine that they'd be anxious. Matthew an' Jenny are in an awfu' way."

"Ay. I believe they will," he replied, and a deep silence followed.

After a time, as the silence seemed to become oppressive, and for the sake of saying something, Mrs. Sinclair said: "What kin o' a meetin' had you the night?"

"My! we had an awfu' meeting, mither," he said in reply, his eyes kindling with enthusiasm at the memory of it. "Smillie was askin' for you, an' he's comin' owre to see you the morn afore he goes awa'."

"Oh, he had mind o' me then," she said, pleased at this information.

"Ay, an' he talked rale kindly aboot my faither to Hardie, mither. Smillie's a fine man, an' I like him," he said with simple enthusiasm.

"He is that, Rob. I've aye liked Bob for the way he has had to fecht. Lod, I dinna ken hoo he has managed to come through it a'. He's been a gran' frien' to the miners. What kin' o' a man is Hardie?"

"He's yin o' the finest men I ever met," he answered in quick enthusiasm. "You would hae enjoyed hearin' him, mither. It's an awfu' peety that the weemin dinna gang to the meetin's. I'm shair there's no' a woman in the place but wad hae liket him. My! if you had jist heard him, strong, sturdy, and independent. Efter hearin' him, it fair knocked the stories on the heid aboot him bein' oot to smash the hame, an' religion an' sic like. He's clean and staunch, an' a rale man. Nae sham aboot him, but a rale human bein', an' after listenin' to him tellin' what Socialism is, it mak's you feel ashamed that you ever believed things that you did believe aboot it. It's that simple an' Tam Donaldson is fair carried awa' wi' it the night."

"I'm glad you had a guid meetin'," she said, her interest kindled too. "Tell me a' aboot it," and Robert told her, sketching the fine picture which Hardie had given to his memory to carry, as long as life lasted for him.

"I've been appointed delegate to the Miners' Council," he said after a while. "I'll hae to gang to Hamilton once a month to attend the conferences."

"Oh!" she said in surprise, and with pride in her voice. "What way hae they sent you?"

"I don't ken," he answered, "but I was a wee bit feart to take it. It's only the very best men that should be sent there to represent the branches, an' I thought they might hae sent an older man, wi' mair kind o' thought about him, an' mair experience."

"Oh, weel, Rob," she said with pride, "ye are maybe as guid as ony o' them, and a hantle better than some o' them. I hope you'll dae well and aye act fair."

"I'll dae my best," he said simply. "Mony a time we hae been selt wi' place-seekers, an' maybe there are some still at it," he went on, "but I can say this, mither, if ever I get an inklin' o' it, I'll expose them to every honest man. We want men who can look at things withoot seem' themsel's as the center o' a' things. My, if you had only seen Hardie," he broke off. "He was grand."

Thus they talked for an hour before retiring, but all the time Robert's mind occasionally kept wondering about Mysie, and he went to bed, his heart troubled and aching to know the fate that had overtaken the girl he had loved and lost.

All night long he tossed unable to sleep, as he tried to think what had happened to her, his mind and heart pained at the thought of something that boded no good to her.

He again lived over in his mind all that had happened that night upon the moor, when he saw the man going to meet her after his own meeting with Mysie.

He was pained and puzzled what to do. Had the stranger any connection with her disappearance, he asked himself? Should he tell of that? And yet she had been to her father's house since then, so that it would be of little value to mention it, he thought.

Perhaps she had run away with the man. That was quite a likely thing to happen, and if Mysie wanted him no one else had anything to do with it.

Still, she might have told her people, he thought. But perhaps she might do that later on.

But Mysie and her fate would not be banished from his mind, and he lay and tumbled and tossed, a terrible anxiety within him, for youth is apt to pity its own sufferings, and give them a heroic touch under the spell of unrequited love.

Thus the night passed and morning came, and he had not slept, and he went to his work debating as to whether he should inform the police or not about the man he had seen in the company of Mysie. But no decision was ever come to.

CHAPTER XVII
MYSIE RUNS AWAY

It was a gray, sultry summer night, with one small patch of red near the western horizon when Mysie, making the excuse of going to the village to visit her parents, had stolen over the moorland path on her way to join the evening train for Edinburgh at a neighboring village station.

She had left early, so as to have plenty of time on the way, and also because she was really ill, and could not hurry.

She had forced herself to work, so as not to attract attention to her weak state during the past few weeks. Peter, who had already gone some days before, had now everything ready for her, and this was her final break with the old life.

She knew she was ill, but thought that when she got to Edinburgh, with good medical attention and treatment, she would soon be all right again. Perhaps a rest and the change would help her as much as anything; and she'd soon get well and strong, and she would work hard to fit herself for the position she was to occupy as Peter's wife.

But her legs did feel tired, as she trudged over the moor, and her steps dragged heavily. She sank down for a few moments upon a thyme-strewn bank to rest; the scent of the wild moorland bloom brought back the memory of that evening in the copse. She shut her eyes for a moment, and heard again the alarmed protest of the whaup, and the grumble of the burn; saw again the moonlight patterns upon the ground, as it flittered through the trees, like streams of fairy radiance cast from the magic wand of night and, above all, heard Peter's voice, praising her eyes, her hair, her figure.

Her cheeks burned again, and her heart throbbed anew—she heard his tones, hoarse, vibrant and warm, as his breath scorched her cheek. She felt his arms about her, the contact of his burning lips upon her own.

Then the calm which follows the wake of the storm, the consciously averted eyes, and the very conscious breathing, which had in it something of shame; the almost aversion to speak or touch again, and over all, the deep silence of the moor, broken only by the burn and the whaup, and the thick cloud, kindly dark, that came over the moon.

But, behind it all, the remorse and the agony that would never die; the anxiety and uncertainty, and the secret knowledge for which each had paid so high a price.

She rose from the bank and went slowly along the lovely moorland path. Her breath was labored and the cough troubled her. She was hot, and besides the tired sensation in her limbs, there was a griping feeling about her chest that made breathing difficult.

She reached the station just a minute before the train was due, and entered an almost empty compartment, glad to be seated and at rest.

The train soon moved out of the station, and an intense desire took hold of her to go back. The full consciousness of her action only seemed to strike her now that she had cut the last tie that bound her to the old life, and involuntarily she rose to her feet, as if to get out. A man sitting in the opposite corner, thinking she was going to close the carriage window, laid a restraining hand upon her.

"Don't close it," he said, "fresh air is what we all need, though we may not in our ignorance think so. But you take it from me, miss, that you can't get too much fresh air. Let it play about you, and keep it always passing through your room, or the railway carriage when traveling, and you'll never be ill. Look at me," he continued aggressively, almost fiercely, and very pompously, "the very picture of health—never had a day's illness in my life. And what is the reason? Why, fresh air. It is the grand life-giver. No, miss, leave the window open. You can't get too much of it. Let it play about you, draw it deeply into your lungs like this," and he took a great deep draught, until Mysie thought he was going to expand so much that he might fall out of the carriage window, or burst open its sides. Then, he let it out in a long, loud blast, like a miniature cyclone, making a noise like escaping steam; while his eyes seemed as if they had made up their minds to jump out, had the blast and the pressure not eased them at the last critical moment.

Then he stood panting, his shoulders going up and down, and his chest going out and in, like a pair of bellows in a country blacksmith's shop.

"Nothing like fresh air, miss," he panted. "You take my tip on that. I've proved it. Just look at me. I'm health itself, and might make a fortune by sitting as an advertisement for somebody's patent pills, only I feel too honorable for that; for it is fresh air that has done it. Fresh air, and plenty of it!" and he turned his nose again in the direction of the window, as if he would gulp the air down in gallons—a veritable glutton of Boreas.

Mysie could not speak. She was overwhelmed by the blast of oratory upon air, and a woman who sat on the far side of a closed window, with tight-drawn lips and smoldering eyes, looked challengingly at this fresh air fanatic, observing with quiet sarcasm: "A complexion like that might make a fortune, if done with colors to the life, in advertising some one's 'Old Highland'!"

The fresh air apostle gasped a little, looking across at the grim set mouth and the quiet, steady eyes, as if he would like to retort; but, finding no ready words, he merely wiped his forehead, and then subsided helplessly in his corner seat, as the lady rose, and, going over to the window, said to Mysie, as she closed it: "It is a little cold to-night, after the scorching heat of the daytime, and one is apt to catch cold very readily in a draught at an open carriage window. There, we'll all feel more comfortable now, I fancy. It is a little chilly." The poor worm who had always lived and thrived upon fresh air felt himself shriveling up in the corner, and growing so small that he might easily slip through the seam at the hinges of the carriage door.

Mysie merely lay back in her corner without speaking. She had never traveled much in the train; and this journey, apart from its eventfulness, was sufficient in itself to stupefy her with its newness and immensity. She had never before had a longer journey than to the county town, which cost sixpence; and here she was going to Edinburgh! a great city, of which she had all the dread of the inexperienced, unsophisticated country girl. A slight shiver soon began to creep down her back, and gradually she became cold; but she sat never speaking, and the other two occupants were so engrossed in thinking out maledictions against each other, that they had no thoughts to bestow upon her.

The wild, bleak moors rolled past, as the train rushed onward, and the telegraph poles seemed to scamper along, as if frightened by the noise of the train. She gazed away to the far horizon, where the sun had left a faint glow upon the western clouds, and she tried to think of something that would not betray her nervousness, but her mind was all chaos and excitement, and strange expectation.

What would be waiting for her at the end of the journey? Suppose Peter failed to be at the station, what would she do in a strange city? What if he were ill, and would not come? Or if he was doing this deliberately, and did not mean to meet her? Thus, torn by anxiety, and worried almost to death by nameless other fears, she spent the hour-long journey which seemed like a day, making herself ill, so that she could scarcely leave the carriage when the train steamed into Princes Street Station.

"Have you any luggage that I can assist you with?" asked the fresh air man, as Mysie seemed reluctant to get out, now that she had arrived at her destination.

"No," she replied simply, forgetting to thank him for his kind consideration, and rising slowly to her feet, she followed the stream of passengers down the platform, keeping a keen look-out for Peter.

"Here we are, Mysie," he said cheerily, striding towards her, with real welcome in his voice, and she clung to him like a child, so glad that he had been true to his word. "I have a cab waiting," he rattled on brightly. "Just come along, and we'll soon be at your digs, and we'll talk as we drive along," and he piloted her to a waiting cab; and getting in beside her, it moved off, as she heard him say "Grassmarket" to the driver.

But she had little interest in anything, now that Peter was here. She felt a sense of security in his company that she had never felt before. She trusted him, now that all her bearings were lost. The fear of the city, and the strangeness of her experiences, made her turn to him as her only prop upon which she could lean; and she clung to his arm as they drove along, the cab rattling over the stones and through what seemed to Mysie interminable streets of houses.

"Did you manage to get away all right, without anyone knowing?" he asked, as he felt her trembling hands upon his arm.

"Yes, I think sae," she replied. "I never saw onybody. I jist let on that I was gaun hame, an' gaed owre the muir, an' got the train. I didna see onybody that I kent."

"That was right, Mysie," he said. "I was afraid you might decide at the last moment not to come."

"I did feel awfu' frightened," she confessed, "an' I could fain hae bidden at hame; but I can never gang hame noo," she added with a slight tremor in her voice, at the realization of all it meant. "I can never gang hame noo!" and the tears gathered in her eyes as she spoke.

What a noise, and what a multitude of houses, she thought. She would never be able to go out and find her way back. She would get lost in all this noise and hurry and confusion.

"I have taken a little house for you, Mysie," said Peter, in explanation of his plans. "I have also a woman engaged to help you for a time, to look after you till you get acquainted with the place; and I'll come home to you every evening, and spend as much of my time with you as I can, superintending your lessons. I am going to teach you myself for a while, and we'll live together and be as happy as we can. But first of all, you must get better," he said, as a fit of coughing seized her. "You've got a bad cold. Luckily, the old man allows me plenty of money, so that we need not worry."

Mysie sat lost in wonder at it all, and presently the cab stopped, and Peter helped her out, paid the fare and, taking her arm, led her up a long flight of stairs—stairs that seemed to wind up and up till she felt dizzy, before he came to a halt at one of the many doors opening on the landing, entering which she found herself in a neat little room and kitchen, simply furnished, but clean and tidy.

"This is Mrs. Ramsay, my landlady," he said as they entered, leading Mysie forward to where a middle-aged woman of kindly demeanor stood with a smile of welcome for them. Mrs. Ramsay stepped forward and began to help Mysie to take off her hat. With a few words she soon made the girl feel more at ease, and then left them to get tea ready.

"Is that the woman you stay wi'?" asked Mysie, as Mrs. Ramsay went to the other room.

"Yes, she's my landlady," he replied.

"An' does she bide here too?"

"Well, she'll stay just as long as you think necessary. Whenever you think you can get on without her, let me know. Her daughter is looking after her own house till she returns. She's a good, kindly soul, and will do anything to help you."

"Are you gaun to stay here now, too?"

"Well, that is for you to say, Mysie," he said seriously. "Certainly I should like to stay with my wife, for we'll be married to-morrow. But if you would rather stay alone, I can easily remain in my digs, and just attend to your lessons In the evening."

"If you stay here, will she need to stay too?"

"Of course that will all lie with you, Mysie," he replied. "Perhaps it might be better for her to stay and help you for a few weeks, and by that time your cold may be better. But you can think it over to-night and tell me your decision in the morning."

Mrs. Ramsay's return cut short any further conversation, and they all sat down to tea, a strange little party. Mysie did not eat much. She was too tired, and felt that she would rather go to bed. She looked ill and very wretched, and at last Peter went out, leaving the women together.

"I'll be round for you by half-past ten in the morning, Mysie," he said, as he was going. "So you must be up, and be as bright as you can. So take a good long sleep, and you'll feel ever so much better in the morning. Mrs. Ramsay will see you all right," and he was off before Mysie realized he was going.

It was all so strange for Mysie. She was lost in wonder at it all, as she sat quietly pondering the matter while Mrs. Ramsay washed the dishes and cleared the table. The noises outside; the glare of the street, lamps, the tier upon tier of houses, piled on top of each other, as she looked from the window at the tall buildings, and the Castle Rock, grim and gray, looking down in silence upon the whole city, but added to Mysie's confusion of mind.

Shouts from a drunken brawl ascended from the street; the curses of the men, and the screams of women, were plainly audible; while over all a woman's voice, further down the street, broke into a bonnie old Scots air which Mysie knew, and she could not help feeling that this was the most beautiful thing she had heard so far.

The voice was clear, and to Mysie very sweet, but it was the words that set her heart awandering among her own moors and heather hills.

> Ca' the yowes tae the knowes,
> Ca' them where the heather grows,
> Ca' them where the burnie rows,
> My kind dearie, O!

This was always the song her father sang, if on a Saturday night he had been taking a glass. It was not that he was given to drinking; but sometimes, on the pay night, he would indulge in a glass with Andrew Marshall or Peter Pegg—just a round each; sufficient to make them happy and forgetful of their hard lot for a time. She had seen her father drunk on very few occasions, as he was a very careful man; but sometimes, maybe at New Year's time, if things were going more than usually well, he might, in company with his two cronies, indulge in an extra glass, and then he was seen at his best.

On such occasions Mysie's mother would remonstrate with him, reminding him with wifely wisdom of his family responsibilities; but under all her admonishings Matthew's only reply was:

> As I gaed doon the water side,
> There I met my bonnie lad,
> An' he rowed me sweetly in his plaid,
> An' ca'd me his dearie, O!

and as he sang, he would fling his arms around Mysie's mother and turn her round upon the floor, in an awkward dance, to the tune of the song, and finally stopping her flow of words with a hug and a kiss, as he repeated the chorus:

> Ca' the yowes tae the knowes,
> Ca' them where the heather grows,
> Ca' them where the burnie rows,
> My kind dearie, O!

So that, when the words of the old song floated up through the noise of the street, Mysie's heart filled, and her eyes brimmed with tears; for she saw again the old home, and all it meant to her.

"There now," said Mrs. Ramsay, noticing her tears, and stroking her hair with a kindly hand. "Mr. Rundell has told me all about it, and I am your friend and his. I deeply sympathize with you, my dear, for I know how much you must feel your position; but Mr. Rundell is a good-hearted young man, and he'll be good to you, I know that. Don't cry, dearie. It is all right."

Thus the words of an old song, sung by a drunken street singer, brought a stronger and deeper stab to the heart of this lonely girl, than to the exile in the back-blocks of Maori-land, or on the edge of the golden West, eating his heart out over a period of years for a glint of the heather hills of home, or the sound of the little brook that had been his lullaby in young days, when all the world was full of dreams and fair romance.

In a sudden burst of impulsiveness, Mysie flung her arms round the neck of the older woman, pouring out her young heart and all its troubles in an incoherent flood of sorrow and vexation.

"There now, dearie," said Mrs. Ramsay, again stroking Mysie's hair and her soft burning cheek. "Don't be frightened. You must go to your bed, for you are tired and upset, and will make yourself ill. Come now, like a good lass, and go to your bed."

"Oh, dear, I wonner what my mither will say aboot it," wailed the girl, sobbing. "She'll hae a sair, sair heart the nicht, an' my faither'll break his heart. Oh, if only something could tell them I am a' richt, an' safe, it would mak' things easier."

"There now. Don't worry about that any more, dearie. You'll only make yourself ill. Try and keep your mind off it, and go away to bed and rest."

"But it'll kill my mither!" cried Mysie wildly. "Her no' kennin' where I am! If she could only ken that I am a' richt! She'll be worryin', an' she'll be lyin' waken at nicht wonderin' aboot me, an' thinkin' o' every wild thing that has happened to me. Oh, dear, but it'll break her heart and kill my faither."

It needed all Mrs. Ramsay's tact and patience to quieten and allay her fears; but gradually the girl was prevailed upon to go to bed, and Mrs. Ramsay retired to the next room. But all night she heard Mysie tossing and turning, and quietly weeping, and she knew that despair was torturing and tearing her frightened little heart, and trying her beyond endurance.

Mysie lay wondering how the village gossips at home would discuss her disappearance. She knew how Mag Robertson, and Jean Fleming, and Leezie Johnstone and all the other "clash-bags," as they were locally called, would talk, and what stories they would tell.

But her mother would be different—her mother who had always loved her—crude, primitive love it was, but mother love just the same, and she felt that she would never be able again to go back and take up her old life—the old life which seemed so alluring, now that it was left forever behind.

Thus she tossed and worried, and finally in the gray hours of the morning her thoughts turned to Robert, who had loved her so well, and had always been her champion. She saw him looking at her with sad eyes, eyes which held something of accusation in them and were heavy with pain—eyes that told he had trusted her, had loved her, and that he had always hoped she would be his—eyes that told of all they had been to each other from the earliest remembered days, and which plainly said, as they looked at her from the foot of her bed: "Mysie! Oh, Mysie! What way did you do this!"

Unable to bear it any longer, she screamed out in anguish, a scream which brought good Mrs. Ramsay running to her bedside, to find Mysie raving in a high fever, her eyes wildly glowing, and her skin all afire. The good lady sat with her and tried to soothe her, but Mysie kept calling on Robert and her mother, and raving about matters of which Mrs. Ramsay knew nothing; and in the morning, when Peter arrived expecting to find his bride ready, he found her very ill, and his good landlady very much frightened about the whole matter.

CHAPTER XVIII
MAG ROBERTSON'S FRENZY

"I want to ken what has gone wrong with you?" said Mag Robertson, speaking to Black Jock, whom she had called into her house one morning as he returned from the pit for his breakfast.

"There's naething wrang wi' me," he said with cool reserve. "What dae you think is wrang?"

"Ay, it's a' right, Jock," she said, speaking as one who knew he understood her question better than he pretended. "I can see as far through a brick wall as you can see through a whinstone dyke."

"Maybe a bit farther, Mag," he said with a forced laugh, eyeing her coolly. "But what are you driving at?"

"You'll no' ken, I suppose?" she retorted. "Sanny has told me a' aboot it this morning afore he gaed to his work. My! I'd hardly hae looked for this frae you," she went on, her voice suddenly becoming softer and more soothing as if she meant to appeal to his sense of gratitude if any remained within him. "Efter what we've been to yin anither, I never expected you'd dae this. I aye thocht that you'd be loyal as we hae been tae you. We hae made oursel's the outcasts o' the district for you, an' noo you wad turn on us like this. No, I never thocht it o' you at a'!"

"What are you ravin' at this morning?" he asked, in a quiet voice, as if he meant to force her into being more definite. "I don't ken I'm sure what you are drivin' at."

"Dae you no?" she broke in quickly, loosing hold of herself as she saw that her method of attack was not going to succeed. "I hae been suspectin' something for a while. You hinna been in owre my door for three weeks an' that's no your ordinar. But I have seen you gaun in tae Tam Granger's nearly every nicht in that time. An' I can put twa an' twa together. Dae you think we dinna ken the reason that Sanny has lost his contracts an' the reason why Tam Granger has stepped into them? Oh, ay," she cried, her voice rising as she continued. "I can see hoo things are workin'! I ken a' aboot it. Wee Leebie, I suppose, will be afore some o' us noo. The stuck-up limmer that she is. She gangs by folk as brazened as you like, wi' her head in the air, as if she was somebody. You wad think she never had heard o' Willie Broonclod, the packman, that she sloped when she left doon the country. Nae wonder she has braw claes to glaik aboot in; for they were gey easy paid. The dirty glaiket limmer that she is. I wonder she disna think shame o' hersel'."

"What the hell's a' this to me?" asked Walker abruptly breaking in upon her tirade.

"I suppose it'll no' mean onything to you," she returned. "But I just wanted to tell you, that you're no her first, for Willie Broonclod gaed to her lang afore she cam' here, an' she's left him wi' a guid penny that he'll never get. But her man's a contractor noo, makin' big money, an' Jock Walker ca's in to see her whenever he's needfu' an' there's naething sae low as a packman noo for her. The brazen-faced stuck-up baggage that she is. Does she think I dinna ken her? Her, with her hair stuck up in a 'bun' an' her fancy blouses an' buckled shoon, an' a'!" Mag was now very much enraged and she shouted and swore in her anger.

"Ach, gang to hell," he said with brutal callousness. "You're no' hauf a woman like Leebie. She's a tippy wee lass, an' has a way wi' her. She has some spirit, an' is aye snod and nate," and there was a tantalizing smile about his lips that was plainly meant to irritate Mag.

"I was guid enough a gey lang while, an'—"

"Ay, but you've haen a damn'd guid innins," he interrupted. "A dam'd guid innins, an' I canna see what the hell you hae to yowl at."

"A guid innins, you muckle black-hearted brute!" she cried. "By heavens, an' I'll see that you get yours afore I hae done wi' you. Dinna think though I hae been saft wi' you a' along, that I'll ay be like that. Oh, no, I can stand a lot; but you'll find oot that Mag Robertson hasna selt her a' tae you, without driving a hard bargain afore she lets you alone. You can gang back to your tippy wee baggage! Gang to hell, baith you an' her, an' joy be wi' you baith! But I'll put a sprag in your wheel afore you gang far. Mind that! By — — I will! She'll nae toss her heid as she gangs past me as if I was dirt. Her, an' her fine dresses that she never payed for wi' money an' her fal-lals. By heaven! But you hae a fine taste!" She finished up exasperated beyond all control by his coolness.

"Ay, it wad seem so," he laughed brutally. "When I look at you, I begin to wonder what the hell I was lookin' at. You're like a damnationed big lump o' creesh," and he laughed in her face, knowing this would rouse her more than ever. Then as she choked and spluttered in her anger he said: "But what the hell odds is't to you, you baggage?" and his eyes and voice were cold and brutal beyond expression. "Leebie Granger is young," he went on insultingly, in a collected even voice which he strove to make jaunty in tone. "She's as fresh an' young. An' you're auld, an' fat an' as ugly as hell, an' if I dae gang to Leebie you hae damn all to dae wi' it. As I said, you've had your innin's, an' been gey well paid for it, an' I dinna gie a damn for you."

"Dae you no'?" she cried now livid with anger and losing all control over her words and actions, her eyes flashing with maddened rage and the froth working from her lips. "I'll let you ken or no'. I'll tear the pented face off your new doll; and I'll sort you too, you dirty black brute that you are."

"Gang to hell!" he shouted, starting out of the door so suddenly that he almost ran into the next door neighbor who hearing the noise had crept noiselessly on tiptoe to the door the better to hear all that was going on.

"What the hell's wrang wi' you?" he demanded turning in rage upon the eavesdropper. "Have you naething else to dae than that? Gang in an' get your dirty midden o' a hoose cleaned an' I'll see that you don't stay lang in Lowwood to spy on ony mair folk!" and cowering in shame the poor woman backed into the door and shut it, making up her mind that her man would be sacked that day, and wondering where they would flit to, so as to find work and a house.

Walker strode up the row with Mag Robertson shouting behind him and the neighbors all coming to the doors as they passed, and craning their necks, while keeping their bodies safe hidden within the doorways of their homes.

"We're surely gettin' an entertainment the day," observed one fat old woman to another woman two doors away, as they both looked after Mag as she followed Walker up the row, shouting her worst names at him, and vowing what she'd do with Leebie Granger, when she got hands on her.

"Ay," replied the other woman stealing along the wall to the doorway of the older woman, and slipping inside as if she were afraid of being detected. "It's a hell o' a business when blackguards cast oot."

"Wheest, Annie, dinna swear," remonstrated the old woman. "I dinna like to hear folk swearin' at a'. I wonner the Lord disna open the grun' to swallow the half o' the folk noo-a-days; for I never heard sic swearin' a' my life."

"Och, there's nae harm meant," returned Annie, taken aback by the old woman's admonition. "It's jist a habit that folk get into an' they canna help it. But listen to her," she broke off, alluding to Mag Robertson again. "She micht think shame o' hersel', the shameless lump that she is. She'd hae been faur better to hae keepit her mouth shut, Phemie."

"That's true, Annie," replied Phemie. "Listen to her. My, she's no' canny an' she's fairly givin' him a bellyfu'. But they're a' yae swine's pick an' no' yin o' them decent. I wadna be in her shoon for a' the money that ever was made in Lowwood. She micht hae kent hoo it wad end. Hark at her. My, but it's awfu'."

"Keep in, Annie," Phemie admonished as they both craned their necks to look up the row as she saw Walker turning to face Mag. "Dinna let him see you or your man will get the sack. My! but she's layin' it in tae' him. What a tongue."

"Lord bless us! He's strucken her, Phemie," said Annie, clutching her neighbor's shoulder as she spoke. "My, he's gaen her an awfu' blow on the mouth an' knocket her doon. Come inside for as sure as daith it'll end in a coort case, an' I'm no wanting to be mixed up in it," and they went inside and shut the door, looking at each other with frightened eyes. Then Annie, stealing to the window and lifting the curtain a little at the side, gazed sideways up the row, reporting to Phemie everything that happened.

"He's kicking her, Phemie. Eh, the muckle beast that he is. My God, he'll kill her afore he's finished wi' her. He's hitting her on the face every time she tries to rise an' gaein' her anither kick aye when she fa's doon again. Oh! my God, will naebody interfere. He'll kill her as sure as death," and she stepped back with blanched face sickened at the spectacle she had described.

"Here she comes, Annie," said her neighbor after a few moments. "My! what a face. Dinna look you at her," cried Phemie in alarm pushing back Annie who had moved near to the window to get a better view. "In God's name, woman, dinna you look at her. You shouldna ha' looked at onything that has taken place. If onything is wrang wi' your bairn when it is born I'll never forgi'e' mysel' for lettin' you look at this business at a'. Gang awa' back an' sit down an' try an' forget a' aboot what you hae seen. Dinna look up till she gangs back intae the hoose," and the old woman kept Annie sitting back at the bedside in the corner farthest from the window until Mag staggered to her home, her face streaming with blood.

Not a soul was in sight as Mag returned; but many a pair of eyes watched her from behind curtained windows, and expressions of sympathy were common even though her relations with Walker were common knowledge in the village, and had been censured by everyone in consequence for her misdeeds. They all knew why Mag had "opened out" on Walker that morning and the reason she had been set aside for another who pleased his fancy.

Tam Granger and his wife had recently come into the district from a neighboring village, where Leebie's name had been coupled with a local draper's or packman's in some scandal. Black Jock had soon got into contact with them and finding them willing tools he had deserted Sanny and Mag Robertson. All the contracts were taken from Sanny and given to Tam, and it was this that had made Mag watch for Walker coming in for his breakfast, determined to have it out with him, with the result which is chronicled above.

The encounter between Mag and Black Jock was the talk of the village. Mag was mad with rage, and having washed her bruised face, she ramped out and in all day, washing the floor, clattering among dishes and scouring pots and pans. She was working off her anger and swearing and threatening, until most of the other women in the row grew afraid, and kept as much as possible within doors the rest of the day.

When the men returned from work the whole episode had to be gone through and described to them by their wives.

When Sanny Robertson came home that afternoon, he found Mag with swollen lips and half closed eyes and a face bruised all over. He did not have to wait long for explanations. She railed and swore and raged until one wondered from where she got all the energy, and all the strength. It was amazing why she did not collapse altogether.

Sanny sat quietly listening without comment, then washed himself and sat smoking by the fire for a time. He was a quiet go-as-you-please man, not given much to talking. But finally he could stand it no longer, and he took hold of his wife by the shoulder, saying.

"Noo, jist you listen, an' for God's sake shut your mooth. It'll no dae a bit o' guid ravin' like that. We are in a bigger hole noo than ever we hae been in a' oor lives, an' mind that. I've made up my mind what I am gaun tae dae. Sae listen. I'm gaun straucht awa' ower to Rundell's the morn, at the time when Mr. Rundell gangs hame frae the office for his breakfast, an' I'll tell him everything aboot the contracts. Then I'm gaun awa' doon the country tae look for work, an' I'll flit oot o' here an' tae hell wi't. Noo shut up an' gae me peace and quateness for an hoor, so that I can think oot things. You get awa' tae bed. Maybe by richt I should gang doon tae Black Jock an' stap a knife in him—if for nae ither thing than the way he has treated you the day, I should dae that. But I'm no gaun to dae it the noo. I'm no' blaming you for what has happened; for I'm mair to blame than you are. But I'll be even wi' that black beast, an' put an end to his rotten career, someway or another. Sae aff you gang to your bed, an' gie me a quate hoor tae mysel'," and there was such a quiet authoritative ring in his voice that Mag dared not disobey it, and she went quietly off to bed while he sat by the fireside smoking and thinking, and feeling that his home that night must surely be the most unhappy place on God's earth.

About midnight he knocked the ashes from his pipe, and placing it on the mantelpiece, went to bed and soon fell asleep, but Mag, an insane decision taking shape in her brain, lay and brooded and tossed till well on in the morning, when she rose, kindled the fire, "redd up" the house, prepared the breakfast and awoke her husband to partake of the meal she had prepared.

Never a word was spoken between them, and at last Sanny, after washing and dressing, walked out without a word, but fully determined in his heart to get equal with Walker before the day was over.

He went straight to Rundell House, and ringing the bell asked to see the mine owner.

He was shown into a room and Mr. Rundell came to him almost before he had been comfortably seated.

"Well, Sanny," he began genially. "What brings you here this morning?"

"A business that I'd rather no' been comin' on," replied Sanny uneasily shifting on his chair.

"Oh, nothing serious, I hope, is it?"

"Ay, it's serious enough," returned Sanny. "Mair serious than you think, Mr. Rundell; an' I dinna ken what you'll think o' me after I hae telt you."

"Oh, well, in that case," said the mine owner, becoming serious, and speaking with slow deliberation. "Just let me hear what it is all about, and we'll see how matters stand after you have told me," and he sat down in a chair opposite Robertson as he spoke.

"I hae lost my contracts, sir," began Sanny, not knowing how else to open up the subject. "But I'm gaun to tell you the hale story just in my ain way, so I want you to sit quate and no' interrupt me; for I hinna jist the knack of puttin' things maybe as they should be put. But I'll tell you the hale story an' then leave you to do as you like, an' think what you like."

"Very well, Sanny. Just go on. I did not know you had lost them. But just let me hear about the trouble in your own way."

"For gey near twenty year," began Sanny, "I've had maist feck o' the contracts in your pits back and forrit—me an' Tam Fleming. Walker an' us were aye gey thick, an' though it maybe was putten doon to you that oor offer to work ony special job was the cheapest, I may tell you that I never put in an offer in my life for yin o' them. Walker an'—an'" here Sanny stammered a little, "Walker an' oor Mag were gey thick, an' I'm ashamed o' this part o' the story; for I should hae been man enough to protect her frae him. But the money was the thing that did it, Mr. Rundell, an' I'm no' gaun to mak' excuses noo aboot it. But every bargain I had, I had to share the pay, efter the men was payed, penny aboot, wi' Walker. That was ay the bargain. He gaed us the job at his ain feegure, an' we shared the profits wi' him.

"Noo, jist keep yoursel' cool a bit," he said, holding up his hand as Rundell made to speak. "We did gey well," he resumed in his even monotone, like a man who was repeating something he had learned by heart. "But gey soon I found that I was expected to spend a good share o' my pay in drink, while Walker took a', an' never spent a penny. So it was, that for a' the money we made we've been gey little the better o't, an' very much the worse o' it. Without exception we shared penny aboot with Walker on every bargain we got, an' I ken he has a guid bank balance, while I hae nane.

"Noo, this is a rotten story frae end to end o't," he went on after a short pause to wipe his face with a handkerchief. "I allowed him to ruin my wife's character. I kent it was gaun on a' the time; but like mony mair I hae kent, a manager's favor was mair to me than the honor o' a wife. I let him tak' a share o' the money I made, an' spent my ain to keep him up on drink. But noo it's ended a'. A wheen o' weeks syne, a man ca'd Tam Granger came to the place and his wife being young an' fresh, an' guid-looking, besides being free, Walker's fancy was ta'en wi' her. So you ken what it means, when a gaffer carries on like that, an' the man is saft enough as weel as the woman being willin'. Tam got my contracts this week, an' I have to gang back into a common place and howk coals.

"Weel, the wife couldna' stand being slighted like thet, an' Granger's wife had been tantalizin' her too, you ken hoo women rave when they are slighted. So she opened oot on Walker yesterday mornin' an' followed him up the row, the hale place being turned oot to hear her exposure o' him. She fair gaed mad wi' anger I think, an' lost a' control o' hersel' an' she followed him shouting so that a' the neighbors could hear her tauntin' an' jibin' at him, till he could staun it nae langer, an' he turned an' struck her, knockin' her doon on the green, an' then kickin' her, till she's a' bruised ower the body. She has an' awfu' lookin' face too, an' she came in bleeding like a sheep.

"So that's the hale ugly story, Mr. Rundell. As I said I'm gaun to mak' nae excuses. There's nane tae mak'; an' I'm cheap served for it a'. I should hae stood by the wife and protected her. But I'll dae it noo. She's mine, an' if she's no guid it is me that is to blame. I'm leavin', an' I'm gaun awa' doon the country the morn to look for work; but I thocht I'd tell you the whole rotten story first, then I'll get Walker, an' hae a reckonin' wi' him an' be off the morn. I'll pay off that black-hearted brute this day afore I leave Lowwood an' then my conscience will be easier."

Mr. Rundell sat stupefied and amazed at the story just told him by Robertson, and just as both men sat staring at each other and before another word could be said, a miner burst into the room, almost exploding with excitement, crying:—

"Oh, Mr. Rundell, you've to come to the pit at once. A woman has flung herself doon the shaft."

"Guid God! That'll be oor Mag," cried Sanny, starting up and out at the door, running in the direction of the pit and stumbling every few yards in his excitement.

When Sanny had left the house that morning to go and interview Mr. Rundell, Mag, with the insane decision she had made overnight still holding her mind, dressed herself in her best clothes, and without hesitation set off to the pit.

On her way down the row she stepped into Leebie Granger's house very excited though she had been fairly quiet all morning; so quiet in fact that Phemie Grey and Annie Watson could not help remarking upon it.

"She's been awfu' quate a' mornin', Phemie," said Annie, going into her neighbor's house. "She has worked away there as if she was gaun to clean the hale place, scrubbing oot the floor, although she washed yesterday; an' noo, she has on her Sunday best, wi' her new hat on too, an' she's awa' into Leebie Granger's. I wonner what'll hae ta'en her noo."

"Guid kens," replied Phemie, "but she's fair off her heid. Dae ye ken she's just like a daft body. Did you see the look in her e'en?" and so they discussed poor Mag, who had drawn their attention by the strangeness of her behavior.

"Oh, dinna be feart, Leebie," began Mag as she saw Leebie's apprehensive look. "I'm no' gaun to meddle wi' you, although I swore yesterday that I would. You've only done what I did before you. You are young, an' mair pleasin' than I am noo, an', as he said, I hae had a good innins. But, Leebie, you'll hae to look for another fancy man. He'll no' be lang yours. I'll see to that. Him an' me will gang oot thegither, if I can manage it. We've baith been rotten, an' it's richt that we should gang baith at once, an' rid the place o' a dam'd bad sore. Guid day, Leebie. It's a dam'd puir life to leave, an' while it maybe is a woman's lot in life to sell hersel' for ease and comfort, it's a' bad for her when she does it in a way that the world says is a wrang way; for she soon finds that her life isna worth a tinker's curse. She sells hersel' an' it's no worth while complainin' if the bargain turns oot a rotten yin.

"If every woman had plenty of honest work, there wad be nae fancy women, for they wadna ned do it. Guid day, Leebie. Maybe you'll think I'm strange a wee an' maybe so I am. You micht think I'm daft; an' maybe so I am. But after a while when you get time to think, you'll maybe feel that you hae heard mair soond sense oot o' Mag Robertson when she was mad than ever she spoke when she was supposed to be wise. Guid day, Leebie. Think ower a' I have said. I'm no gaun to hurt you; but I'm gaun to tak' Black Jock oot o' your clutches as shair as daith. You've had your innins too; but it has been a dam'd short yin. I've had mine, an' the game is feenished noo. It's time the hale thing was totaled up so that we can see wha is the winner. I've been maybe playin' a losin' game, Leebie, but noo we'll ken afore lang. Guid day, Leebie. I'm off," and she was out of the door leaving Leebie speechless with fear and amazement.

Mag flew down the brae to the pit almost running, while Leebie and other neighbors looked after her with a strange dread at their hearts.

When Mag arrived at the pit she asked a boy if Walker was up the pit yet for his breakfast.

"I dinna' think so," replied the boy. "He's kind o' late this mornin'; but there's the bell chappit three," he said as the signal was made from the bottom that men were about to come up. "That'll likely be him coming up."

The boy had no sooner spoken, than with a mad rush Mag darted forward, and opening the gates at the "low scaffold," where no one was near, being situated below the pit-head proper, with a loud scream she hurled herself down the shaft.

"God Almichty!" roared the engineman who saw all from the engine house, as he rushed out of the door, calling to the pit-head workers. "Mag Robertson has flung hersel' doon the shank!" and immediately all was consternation.

The engine keeper had just been in the act of signaling down to Walker, who was ready to ascend when he saw the flying figure dart forward and fling herself into the yawning abyss.

Walker, standing at the foot of the shaft waiting for the answering signal from above, heard the noise and the rush of Mag's body as it bumped from side to side in its mad descent, and starting back, he was just in time to get clear as the mangled mass of rags and blood and pulpy flesh fell with a loud splashy thud at the bottom, the blood spattering and "jauping" him and the bottomer, and blinding their eyes as it flew all over them.

"In the name o' Heavens what's that?" yelled Walker, screaming in terror and jumping aside from the bloody upturned face, with the wide, staring eyes, which he seemed to recognize, as the other parts of the body lay about, still quivering and twitching, and a horrible sickness came over him and terror flooded his mind.

"Bell, three, quick!" cried Walker, frantic with desperation in his voice. "Bell three, dammit. An' let us up out o' here. Hurry up, hell to you," and he drew the bell himself, and without waiting on the signal back from above, jumped into the cage, averting his face from those horrible eyes, which lay staring at him out of the darkness.

"Chap it awa', man!" he yelled at the bottomer, his voice rising to a scream. "Chap it, an' let us up to hell oot o' this," and the bottomer, no less frightened than he, tore at the bell, and jumping in himself just as the cage began slowly to ascend, clung to the bar, shivering with terror.

CHAPTER XIX
BLACK JOCK'S END

When Walker reached the surface, he was like a madman. He raved and swore and frothed like a churn, running here, there and everywhere nearly collapsing with rage, which sprang from terror.

Usually cool and calculating, steady and active-minded, he seemed to have lost all grip upon himself. He had been drinking heavily the night before and was none too sober in the morning when he was called upon to go to work. Mag Robertson's attack the night before had sent him to the drink, and being a heavy drinker he was in a bad state the following morning. Mr. Rundell found him swearing and raving in a great passion, sacking men and behaving like a maniac.

"Look here, Walker," he began at once, his quick temper rising anew as he thought of the story Sanny Robertson had told him. "I'll give you twenty-four hours to get out of here and away from the place; and if you are not gone in that time I shall inform the police. I know the whole story regarding the setting of the contracts. Sanny has told me, and if I was doing right I would not give you a single minute."

Walker seemed to calm down all at once, and his eyes became cringing as those of a kicked cur as he stood before the angry mine-owner.

"But I hinna telt you a' he has done," said Sanny Robertson, who came up just then in time to hear Mr. Rundell's words. "The dirty black-hearted brute murdered Geordie Sinclair. He telt me himsel' one nicht at the time when we were drinkin' together. He kent a' aboot Geordie workin' on the boss ground an' sent him to his death to get rid of him because in a soft moment I had telt Geordie hoo the contracts were set. He was feart Geordie wad tell you. He's a black-hearted murderer, an' noo he has added Mag's death to his list o' damnation. Tak' that! an' that! you dirty villain! I'll save the hangman the bother o' feenishin' you!" and Sanny was upon Walker tearing at him like a cat, and clawing his face with his nails, punching, biting and kicking him as hard as he could drive his hands and feet.

The attack was so sudden that Walker went down, and Sanny was on top of him before anyone could intervene.

"I'll tear the thrapple oot o' you, you dirty swine!" he squealed, as he tugged at Black Jock's throat.

Mr. Rundell and a couple of laborers soon pulled Sanny up, though he struggled to maintain his hold upon the throat of his adversary.

"Let me at him," he yelled, striving to get free. "Let me at him, an' I'll save the hangman a guid lot o' bother stretchin' his dirty neck! Oh, you swine! You dirty murderin' beast!" he shrieked, as he tried to break away from the restraining hands which held him.

But Sanny was soon overpowered, and Walker, bounding to his feet, was off up the railway towards his home, terror filling his heart, and his mind reeling with fear.

Mr. Rundell quickly organized a band of men to descend the shaft and recover Mag's body, and soon the whole village was in possession of the news, and the excitement was intense.

They gathered her up, a mass of dirty, pulpy flesh, scraping the remains together and shoveling them into a rude improvised box, the head and eyes being the only part of the body that resembled anything like a human being.

"Hell to my sowl, but this is the warst job that ever I got," said Archie Braidhurst, as he scraped a mass of blood and bones, mud and rags, together. "It's a hell o' a daith to dee."

"Ay, puir lassie," replied Adam Lindsay. "She's made a splash at the hinner end. Mag ay cried that it was best to mak' a splash aboot the things you did; but, by sirs, she has made yin this time. What an awfu' mess!"

"Splash!" echoed Archie with a grim laugh. "She's gane a' into jaups. She maun hae thocht she was a juck-pool. I would like to dee like a Christian when I dee, and no' shuffle oot like a scattered explosion, or a humplick o' mince."

"Oh, for Heaven's sake shut your mooth, an' let us get her gathered up an' get oot o' here. Dammit, hae ye nae common sense, swearin' an' jokin' about sic a thing! It's enough to tempt Providence, an' had it no' been for the tumblerful o' whisky that Mr. Rundell gied us I dinna think I could hae faced it. It's awfu'!"

"What the hell are ye girnin' at?" asked Archie, turning round on him. "Are ye feart Mag bites ye? Man, she's got a' her bitin' by noo, although I admit she's made a hell o' a mess at the end. Pit your shovel in here an' lift this pickle, an' no' stand there gapin' like a grisly ghost at the door o' hell! Fling it into her gapin' mooth, if you think she's goin' to bite you!" and the others laughed uneasily at Archie's sardonic humor.

It was a nerve-trying experience for most of them, and they felt sick with horror of it, in spite of the whisky and their grim jokes. The pit was put idle, and the men went home. A gloom brooded over the whole place.

Black Jock saw Mag Robertson's eyes staring at him, as he hurried over the moor. He had not even stopped to wash himself, but merely stowing some money into his pocket, was off, not deigning to answer his daughter's enquiries as to what was wrong, or where he was going. Every wild bird upon the moor seemed to shout at him in accusation; every living thing seemed to scream out in terror as he approached.

He laughed a harsh laugh, like the cry of a wild beast, and the sheep scampered away in fear. The wind moaned out of the gray clouds, which lay thick upon the hidden hills, and there was an early iciness in its breath as it groaned past; A soft, slushy sound rose from the moor at every step, until it seemed that even earth protested. Eerie and sad the moor was, gray and threatening the hills. Laughing at intervals that low gurgle which sprang from fear, as some wild bird would start up at his approach, he plodded on.

He did not know where he was going. He had no particular objective. He did not know what line he would pursue. He only wanted to get away from the scene of the tragedy, and those terrible eyes staring, which seemed to follow him from behind every bush or clump of heather, till in the gray mist it seemed as if the moor were alive with them.

Eyes everywhere. Eyes that never winked or moved. Eyes that never trembled with recognition or glimmered with life. Dead eyes, cold eyes, immovable and clear—horribly clear they were—eyes that simply stared, neither showing accusation nor denunciation; but there they were at every tuft of yellow grass, behind every moss-hag, and staring like pools of clear silent death, which struck horror to his heart. He bounded sideways as a partridge on whirring wing flew away at his approach, and almost dropped dead with fright as a muircock, with loud protesting voice, seemed to scream: "'way back! 'way back! 'way back!" and then, drawing out into a low grumbling command, as it came to earth a few hundred yards away, still muttering its orders to him, as he momentarily stood to recover from his fright.

The whinny of a horse upon the hillside, the low cry of a young cow, the bleat of a sheep, all added to his feeling of dread, until the sweat streamed down his body, as he swung along the moor.

At last he came to a little village, about six miles from Lowwood, and, entering the inn, he called for a supply of whisky.

"It's kind o' cauld the day," the landlady said in an affable way, as he stepped into the bar.

"Warm enough where I have been," he replied bluntly. "Gie's something to drink in whusky!"

"So it wad seem," she said in reply, noting his beaded forehead, as he wiped it with a colored handkerchief.

"You've surely been gey hard ca'd wherever you hae been," and there was a note of curiosity in her voice.

"I want a drink," he broke in abruptly, "an' it doesna matter a damn to you whether I hae been hard ca'd or no'. You're surely hellish keen to hae news. Dis a' your customers get the Catechism when they come in here?" he queried. "If they do, I may as well tell you to begin with, that I came in for whusky, an' no' to staun' an examination."

She saw at once that he resented her leisurely way and her attempt at affability, and she hastened to apologize.

"Look dam'd sharp," he growled, as she attended to his order. "I want whusky and plenty o' it."

"You are in an unco' hurry," she replied, getting nettled, as she filled a glass. "It doesna' do to be so snottery as a' that."

"Well, dammit, look alive. I'm dying for a drink. Bring in a bottle," as she placed a glass before him filled with whisky, "an' tak' the price o' your dam'd poison aff that!" and he flung down a sovereign upon the table.

"Look here," said the landlady, "I'll tak' nane o' your snash, so mind that. If folk come in here to be served, they've got to be ceevil."

"Oh, there's nae harm," he said apologetically, with a forced laugh, "but I'm in a hurry, and I want a drink."

"Weel, I maun hae ceevility. So if you don't gi'e the yin, you'll no' get the ither."

"That's all right," he said. "Keep the sovereign. I may need more. Tell me when it is all spent," and he filled a bumper and drained it without halt.

"Weel, ye may be dirty at many a thing," she observed, as she noted his action, "but you're a gey clean drinker o' whusky anyway," and she left him with his bottle to fuddle alone.

"A gey queer body that," she mused, as she returned to the bar. "Lod! he's like a wannert thunder-storm, growlin' and grumblin', as if he had got lost frae the rest o' his company. But he seems to hae plenty o' siller anyway," she concluded, "an' he can drink whusky wi' anybody I ever seen try it."

By and by a village worthy came in, and he was at once hailed by Black Jock, and invited to have a glass.

"What are you drinkin', chappie?" he enquired.

"Same as you," was the reply, while a smile of pleased anticipation hovered round the worthy's face at this unexpected good fortune. "I jist ay tak' a moothfu' o' whusky. As a maitter o' fact, I was brocht up on the bottle, and I hae never been spained yet."

"Right you are, cocky! Drink up! You're the man I am lookin' for to help me to spend an hour or twa."

"That'll suit me a' to bits," was the reply, "an' you are jist the man I hae been lookin' for. It's a guid thing we hae met, or we'd baith hae been unhappy."

So the hours passed, and each newcomer was invited to join the company, until it grew so large that the "big room" was requisitioned, and it soon held a laughing, joking, drinking, good-natured set of as drouthy individuals as ever met together in company. Every worthy for miles around seemed to get the news of the free drinks, and whisky and beer flowed like water, and the company grew more and more cheerful and happy.

Bottle after bottle of drink was consumed, and as the company got hilarious, a song was sung or a story was told, until the whole place had the air of a fair day about it.

Jock spent his money freely, and his company drank his health as freely as he paid for the drinks. So the merry hours went past, and the darkness came on. Yet for all the whisky that Walker consumed, he never seemed to get drunk. He was certainly a bit intoxicated, but was in that condition described by one of the company next day as being "sensibly drunk."

"Come on, damn you, you son of a tinkler," he urged. "Drink up, an' let us mak' a nicht o't," and thus urged they drained their glasses, and had them refilled again and again.

"Gie's a sang, Geordie," cried one of the company across the room to an old shaggy-faced individual, who sat and laughed and drank with happy demeanor, rubbing his bristly chin, which resembled the back of a hedgehog, with dirty gnarled fingers which seemed made for lifting glasses, having a natural crook in them, into which the glass as naturally fitted. "You hinna sung anything yet. Gie's yin o' your ain makin'."

"Lodsake, I canna sing," said Geordie, with the air of a man who wanted to be told he could sing.

"Ach, you can sing fine," was the chorused reply from nearly everyone in the company.

"Come on, Geordie, you ken you can sing fine. Man, there's no' a better singer in the place, auld and a' as ye are."

"Och, I canna sing noo, Charlie," replied Geordie, clearing his throat, "but I'll confess that I hae seen the day when I could lilt it wi' the best o' them."

"Oh, but we a' ken fine that you can sing. Man, it's a treat to hear him," said Charlie, turning to Black Jock. "He could wile the bird aff the bush. Gie's yin o' your ain, Geordie. It's aye best to hear you at yin o' your ain."

"Oh, weel," said Geordie with a show of reluctance, as he rose to his feet, making a noise in his throat, like the exhaust pipe of an engine, "seein' that you are all so pressin' on the maitter, I'll gi'e ye a bit verse or twa."

A roar of applause greeted Geordie as he sat down, and words of appreciation broke from everyone in the room.

"Dam'd guid, Geordie! Fill up your glass. That deserves a richt guid dram!" cried Black Jock, as he reached across the table and poured a bumper for Geordie. "Wha's gaun to sing next? Come on, chaps; let us mak' a nicht o't!"

"Hear, hear," said Geordie. "I'm just feelin' in gran' fettle for a nicht. Tammas Fairly will gie's a bit verse maybe. He can sing a fair guid song."

"Me sing!" exclaimed Tam. "Gae awa'! Ye ken fine I canna sing like you, Geordie," and there was a hint of assumed bashfulness in Tam's voice as he spoke.

"Come on, Tam. There's to be nae jookin' oot o' it. It's to be a sang roon' aboot, so you micht as weel begin noo, an' get your turn by."

"Ay, come on," chimed in Walker. "Let us enjoy oorsel' the nicht, when we are in a mood for it. Guid kens when we may ever spend a nicht thegither again. Come on, Tam, get up!"

"Oh, weel," said Tam with bashful reluctance, "I'll do my best," and clearing his throat, Tam sang.

"Hear, hear!" roared Black Jock. "That deserves a bumper too, Tammas. Fill up your glass. An honest dram's afore a' the simperin' Judies that ever held up their gabs to be kissed!" and filling another round, they drank, and roared, and cried their appreciation.

The fun waxed fast and furious, as song after song was sung, which sometimes were capped by a rough story or a questionable joke from someone in the company.

"But you havena gi'en us a sang yoursel'!" observed Charlie, turning to Black Jock, after most of the company had obliged with an effort.

"No, I havena gi'en you a sang," he replied with a coarse laugh, "but I hae paid for a' the drinks, an' I suppose that'll please the maist o' you better than a dizzen sangs frae me."

"Quite true," said Geordie. "You're a gentleman, an' I never met a better. I only hope we'll hae the pleesure o' meetin' you here again afore lang. It's been yin o' the best nichts I hae spent for a lang time."

"That's true, Geordie," said Charlie. "He has gi'en us yin o' the best nichts I hae ever spent. In fact I never min' o' haein' a better, an' to celebrate it, if nane of you hae ony objections, I'll sing anither sang."

"Hear, hear," cried Walker heartily. "Order for the sang," and he tapped the table loudly with a bottle, as he called for quietness amid the din.

"Order for the sang, boys!" bawled Geordie, "Charlie is gaun to favor the company," and as the noise immediately ceased, Charlie sang a song about the fascinating women.

"That's a guid yin, Charlie," roared Walker, thumping the table as he roared. "I hae had a lang experience o' weemin' bodies," and he winked across to Geordie as he spoke, "an' I can say they are rale blood-suckers. They're like whisky, gran' at the time, but you sing sorry next day, an' fin' oot what a fool you hae been. They hing on to you like leeches, an' mak' a mess o' things at the en'. Though you had a face like a crocodile as long as you had plenty of cash, they'd lick your feet; when your money's done, they're awa' like swallows at the first nip o' autumn frost!"

"Ay, it's a dam'd funny world," he went on in a lower tone, as if half speaking to himself. "A fu' purse an' you've plenty o' frien's, an' a woman when you need her, but if your purse is toom, your heart may grien a hell o' a lang while afore yin wad ever come near you."

Thus the evening passed till some were lying below the table, unable to sit up and take their round; and finally the closing hour arrived, and all had to disperse.

Black Jock, again left to himself, deserted by all his company, and in spite of all the drink he had consumed walking fairly steadily, stepped out upon the country road, neither caring nor knowing in which direction he went. His head bent forward upon his breast, or rolling occasionally from side to side, seemed too heavy for his neck to support, as he swayed from the center of the road to its margin.

The horrible staring eyes began again to infest his journey, and seemed to accompany him wherever he went. He could not get away from them. Out in the lonely night, the whole sky merry with stars, was alive with staring eyes, that glared down upon him from above with a cold sinister light. They looked at him from the hedgerows; they glared at him from behind every bush or knoll by the wayside; they glowered at him from behind the trees; and they even perched upon his shoulders and peeped at him in accusation.

"Damn you!" he growled, striking at them as if he would brush them from his sight; but still they followed and accused no matter where he turned. He grew more and more irritated and alarmed, as they seemed to multiply with every minute that passed; and he quickened his pace, but in spite of his speed, they still pursued and multiplied.

Driven mad by the persistence of their stare, he rushed from side to side of the road, striking at them, hitting out with his hands, and kicking with his feet; but still they grew in numbers and in immensity.

He shook himself as if to free his body from them; he rushed ahead, swearing and muttering; he growled and shouted, sometimes pleading to be let alone, and sometimes roaring defiance to the night air; but still the eyes held him relentlessly, implacably, and ever growing in numbers, until it seemed as if the whole countryside were alive with them. They came nearer and receded again; they swarmed round him in legions, then withdrew behind the hedges to stare at him with wide-open lids. They drew him onward, and he advanced cautiously. Then they rushed at him, and retired again, as if driven back; but still they were there, just round the bend of the road, just behind that bush, just over that hedge, and behind that tree, glaring and looking at him, and ready to rush forth again as soon as they thought he was sufficiently off his guard.

"Back!" he roared again, striking out with his fist as they rose only a couple of yards ahead. "Back! an' be damned to you," as a whole swarm larger and larger, so that they lighted up the night, came rushing round him.

They were hissing and roaring at him this time. They had hitherto been silent, and he seemed to hear at first a low murmuring whisper, as if they consulted together as to the best way to attack him. Then the whisper grew to a louder swishing sound like the noise Mag had made as her body hurtled from side to side on falling down the shaft. It grew louder and louder, like the wind coming through far-off trees, gradually swelling to a roar. The eyes grew in numbers and got larger with the noise; and finally, with terror clutching at his heart and an oath upon his lips, he turned to run back, only to find that they had all merged into two wide, horribly glaring fiery eyes which were bearing down upon him with the speed and noise of an express train. They were on him before he could turn, as if they now realized that he was fully at their mercy, and with the courage of desperation he flung himself bodily upon them and went down crushed beneath the heavy mass of a motor driven with reckless speed by a young man rushing to catch a train.

Walker was down before the young man realized what had happened and the hoot of the horn had merely spurred Black Jock to the last desperate leap to death, the lights of the motor having taken on the shape of all the pursuing eyes that had followed him that night.

When he was taken from beneath the wheels, his neck broken and his body smashed, Black Jock had paid the last penalty, and the eyes which destroyed him flashed out accompaniment to his departing soul. And the winking skies, still merry with the stars of night, looked down unmoved, while the night-birds on the moor answered one another in their flight, and called a last farewell to the spirit of Black Jock.

CHAPTER XX
THE CONFERENCE

The storm which had been brewing in the industrial firmament grew more threatening and the clouds grew blacker until it seemed as if nothing could prevent a commotion on a big scale.

The demand for a fuller life and more security was being made by the miners all over the country. Organization was proceeding apace, and a new idea was being glimpsed by the younger men especially, which filled their hearts and fired their imagination.

"Do you think the time has come now, Bob?" asked Robert Sinclair, speaking to Smillie one day, as they proceeded by rail to a conference together, "when the whole Federation can try its power in a demand for something real?"

"What do you mean by something real, Robert?" asked Smillie, with a keen look at the young, eager face turned towards him.

"Some guarantee of comfort in our lives," was the reply. "You know that we have none now. You and others of us have been teaching the miners to work towards the day when a standard of ease and comfort will be assured to all. We have worked for it, and the miners now are looking for something tangible."

"Yes, I know; but do you think, Robert, that the time has come to put it to the test?" and Smillie had gone on to tell of some of the difficulties they were faced with.

So they talked and discussed, exchanging opinions and hopes; and all over the mining world their dreams were being voiced, and had helped to make the coming crisis.

Conferences were held, and the whole matter threshed out from every angle. The miners were united as they had never been before and the whole of the British miners were determined to use their organization to enforce their demands.

It was a triumph for Smillie's genius, the climax of his dream, to have them united as one body to fight what he called their real enemies. One federation linked together by common ideals, with common interests bound by common ties, united by traditions, by creed, by class, by common tastes shared, by suffering and hardship. It was his monument, and perhaps he regarded it with no little pride.

When Robert was appointed delegate to the council of his Union from his branch, he set himself to master thoroughly, in every detail, its machinery, and very soon his voice was raised in the debates, and it amazed even himself to find what a power he seemed to possess over his fellows. He soon learned to state his case in simple unaffected language which took a marvelous hold upon his hearers, while at times his warm glowing imagination would conjure up a living picture that hit with irresistible force, and made a lasting impression upon those who listened.

He gradually became more fluent, and studied how best to impress his comrades. His earnestness and enthusiasm were unquestioned, and sometimes were even found to be a serious obstacle to the older type of leader, men for the most part lacking imagination, and whose older and more prosaic outlook could not understand the younger man, whose zeal they regarded with impatience.

But Smillie soon recognized Robert's talent and his worth, and gave him more scope than he otherwise might have done.

Robert's admiration for his chief was unbounded, though it did not keep him from differing from Smillie at times on matters of detail. On principles they were generally at one with each other and while it was rarely that they differed, the occasions upon which they did so were remembered by all who heard. Smillie soon realized that there was an unshakable will behind the young man, and watched him under every difficult occasion with a certain amount of pride, as he grew in individuality and resource. Robert was not a frequent speaker, but was always listened to with respect when he did speak.

An industrial crisis was upon the country and everyone was expectant, and wondering how it would all end. Keir Hardie's preaching of the working class gospel was a big factor in Robert's development and the latter was soon in demand for platform lectures, stirring up the workers and pleading with them to organize, and teaching them economics through historical allusion and industrial evolution until he soon became recognized as one of the coming forces in the working-class movement. He was as yet very impulsive, and while such a trait had generally a powerful appeal on the average audience of the working class type, it often put him into somewhat compromising situations, when dealing with the more sober and serious work of the organization. Still he was showing up well, and only time and experience were needed to cure his defects. So the year ended, and the cloud grew more and more threatening.

January brought the crisis to a head, and the Government, recognizing that nothing could avert a strike and as the foreign situation was passing through a critical period, requested that a conference should be called in London, and invited the miners and the mine-owners to come together so that the Prime Minister and other statesmen could be present to try and adjust the grievance. It was a historic gathering and one that marked an epoch in the history of the industrial movement.

Delegates were present from almost every Miners' Lodge in Great Britain, while the owners were also fully represented.

The Prime Minister acted as chairman of the gathering and he was supported on the platform by other members of the Government, while Smillie and other well-known leaders represented the men and a number of the owners represented the Coal Masters' Association.

The platform party was an imposing one. Men of big reputation were there, and Robert felt himself wondering, as he looked at them, how ordinary they looked after all, and he began to speculate as to the qualities they possessed which had given them such importance.

"That's the Chancellor o' the Exchequer," said one of the delegates to Robert, pointing out the individual named. "He's a wee eatin'-an'-spued' lookin' thing when you see him sittin' there, isn't he?"

"Ay," answered Robert casually, as he surveyed the group. "I was just wondering how it was they had a' gained such reputations. In appearance they are not much to boast about."

"Ach, they're jist a lot o' oily tongued wheedlers," was the reply, "an' that wee ferrit-eyed yin is the worst o' them a'. Just wait till he begins to speak, an' you'll think he's a showman. He can fairly pit on the butter, an' he'll send us a' away hame in the belief that we're the finest set o' men he ever met, an' mak' us feel that if we decide to do anything against what he recommends, the hale country will gang to ruin."

"Oh," said Robert, as his fellow delegate paused, "I've read aboot him."

"Ay, but wait till you hear him. We can a' come up here as angry as hell, ready to string him up to the nearest lamp-post; but after he has spoken an' slaivered ower us for a while, we begin to feel differently, an' finally gang awa hame wi' our minds made up that we are the salt o' the earth. Man, it tak's a' the sting oot o' bein' dune, to be dune sae well an' sae completely."

"Yes, but when you know that why do you allow yourselves to be wheedled?"

"Ach, man; it's a' right askin' that question; but efter thae chaps get round aboot you, wi' their greasy tongues, an' their flatterin' ways, you jist begin to think that it's nae use to bother ony mair aboot resistin'. Look at that auld fermer-collier lookin' chiel, wi' his white heid an' his snipe-nose an' a smile on his face that wad mak' you believe he was gaun to dae you some big service. That's the smile that has made him Prime Minister. You'd think frae his face that he was just a solid easy-gaun kindly auld fermer, who took a constant joy in givin' jeelie-pieces to hungry weans. But when he speaks, and gets a grip o' you, he's yin o' the sooplest lawyers that ever danced roun' the rim o' hell withoot fallin' in. He'd do his faither, that yin. He wad that."

Robert looked at the various individuals as they were described, keenly interested and feeling that this comrade of his was describing much of what he himself had felt about these men, and wondered more and more as to what it was that had given them their power.

"They're a fine rogues' gallery when you see them a' sittin' there," went on the other. "They ken we are up here the day determined to demand our terms, an' that's the way they are a' turned out. Just you wait till they begin, an' you'll see a fine bit o' play actin'. They'll play us aboot as auld Tom Tervit wad play a trout in the Clyde. They hae ony amount o' patience, an' they'll gae you onything but the thing you want. They'd promise us the kingdom o' Heaven; an' they'll give us plenty o' line to run wi'; but a' the time they'll be lookin' for a chance to land us. An' they'll do it. Jist you wait."

"Well, it will be our own fault if we let them," said Robert, shortly, as he listened. "I would not let any of them do that. If we have our minds made up on what we want, I can't see why we should be wheedled like that."

"Neither do I," was the reply. "But it is aye done for all that. Then there's that ither chiel—I think he's on the Local Government Board or something. He's a corker, wi' a face like yin o' they pented cupids that the lasses send to the young men on picture postcards. Look at his nice wee baby's mooth, an' the smile on it too. It wad dazzle a hungry crocodile lookin' for its denner. His e'en are aye brighter than ony I ever saw—an' speak! Guid God! He could speak for a hale June day. He's gran' at makin' your flesh creep. He blinds you wi' sparks, an' fire-works, his words are that hot an' glowin', an' he fair dumbfounders you wi' fine soundin' sentences an' lang words. He's a corker I can tell you! But here, they are gaun to begin," he broke off hurriedly as the Prime Minister rose to his feet. Then in a sly whisper, he added:—"Just you pay attention, an' tell me after if you can tell how we hae been dune. They are here to do us the day, as sure as daith."

The Underworld | 171

The Prime Minister's speech was a masterly plea for compromise; but through it all, it seemed as if he was laying the blame upon the miners for the critical stage which had been reached. He appealed and cajoled, asked them to take long views, and talked fine platitudes about self-sacrifice, and the spirit of brotherhood, which could alone bring peace and contentment. The country was in danger, and it would be a terrible crime if the miners forced a strike; for only upon the great white solitudes of self-sacrifice and mutual help, whose peaks towered away into the realms of eternity, could real satisfaction be gained, and much more of a like kind.

Then followed other ministers, who took their cue from their chief; but there was no hint that any of them had ever made a serious attempt to understand the problem which has arisen to confront them so seriously.

They talked, or so at least it seemed to Robert, who sat in the body of the hall with the rest of the delegates, to the miners as if they were children, naughty and spoilt; and of course such an attitude could never bring about any form of agreement to sensible men, who deal every day with the life at the rough, raw edges of things.

So it was, when four of them had spoken after the Prime Minister, and none of them had shown any attempt to grapple with the subject under dispute, Robert felt more and more the truth of his fellow-delegates' description. It was all a masterly bit of wheedling and the Chancellor's effort especially was designed to win them over to a compromise settlement.

He began jocularly with a broad jest which set the delegates all rocking with laughter, telling how glad he was to be there to talk over with them the difficulties which had arisen. It always gave him pleasure to meet them and to get to know their point of view; because usually their good sense and their large stock of prudence made them amenable to listening to a reasoned argument.

He was glad they always recognized there were two sides to most disputes, and he felt sure whatever the outcome of this conference might be they would not allow their good sense to stand in the way of a possible settlement. Gradually he worked into more serious lines, and with vivid language, putting the case for the opposite side, gently bringing their minds by degrees further and further away from the point—the real point of issue.

Then finally when sufficiently developed, he gathered all the threads together, and in a great burst of poetic eloquence and fiery fervor he swept along like a tornado in a grand burst of superb oratory, his eyes rolling and flashing, his hands and head poised into beautifully effective gesture, and appealed to them in great rolling, fiery sentences that completely swept the conference like a whirlwind, and sat down amid a great burst of applause which broke with splendid spontaneity from the assembled delegates, and the winning golden smile upon his face which Robert's companion had described earlier in the day.

Robert could hardly analyze his feelings. He felt he did not know whether to admire or condemn, but all the time he felt a slow rising indignation within him, and that the Conference was being swung away from what they had met to discuss. Perhaps it was his companions' conversation that did it. He could not tell; but unable to contain himself longer his impulsive nature getting the upper hand, he bounced to his feet, pale and excited, though trying hard to curb and control himself, and in a low tense voice, which at first halted a little, electrified the gathering by a speech wrung from his very soul.

"Mr. Chairman," he began, in this unexpected incident, "I have listened very attentively to the speeches just delivered by yourself and the other honorable gentlemen."

Here some of the other delegates intervened to tell him that he was not expected to speak, but the Prime Minister, for some reason unknown, told him to go on and so he proceeded.

Then Robert proceeded to pour out his soul, stating the miners' grievances and their rights as men. How they were always put off with promises, and defeated in dialectics and the game of wits. As he spoke he felt the assembly gradually thaw, then become liquid, finally it seemed to join the torrent of his eloquence, and sweep on, blotting out all resistance.

When at last he sat down a wild burst of applause rent the air, as he sat down pale and excited; but glad that he had got the chance at last of speaking what he felt to the enemies of his class.

For fully five minutes the delegates went wild in their cheering and applause. Again and again it broke out afresh, when it had spent itself a little, and seemed to be dying down, but the memory of it always stirred them to fresh outbursts until at last, taking advantage of a lull, the Prime Minister suggested that he and his colleagues would prefer that the conference should stand adjourned till the next day, and this was agreed to by the delegates, who were not averse to the holiday.

Congratulations were showered upon Robert from all sides. Even men who differed from him on most things grasped his hand and shook it, and told him how proud they were of his little speech.

Robert heard and saw all their pleased enjoyment but was vaguely troubled in his heart, wondering how Smillie would have taken it, and this pained him more than the pleasant things the other delegates said to him.

"Man, Sinclair," said the one who had sat next to Robert in the Conference, when they got out on to the street, "you've fairly upset the hale jing bang o' them the day. Lod! But I was like a balloon in a high wind, fair carried away wi' you. I never thocht you could have done that. I was in the opinion that Smillie was the only yin that could stand up to that set o' rogues. It was great. It was that."

Robert laughed uneasily and bashfully as he answered, "I couldn't help it, Davie," then adding as an afterthought, "Maybe I hae put my fit in it. I wonder how Smillie took it a'."

"Ach, well, it disna matter a damn, onyway. You did fine, an' I canna see how Smillie has onything ado wi' it. However, we hae a hale day to oorsel's now, what dae you say to gaun to the length of Kew Gardens? It's a gran' place, an' I hae a sister oot there in service."

"Oh, I don't mind. I don't know onything aboot London and as you are nae stranger, I might as well gang wi' you, as bother onybody else to show me roun'."

"There's some of thae chaps'll fairly enjoy this," said Davie, nodding in the direction of some of the delegates. "That's the way they agreed to adjourn sae already. They jist leeve for the conferences. It's the time they like. They booze and get their horns oot for a day or two, an' I can tell you, Rab, it's maybe jist as well that they dinna bring their weemin folks wi' them. However, it tak's a' kinds of folk to mak' a world, I suppose, so let's off, and see as muckle o' London as possible," and they set off and were soon swallowed up in the great Metropolis.

CHAPTER XXI
THE MEETING WITH MYSIE

When the London Conference ended, the delegates hurried back to put the terms of the suggested agreement before the men, and as they journeyed the whole topic of conversation was of the Conference, and of the terms which had been suggested as a basis for settlement of the dispute.

"Well, you can a' say what you like," put in Davie Donaldson, who had sat beside Robert in the Conference, "but in my opinion we hae been diddled again. The wee showman wi' the ferret een was too mony for us, an' he jist twisted us round his wee finger as he liked."

"Ach, but you are never content," replied another who was of an opposite opinion. "It doesna matter what kind o' terms you get, you're never content."

"I'm no' content wi' thae terms ony way," persisted Davie stubbornly. "What the hell's the use o' makin' a demand for something, an' sayin' afore you gang that you mean to hae it, an' then to tamely tak' the hauf o' it, an' gang awa' hame as pleased as a wheen weans wha have been promised a penny to tak' castor oil? I'd be dam'd afore I'd tak' that."

"You're owre ill to please," said the other. "You're never satisfied wi' a fair thing. Didn't you hear as weel as me that there was a danger o' war breakin' oot at the present time, an' we couldna possibly hae a strike at a time like this."

"War!" retorted Davie, heatedly. "They'll aye hae a war or something else to fricht you wi', when you show that you mean business. Wha the hell hae we to quarrel wi' onyway, I'd like to ken?"

"Oh, it micht be France, or Germany, or Russia, or some ither o' thae cut-throat foreign nations."

"An' what are you gaun to quarrel aboot?" yelled Davie still more heatedly.

"What the hell do I ken?" was the answer.

"Then, if you don't ken, why the damn should you quarrel? It's a dam'd silly thing to fecht at ony time, but it's a dam'd sicht sillier to fecht withoot haein' a quarrel at a'," cried Davie, now fairly roused. "That's jist hoo they diddle us. They diddle the workers o' France an' ither countries in the same way. Maybe the French Government is telling the French colliers that there is a danger o' a war wi' Britain at this minute, to keep them quate; an' if they are, do you an' me ken anything aboot what the war will be for? No' a thing does yin o' us ken. Wars are no' made by workin' folk at all! They are made wi' the ither crowd, an' they laugh in their sleeves when they hae sent us awa' back to our work an' oor hames as quate as mice," and Davie looked round in triumph, asking with his eyes, and in the tones of his voice, for confirmation of his views from the others.

Thus they talked and discussed, exchanging opinions about all things in strong but expressive language, as the train sped northwards bearing them home. District meetings were organized, and the leaders put persuasively the arguments for the acceptance of the terms laid down. All through the crisis the men had behaved admirably, for they had learned to trust Smillie, even when they felt doubtful of his policy. Robert took a big share in the organizing of these meetings and in addressing them. He flung himself into this work whole-heartedly. The terms certainly did not please him; but, as the majority at the London Conference had decided to recommend them to the men, he thought it his duty to sink his personal opinions, and in the interests of discipline and the unity of the organization—as he had already had his say and had been found in the minority—he put all his efforts into trying to get the men to accept the suggested terms, and go forward as one united body. His persuasive powers of appeal, and his straight, direct way of argument, commended him to his comrades. By the time that the ballot had been carried through in the various districts, it was mid-February, and the Scottish delegates met in Edinburgh to give the result of the voting among the rank and file.

Robert attended the Conference, and while he had appealed to the men to accept the terms of the London Conference, he secretly hoped that the ballot vote of the men would decide to fight; for, like Davie Donaldson, he believed they had again been side-tracked. He wondered how Smillie regarded the matter. He had not had an opportunity of talking with Smillie to learn his opinion, but he felt sure that his leaders did not like the terms either.

If, however, the men had agreed on acceptance, he could not help matters; but a direct refusal from the rank and file would, he thought, be an intimation to the more reactionary leaders that the spirit of revolt was growing, and would give the rebels the chance for which they were looking. But he would soon know, he thought, as he hastened to the Synod Hall, where the Conference was to be held; for the result of the ballot was to be announced at the end of the first part of the Conference.

There was some routine business to get over when it opened, and after a while the President rose and gave the result of the ballot, which showed a considerable majority for acceptance, and this brought the adjournment for dinner.

Robert felt that he wanted to spend a quiet five minutes or so before the Conference resumed; so he hurried through with his dinner and then strolled out into Princes Street Gardens, which attracted him very much. His mind seemed to want peace and quietness, and as he walked along, turning over the situation and examining it from all points of view, the fluttering of early mating birds among the shrubs soon shifted his thoughts to other things; and, as they romped and courted, and fought among the bushes, his thoughts went back to the moor at home, and the little wood, and the memories of other things.

The vague stirrings of power within him had become more pronounced during the last six months, and he felt conscious of a growing sense of importance. It was not that he was conceited, but his mental muscles, as it were, seemed to have gained in power from the strenuous exertions which they had lately undertaken.

He knew that he possessed talents far above the average of his class. He was sensible of a certain superiority, yet it was not from the contemplation of this that he drew his elation. He saw the issue quite clearly and knew the pathway which must be trodden. He was not personally ambitious for the sake of making an impression or gaining power. He knew that in too many cases men had in the past made their position a sinecure in the Labor Movement and he condemned their action. The Movement must be served and not lived on. Not personal betterment, but the betterment of the whole lot. Whatever it demanded of service from anyone should be given willingly, no matter in what direction the call were made.

Musing thus, he strolled along among his hopes of the future. His life's work lay here, working for his own class—for humanity. There was nothing else to win him; for like most young men in like circumstances he had already concluded that now, since Mysie was not to be his, there was nothing else to which he could better devote his life.

Where was Mysie, he wondered? What had happened to her? She had completely gone out of everybody's knowledge, and no one seemed to know anything about her.

He moved slowly along and at the thought of Mysie his former decision seemed a cold one and he felt that she still held a big place in his life. Moving towards a seat a little way ahead so that he might enjoy this mood, the figure of a girl started up as if to go, and immediately he rushed forward, all his pulses afire, and his whole being stirred beyond words.

"Mysie!" he exclaimed, jumping forward, "Guid God! where have you come from? Where have you been?" and his hands were holding hers, and his eyes greedily scanning her face as if he would look into her very soul, and read the story of the last few months.

"Oh, Rob," she said, with a gasp, "I didna think I wad meet you here."

"Sit down," he said hurriedly, as he recovered himself. "Sit down and rest. You're ill. What's the matter? Where have you been? Tell me all about it!" There were tears in Mysie's eyes too, as she weakly sat down, unable to do anything else. She had recognized him as he approached, and had started up to get away; but he had also recognized her, and she was too late.

"Hoo is my mither an' my faither?" she enquired, after a short silence, as she tried to recover herself. "Hoo are they a' at hame?" the greedy heart hunger for loved ones drove her to the impatient enquiry. "Did they miss me muckle, Rob? Were they awfu' vexed at what I did? Tell me a' aboot it then, I want to ken."

"But you must tell me first aboot yoursel', Mysie," he replied evasively, searching in his mind the best way to adopt in telling her of the things he knew would wound her. "Come, Mysie," he urged, "you surely can trust me. I have always been your friend, and I only wish now to hear all about you. Why did you go away?"

She saw him look at her, and a quick flush overspread her thin, pale cheeks as she detected his look. He had no need to ask further.

"Oh, Rob, I wish—I wish I had died a year syne!" and a wild burst of sobbing came over her as she spoke.

"Dinna greet, Mysie," he said, as his hand reached out and began to stroke her hair tenderly. Then after a short pause, "Wha was he, Mysie? Tell me, an' I'll tear the black heart oot o' him!"

But Mysie only cried, uncontrollably, and hid her face in her hands; for the homely doric on Robert's tongue touched her and it came readier to him in moments like these, and the tender touch of his hand upon her head gave her comfort, soothing her, and staying her grief, as a child is quieted by the loving hand of a mother.

"I'll tell you a' aboot it, Rob," she said at last after a short time. "An' I hope you'll no' tell onybody. There's naebody to blame but mysel' for a' that has happened, an' I maun bear the punishment if there is punishment gaun," and bit by bit, with many an effort to compose herself as she spoke, she told him the whole sad story from beginning to end.

"There was naebody to blame, Rob—naebody but mysel'! I should hae kent better. But I never thocht it wad hae turned oot as it has done. I hae been gey ill, an' I maun say that Peter has been awful guid to me. He's done his best to get me better, so that he can marry me afore it happens. I lay for nearly six months, an' I wasna carin' whether I died or no'! I was fair heartbroken, an' didna mind what happened. This is the first day I hae been oot. He cam' this mornin' frae his lodgings tae ask me tae gang oot a wee while in the sunshine, seein' that it was sic a guid day, and Mrs. Ramsay brocht me oot here, and warned me to sit till she cam' back. When I saw you comin' I got up to run awa', but I dinna ken whaur to run to; for this big toon is a' strange to me, an' I'm feart."

"Oh, if I had only kent! You maun keep yoursel' as free frae worry as possible, an' try an' get better," he went on, trying to speak as lightly as possible. "Keep up your spirits, an' you'll maybe soon be a' better."

"Aye, Rob," she said, "but it's no' easy. An' I hae been gettin' waur instead o' better. I ken mysel' that I'm no' improvin', an' I often think it wad hae been better if I had died. When folk don't want to live—when they've nothing to be happy aboot they are better to dee!"

"But you maunna talk like that, Mysie," he said again. "You'll get better yet, an' be as happy as ever you were. It is only because you are ill noo an' you sae weak, that mak's you talk like that. An' forby you maun mind that there are ither folk wha'll be vexed if you dinna get better. Your faither and your mither wad like to see you weel an' happy, an' oh, Mysie, Mysie, I want you to get weel!" he broke out passionately—pleadingly, the misery in his voice going to her heart as it cried to her, ached for her, and suffered for her. "Wad you hae married me, Mysie, if I had asked you afore you went awa'?" and his hands were again stroking tenderly the brown hair and patting the thin cheeks as he spoke and plead.

"Ay, Rob," she answered simply, "I wad hae married you. I sometimes think yet that I'll never marry onybody else. As a lassie I aye dreamed in my ain mind that I'd be your wife. It's awfu' hoo the things that folk want maist are aye the things they never get!"

"Mysie, wad you marry me yet?" he asked, impulsively. "Jist this minute? An' I'll tak' you hame, an' naebody will ken onything. I'll take a'

The Underworld | 179

the blame, an' you can say that it was me. I'll nurse you back to health again wi' my mither's help an' naebody need ken the richt wye o' it!"

"No, Rob," she said after a short pause. "I couldna dae that. It wad neither be fair to you or me, nor to onybody else."

"But, Mysie," he went on in the low tender voice that was so difficult to withstand, "you don't like Peter weel enough to be his wife. You say you never intended to be onybody's wife but mine; an' what wye should you no' do as I propose? You ken I'll never do onything else but love you. You ken that, Mysie!"

"Ay, Rob," she answered, "I ken a' that. Naebody kens it better than me noo; and that's what mak's it sae awfu' hard to refuse. But it wadna be richt at a', an' that's a' that can be thocht aboot it. You maunna ask me ony mair."

"But I will ask you," he cried in another burst of passion, "an' I'll keep on askin' you. You ken you are mine, an' naebody else has a richt to you. I love you, Mysie! Oh, can you no' see, lassie, that it wad be a' richt if you'd do as I want you?"

"No, no, Rob. Dinna say that. It wadna be richt at a', an' I'd be doin' anither wrang thing if I did."

"But you said jist the noo, that you sometimes thocht you wadna marry onybody else?"

"Yes, I ken I said that," she replied. Then with pain in her voice as it grew more pitiful, "Dinna ask me, Rob, to do that. I ken it wadna be richt, an' you munna ask me ony mair; for though I said that I sometimes thocht I wadna marry onybody else, I canna marry you noo. Oh! if only my mither kent, it would break her heart, an' my faither wad dee o' the disgrace! What do they think o' me, Rob? Tell me a'—hoo are they, an' if they miss me very much."

"Your faither and mither nearly broke their hearts," he said simply, "an' at nicht your mother lies an' thinks an' wonders what has come owre you. You ken hoo a mither grieves an' worries aboot her bairns. She never thocht o' sic a thing happening in her family. She was aye sae prood o' them a'. I heard her say ane day to my mither that she dootit you maun be deid, or you wad hae sent her word; and that you wadna hae gane wrang. She never, she said, kent o' you takin' up wi' men, an' was sure that naething o' that kind had happened."

"Did she really think that, Rob?" asked Mysie, glad to know that her mother had believed in her virtue, yet pained. "Rob, if only mithers wad be mair open wi' their lassies an' tell them o' the things they shouldna' do, an' the dangers that lie afore them. But tell me aboot them a'. What did my faither say aboot it? How are they a' keepin'?"

This was the question which Robert had feared most, for although Matthew Maitland had said very little, everybody knew that he grieved sorely over his daughter's disappearance, and at the time was lying very ill. He was fast nearing the end, which most colliers of the day reached—cut off in middle life, made old by bad ventilation in the mines, and black damp. His condition was almost despaired of by the doctor, and when Robert left Lowwood that evening for Edinburgh, he was in a very critical state. Two months before, the oldest boy, who was some two years younger than Mysie, had been taken suddenly ill, and had died after a few days' illness.

How was he to tell Mysie of this? How tell her that John was dead, and her father perhaps dying? How tell of her mother eating out her heart in the hungry longing for news of the missing girl, and killing herself with work and worry?

"Your faither's no' very weel, Mysie," he began evasively, his eyes turned away from her, in an attempt at hiding what he felt.

"What's wrang wi' him, Rob?" she asked, the quick alarm in her voice cutting his heart as she spoke.

"He hasna been workin' for fully a fortnicht," he replied.

"But what's wrang?" she persisted. "Is he ill?"

"Mysie, I'd raither onything than be the means o' painin' you, for you are no' in a fit state to be worried."

"You maun tell me, Rob," she cried fiercely, her face showing excitement. "What is it that is wrang? Is he awfu' ill?"

"He's lyin' gey bad, Mysie, an' when I cam' awa' this mornin', I didna like the look o' him at a'. He was kind o' wanderin' in his mind, an' speakin' to you an' John, jist as he used to speak when we were a' bairns thegither. He was liltin' some o' thae auld sangs he used to sing to us. But dinna greet, Mysie, you'll mak' yoursel' waur. You are no very strong, you ken, an' if you worry it'll mak' you waur. You should raither try an' bear up, an' get strong, an' maybe gang an' see him. He'd be awfu' prood to see you, an' so wad your mither."

"No, no," she cried. "I canna gang. It wad kill them to see me noo, an' I couldna bear't, if they should be angry wi' me. I couldna face their anger, Rob."

"Weel, Mysie," he said, drawing a long breath, as if to face a stiff proposition, "there is no other way out of it, but that you'll hae to marry me now—just this minute, an' gang back wi' me. If you do that, I can tak' you back wi' me, an' gang to your faither an' say that it was me that was responsible. It can be done, Mysie, if only you'll agree to it. Come, Mysie!" he cried in a burst of passionate pleading. "I want you. Mysie, Mysie! Say that you'll come."

Robert looked at her pale, thin, emaciated face with greedy pleading in his eyes. He saw the thin-looking, hungry body as it shook with her sobs, and that terrible cough, which seemed as if it would carry her away before his eyes. "Say you'll come, Mysie!" he pleaded, his hands held out appealingly. "Say you'll come, an' it'll be so easy."

"No, no," she sobbed vehemently, "I canna do that. Dinna ask me ony mair, Rob, I canna do that. It wadna be fair."

A hopeless look came into his eyes as he listened to her words, for he knew that Mysie could never consent to his proposal. Frail as she was, and torn by her wish to agree, yet he knew she meant it, when she said no.

"Where do you live, Mysie?" he enquired at last, thinking to find some way of helping her. "Wad you gie me your address, so that I'll ken where you bide?"

"No, I dinna want to tell you, Rob. You'd better gang awa' noo. Mrs. Ramsay will soon be comin' for me. Gang awa' an' leave me. I want to be a wee while by mysel'. Oh, dear! Oh, dear! I wish I could dee an' leave it a'!"

Robert stole away on tiptoe, as if he were afraid longer to intrude upon her grief—his mind in a whirl, and his heart heavy with sorrow. He returned to the Conference to find that the debate was in full swing, and that Davie Donaldson, was laying about him in vigorous style, denouncing the leaders for recommending the terms to the men, and telling them that the "wee chocolate-moothed Chancellor had again diddled them."

But he felt no interest in Davie's denunciation, and could not smile at his picturesque language. His mind would revert to the gardens in Princes Street, and he saw the thin white figure on the seat, the picture of hopeless misery, her frail form torn with sobs; and heard the wail in her voice as she moaned, "Oh, dear! Oh, dear! I wish I could dee an' leave it a'!"

Some of the young delegates wondered why Sinclair remained silent in such an important debate. They had succeeded in raising a question which at any other time would have brought him to his feet; but he sat impassive and silent, and above all the clash and glamor, above the applause and the interruptions, above all the witty sallies which brought unexpected laughter, he saw only the thin, white lonely figure—the dejected and outcast, the poor plaything of fate, and heard the heart-breaking cry, "Oh, dear! I wish I could dee an' leave it a'!" and in every syllable there was a stab of pain.

The Conference ended, and the delegates made homeward. The terms had been agreed to, so far as Scotland was concerned, and all pointed to peace.

"You didna speak the day, Sinclair, and I fairly thocht you wad hae been into the fecht," said one delegate to Robert, as the train moved away from the station.

"No, I wasna feelin' up to the mark," he returned, in a tone that hinted that he did not want to be troubled, and he sat back in his corner in silence. In the gray quick gloaming the moors and the hills, viewed from the train, seemed to him a country without hope. There was sadness in it, and pain, and the gray wintry sky brooded of sorrows to come.

Occasionally a few sheep would start away from where they had been grazing close to the railway, startled by the noise of the train. Thin wisps of gray ragged clouds hung low, as if softly descending upon the hills, in fateful sinister storms, and a fiery flash of yellow left a strip of anger on the western horizon, where the sun had gone down a short time ago.

Gray mists and grayer moors, with occasionally a solitary tree standing out in the distance, as if to accentuate the loneliness and the sorrow of the world in their ragged branches, which seemed ready to pierce the sky in defiance of the anger of the, as yet, unleashed storm.

On rushed the train, and through the mists there kept coming before his eyes the white lonely figure, moaning in fatal grief—grief inexorable and unrelenting, while the flying wheels groaned and sobbed and clicked, with the regular beat of a breaking heart, as if they were beating out the sorrows of the world, and over all they sang the dirge of the broken life of a maid. "Oh, dear! Oh, dear! I wish I could dee an' leave it a'!"

CHAPTER XXII
MYSIE'S RETURN

When Mrs. Ramsay returned she found Mysie in a fainting condition, thoroughly exhausted, and on the point of collapse. Mrs. Ramsay saw, by her red swollen eyes, that she had been weeping. With the help of her daughter the kind woman, who had done so much for Mysie during the past few months, got her to the street, and procuring a cab, got her back to the house, much alarmed by the patient's condition.

All night Mysie tossed and raved in a high fever and delirium, while Mrs. Ramsay sat by her bedside, trying to soothe and quieten the stricken girl. As she seemed to get no better the older woman grew more alarmed.

"Oh, my puir faither!" moaned the girl. "Oh, mither, I am vexed at what has happened. Oh, dear, I wonder what I'll do!"

"There now, dearie!" said Mrs. Ramsay in warm sympathetic tones, as she stroked the burning hands and brow. "Try and quieten down and go to sleep. You were getting on very well, you know, and making fine progress, but you'll make yourself worse than ever if you carry on like that. There now, dearie! Try and get to sleep, and you'll soon be better again!"

But Mysie was silent only for a moment, and the low moan soon broke from her lips again, like the wail of some stricken thing at night upon the moor, and still she tossed and tumbled feverishly in her bed.

In the morning the doctor came and shook his head. Mysie was ill, very ill. Her condition was serious, and it was little he could do. Only care and good nursing and try to keep her from worrying. He left a prescription, and Peter soon had the necessary medicine, and later the patient grew calmer, and finally sank into a deep sleep; and so the old fight had to be fought over again, to get her strength restored and her vitality increased.

Mysie did not mention another word of home. She lay quiet, hardly even moving and seldom speaking; but the burning fire that consumed her was apparent in her hectic cheeks and glowing eyes, and one could see that her mind was away, never dwelling upon her surroundings, but was wandering among the heather hills and quiet valleys, where the call of the curlew and the shout of the lapwing stir the primitive impulses of those who love the haunts of the moorland life, and weave so much romance into the lives and souls of the country bred people, who never grow to love the ugly towns, but whose hearts remain with their first love—the moors, and the hills, and the mountain brooks for ever.

She seemed to grow a little stronger as the days passed. She took her medicines regularly and without protest; but deep down in her heart she felt that she would never get better, and her only desire, that had been shaping itself ever since Robert had told her of her father's condition, was to be strong enough, to go home to Lowwood, just to see her parents, her brothers and sisters, once more; then she could die in peace. If only she could do that, she would not care what happened. Nothing else mattered; but she must get home. Nothing would prevent her from doing that.

It was the instinct of the wounded animal, dragging itself home to die— home to its home in the kindly earth, away from contact with other things— just to be alone, to nurse its suffering and its misery, till the last shred of strength had gone, and the limbs stiffened out, while the glazing eyes looked forward as the pain increased, across the barriers of other worlds to a land of plenty—a land of green shrubs, and sweet waters bubbling from scented hillsides, overhung with blue skies which never brewed storms. A land of bud and bloom and blossom, scented and sweet, with every desirable weed and tasty herb—a land of life full and beautiful, of warm suns, calling up dreams from a blossoming mist of bluebells, creating the freshness and the happiness of youthfulness in every living thing. A land where far vistas and wide horizons, bounded by green hills, brought visions from the inner self, with joyous abundance through lusty life, and glorious passionate being—a land sweet and fruitful, and never-ending in its beauty and its means of happiness!

Slowly the days passed, and her strength gradually increased little by little, until a month had gone past, and she was able to be about the house again; but this determination in her heart to go home grew stronger with every day that passed, and it seemed to give her strength and vitality, and her hope became more definite and more sure.

She pictured her home again, as she had known it; the little kitchen, with its white scrubbed floor and a few newspapers spread over its newly washed surface to keep it clean from muddy feet; the white-washed jambs of the fireside, and the grate polished with blacklead; the clear-topped fender, with its inscription done in brass in the center, "Oor ain fireside"; the half-dozen strong sturdy, well-washed chairs; the whitewood dresser, with its array of dog ornaments and cheap vases, and white crocheted cover; and the curtains over the two beds in the kitchen. All these things she loved to think about, and she saw them pictured in her mind as real as they'd ever been to her when her own life was centered in them, and her fancy took delight in these secret joys. It was her home she saw always, the humble "but and ben" with the primitive conditions of life, the crude amenities, the sweet joys of simple unaffected people; but it was her home.

One day, Mrs. Ramsay had gone out on an errand that detained her some time, Mysie seized suddenly again in a more intense form by her desire to go home, feverishly dressed herself, and hastily scribbling a note of thanks to her good friend and nurse, she stole out on to the street, a poor, forlorn, weak girl, but thoroughly determined to go home to where her heart called her.

Out upon the street, she grew frightened. She did not know anything about the city, nor in which direction to turn. She had no idea how far it was to the station. She was helpless and alone, and very much excited.

A boy passed her, whistling as she had often heard her own brothers whistling, and hastily calling to him she accosted him thus:

"Could you tell me hoo far it is to the station?"

"Whit station?" asked the boy, and she suddenly remembered it was Princes Street, and mentioned it. "Oh, ay; it's no' faur," he said airily, as he pointed in the direction of it. "Jist gang alang that way," and he turned away as if to leave her.

"Wad you tak' me to it, an' I'll gie you a shillin'?" she asked, and he eagerly turned at once to close the bargain.

"Oh, ay," he agreed, "I'll soon tak' you there," and the two set off; and guided by the boy, whose knowledge of the city seemed to her wonderful in one so young, they arrived at the station, with Mysie very tired and half-fainting with excitement.

"Hae you a ticket?" asked the boy, judging from her appearance that she needed to be reminded of such things.

"No, I forgot I hadna got yin," replied Mysie. "I wonder where I'll hae to gang to get yin. Hoo much will it be, think you?"

"Oh, I dinna ken," said the boy. "Come alang here to the bookin' office, an' ask a ticket for the place you want to gang to, an' the clerk will soon tell you the price o't."

Luckily Mysie had a few pounds in a purse which Peter had given her some time ago, in case she might want to go out, he said, and buy something she might want. Going to the booking office, and guided by her little friend, she timorously made known her wants, and a ticket was given her; and she returned under her youthful escort, who enquired the time of the trains leaving of a porter, and conducted her to the platform, and helped her into the train, which soon started off on the homeward journey.

"Thenk you," said the boy, his eyes glowing with pleasure at the two shining half-crowns which Mysie had given him, and he waved his hand to her as the train steamed out of the platform.

"Going home, going home," sang the wheels as the train rushed along. "Going home," with every beat of her heart they answered her with their cheery monotone. "Going home," they gurgled, as they freely ran down the gradients. "Going home, going home," as they ran along the flat moor. "Going home, going home," they panted up the inclines, but still joyous in the thought of getting there.

Home, aye, home, they were taking her. Home to the cheery fireside, with the homely fare and the warm hearts! To the cosy corner by the fender at her father's feet, to the music of her mother's clicking needles as she knitted; to the sweet comfort of the love and kindness of brothers and sisters; to the warmth of glowing smiles and loving hearts. Home! Home! Oh, God! Comfort of weary and battered humanity, dragging its wounded and broken life to the shelter and the sanctity of love. So rose her hopes, and her heart sang as the brooding night lowered and the wind rose, bringing the rain lashing from the spring clouds to burnish the moor with storms. Home to the hearts that loved her first, and would love her to the end.

At last the train steamed into the little station from which she had first gone to the great city, and everything looked just the same as upon that night, when she had stolen across the moor to run away where she expected to hide her shame, and try and redeem that one mistaken impulse, which had been so thoughtlessly indulged, and so terribly paid for in suffering and tears. The station-master looked at her keenly as she passed. She seemed so frail and weak looking to be abroad in such a night; but she passed on and out upon the country road that ran across the moor, where the darkness always lay thickest, and where the terrors of the timid were greatest, and the storms raged fiercest.

On she battled, already feeling weak and tired; but always the thought of home waiting for her impelled her onward. Home was waiting over there—waiting just two miles off, where she could see the twinkling of the lights from the pithead at which she had worked, and where she had been so happy at the dreams conjured by six and sixpence per week. Down rushed the wind from the hills, careering along the wide moor, driving the rain and hail in front, as if he would burst the barriers of the world and go free.

She halted and turned her back upon the blows, as if she would fall; but there were light and warmth, and love and cheerfulness over there, if only she could hold out till she reached them.

She turned again, and a sheep scampered across the moorland path just in front, and the soft bleat of an early lamb soothed the quick excited leap in her heart. The rain ceased, and a pale glitter of the rim of a moon, like the paring of a giant's nail in the sky, glinted from behind the dark cloud, and flung a silver radiance over the bog-pools around, which glittered like patches of fairy silver upon a land of romance.

She was wet, but not cold. The fever in her blood raged and she staggered forward again, slowly and tottering. A smile was playing about her lips and eyes. Her lips were parted, and her breast rose and fell like the heaving beat of an engine. But home beckoned and lured her onward, and the hope of a long dream filled her soul. Again a sharp scurry in front drove her heart to her mouth, as two hares battled and tore at each other for the love of the female which sat close by, watching the contest.

The sharp swish of the wings of lapwings, as they dived towards her, filling the moors with their hard rasping double note, and also battling for possession of a mate, stirred her frightened blood; and at every step some new terror thrilled her, and kept her continually in a state of fear.

Still she plodded on, and another squall of rain and hail followed, giving place soon to the glory of the cold moon, and again obscuring it in a quick succession of showers and calm moonshine. But there was home in front, and she was always drawing nearer. Just a little while now, a few hundred yards or so, and she would be there.

Weak and exhausted, stumbling and rising again, driven by that unrelenting, irresistible desire, this poor waif of humanity, impelled by sheer force of will, staggered and crawled towards its hope, forward to its dream, and at last stood by the window of the home it had sought.

Panting and utterly worn out, she stood holding on to the window ledge, her will now weakened, her strength of mind gone, and her desire forsaking her now that she was there.

The wind fell to a mere whisper, and she stooped to look in at a chink in the shutter, the tears running in hot, scalding streams from her eyes and blinding her vision. The soft stirring of little limbs beneath her heart brought back the old desire to hide herself from everyone she had known.

Oh, God! It was terrible thus to be torn; for she had sung the song of all motherhood in her own simple way—the song of the love that recreates the world. The same song that enables motherhood to commune with God. "I will walk in the pure air of the uplands, so that your life shall be sweet and clean. I shall bathe my body in the sweet waters of the earth, so that you shall be pure; I shall walk in meditation and solitude, so that your thoughts shall be worthy thoughts; I shall dwell on the hillsides, so that your mind shall be lofty; I shall love all living things, so that you shall be godly in the love of your kind; I shall be humble, so that you shall not be proud; I shall be tender, wandering among the sweet flowers, so that you shall never be rough or unkindly; I shall serve, so that you shall be kingly in your service to others.

"Down in the valleys I shall linger, drinking in the music of sweet streams; and the songs of the morning and the eventide shall make you gentle and happy. The tender grass shall be my couch upon the moor, so that you can know the restfulness and comfort of love. The grateful trees shall shade me from the fierce heat of the sun, so that you shall be restful, yet active in kind deeds. Oh, I shall clothe me in the sweetest thoughts, and sing the sweetest songs, speak the kindliest words, and do the friendliest deeds—I shall lie down in gratitude for all that has ever been rendered to me, and shall keep faith with love, so that you—you who are me, you who are my heart and mind, my body and soul shall be ushered into the world as a savior of the race; and the lyrics of the dawn and the dayfall, of the golden, glorious day, and the silver radiant night, shall all be thine to interpret, in spirit and in word and service."

Thus had motherhood sung in all ages, weaving the dreams of hope about the soul which she had called from eternity, after having gone upon that long perilous journey into the land of Everywhere to bring back a new life to the world. Mysie dashed the warm tears from her eyes, and looked again through the chink in the shutter.

She had a full view of the kitchen. It was the same cosy, bright place it had always been, when she had sat there on the corner of the fender o' nights, her head against her father's knee, as he read out the news from the evening paper, while her mother sewed, or darned, or knitted.

Her father sat in the easy chair, pale and thin and weak. He looked ill, and it seemed as if he were merely out of his bed, so that her mother might change the linen, for she was busy pulling off pillow-cases and putting clean ones on, and turning the chaff-filled tick to make it easier for his poor bones to lie on.

He lay back in his chair, his eyes half closed, as if tired.

"The wind has surely gane doon noo," Mysie heard her mother observe, as she spread out the clean white sheet upon the bed.

"Ay, it seems to hae quietened," returned Matthew weakly. "It has been an awfu' nicht, and gey wild."

"Ay, it has that. Peety ony puir body that has been oot in it," said her mother, with a deep sigh, as she folded back the blankets. "It's an awfu' nicht for the homeless to be oot in."

Silence reigned for a short time, and only the whisper of the wind outside prevented the sobs of the poor waif at the window being heard.

"You are lookin' a wee better the nicht, Matthew," said Mrs. Maitland after a long thoughtful pause, as she drew in her chair beside his.

"Ay, I'm feelin' no' sae bad," he answered feebly. Then, as if having made up his mind about something, he went on, as he looked into the glowing fire, "Do you ken, wife, I hae been thinkin' a lot aboot oor Mysie a' day. I wonder what'll be the cause o't? But a' day she has been in my mind, an' I only hope naething has come to her."

"I dinna ken, Matthew," she said; for this was the first time he had spoken about their missing daughter since the day they had learned of her disappearance. He had always remained silent when she had given expression to her thoughts regarding Mysie; but thinking this an encouragement, she spoke about her, and he too, in a way that made her wonder; for he was never talkative at any time, and it seemed as if his heart was hungering to talk of their bairn.

"I wonder what wad hae come owre her, that nae spierin's o' her could be got. Puir Mysie! I liket that wean, wife—liket her maybe owre weel; an' my heart has been sair for her mony a time, wonderin' what has come o' her!"

Mrs. Maitland lifted a corner of her rough apron and wiped her eyes, as she cried softly at hearing her husband thus speak of their missing daughter.

"Do you think she'll be living, Matthew?" she asked looking through her tears at her husband anxiously.

"That's hard to say, wife," he replied, a break in his voice. "Sometimes I think she maun be deid, or she wad hae come back to us in some way. I think we liket her weel enough, an' she kent it, and she was ay a guid lassie at a' times."

"Ay, she was," replied the mother, "a guid bairn, an' a clever yin aboot the hoose; an' I never had an angry word frae her a' my days. Oh, Matthew," she cried out, again bursting into tears, and sobbing pitifully, "what is't we hae done to be tried like this? Mysie gane, an' guid kens where she is, an' John ta'en awa' jist when oor battle was beginnin' to get easier. Noo you hae been laid aside yoursel', an' God kens hoo we are to do, for hinna a penny left in the hoose! Oh, dear, but it's a hard lot we hae to suffer!" and she sobbed in silence, while her husband stroked her pale, thin, toil-worn hands that hid her weeping eyes.

"Wheesht, lassie!" he said brokenly. "Dinna you break doon noo, for you hae been the mainstay o' us a', when we wad hae lost heart often. I used to think that oor lot couldna be harder, when the bairns were a' wee, an' we were struggling frae haun' to mooth, to see them fed an' cled. But wi' a' the hardships, thae days were happy. We were baith young, an' I was aye fairly healthy an' when we locked the door at nicht, we were satisfied that a' that belanged to us were inside, an' in safety, even though their wee stomachs maybe werena' ower fu'. But noo we canna do that, wife. Some hae gane to where want an' poverty canna hurt them, an' that is a consolation; but where will oor lassie be, that never gi'ed us a wrang word a' her days? Is she in want this nicht, the same as we are oorsels? Will she be hungry an' homeless, ill clad, an' oot in the storm? If she is, then God peety her. If only we had her aside us, hunger wad be easier tholed for us a'," and Matthew, unable to control himself longer, completely broke down and wept, mingling his tears with those of his wife, because of their misery and poverty and suffering.

The girl outside could hardly restrain herself at thus hearing her parents speak. She sobbed and held on to the window ledge, her eyes fixed greedily upon the open chink in the shutter, listening to, and looking at her parents in their misery, as they sat and talked so kindly and anxiously about her— talked so that every word was a stab at her heart; for she had never heard them open their hearts like this before.

"Ay, wife," he said after a time, "it was a sair blow to me. I could hae fain dee'd at the time; I was fair heartbroken. It's a gey queer world that brings the keenest pangs frae them that yin likes best. I could hae dee'd gladly to hae saved that bairn frae the slightest hurt!"

"Matthew," said the mother, speaking with all her soul in her eyes, as she looked at him, "if by ony chance it should turn oot that Mysie gaed wrang an' fell into disgrace, wad ye tak' her back, if she should come hame again?" and there was a world of pleading in the mother's voice as she spoke.

"Tak' her back! Oh, God, I'd dae onything to hae her here at this meenit, nae matter though it should be proved that she was guilty o' the warst sin under the sun. Tak' her back! Oh, wife! my heart is breakin' for her!" and he lifted his thin worn hand to his eyes and sobbed in his grief.

"Weel, Matthew," returned the wife, "if ever she does come back, nae matter when it may be, or hoo it may be, I'm glad you'll no be harsh wi' her. You'll just speak to her as if naething had happened; for I ken she'll be mair feart to face you than onybody else. Jist try an' mak' her believe, when you speak, that she had gane awa' to the store a message, or to the well for watter, an' that she had bidden owre lang, as she an' ither weans used to do when they got started the play, an' forget to come hame. Jist speak to her that way, Matthew, an' the hame-comin', if ever it comes, will no' be sae hard for the puir bairn. For God knows, it micht be hard enough for her!"

The girl outside, listening eagerly to every word, tried to cry out with the pain of all this talk by her parents, but her tongue clove to her parched mouth, and her lips were stiff and dry.

"I'll never be harsh wi' a bairn o' mine, wife," he replied brokenly. "I liket Mysie owre weel ever to be harsh wi' her. Oh, if only I could see her afore me this nicht, I wad gie a' I ever had in the world. To hae her sittin' here, as she used to sit, her wee heid wi' its soft hair against my knee, an' my haun clappin' it, an' her bonnie een lookin' up at me, as if I was something she aye looket up to, as bein' better than ony living being she ever kenned, wad be mair pleasure for me this minute than if I got a' the money in the world. I'd swap heaven and my chances o' salvation, wife, jist to hae her sittin' here on the fender, as she used to sit. Hunger an' a' the rest wad be easy borne for that."

There was a soft rustling sound at the window as he spoke, and a slow step was heard, which seemed to drag along towards the door, then a fumbling at the sneck, the handle lifted, and the door opened slowly inwards, as if reluctant to reveal its secret.

It was a tense poignant moment for all; for both the father and mother, weak as the former was, rose to their feet expectantly, their eyes searching the slowly opening door, as a thin pale draggled figure entered and staggered forward with a low pitiful cry of "Faither! Mother! I've come hame!" and tottering forward, fell at Matthew's feet, clasping his knees with the thin fragile hands, while the tears of a heart-breaking sorrow flowed from the appealing eyes, upturned to the amazed parents.

"Mysie! Mysie!" he sobbed, clasping her to his thin worn knees, and kissing the bent head, as she sobbed and cried. "Oh, Mysie! Mysie! but you hae been a lang time at the store!"

CHAPTER XXIII
HOME

"Oh my puir wean! My bonnie bairn!" crooned Mrs. Maitland, as she bent over the figure of her daughter who, clinging to Matthew's knees, was looking up into his face, as he lay back in his chair where he had fallen, when Mysie fell at his feet. "Oh, my puir lamb, you're wet to the skin, an' fair done; for God knows its an' awfu' mess you hae cam' hame in."

"Puir thing," she wailed and crooned, again breaking out after having kissed and fondled Mysie's wet face. "We hae lang hungered for you — hungered for you for a gey lang time, an' noo you hae cam' hame, near to daith's door. But we'll nurse you back. We'll mak' you strong and healthy again. Oh, Mysie, my puir lassie. What ails you? Where hae you been? What has happened to you a' this time? But what am I thinking aboot," she broke off, "sitting here, when I should be gettin' some dry claes for you, an' a bed ready."

She rose and began to busy herself shaking up a bed and diving into drawers, bringing clean clothes forth and hanging them over a piece of rope which stretched across the fireplace, so as to air and heat them, the tears streaming from her eyes and occasionally a low moan breaking from her as if forced by some inward pain; while Matthew, nearly overcome with excitement, could only lie back in his chair, his eyes closed and his hands stroking tenderly the wet young head that lay against his knee.

"Faither," murmured Mysie, brokenly and weakly, "oh, faither, I've come back. Jist let me lie here near you. I jist want you to clap my held, to lean against you, an' gang to sleep. Are you angry wi' me, faither? Are you—" and Mysie's eyes closed in a faint, as she lay limp against his knee.

Just then the door opened and Mrs. Sinclair came in. She always came in, after she had got everyone in the house to bed, to see how Matthew felt. It was her first errand in the morning and her last before retiring at night. She was generally the last visitor, and the door was always locked and barred when she went away.

"Oh, Nellie, come awa' in," said Matthew. "You're a God's send this nicht. I'm glad to see you. Mysie's jist cam' back, an' she has fented. Gie's a bit haun' wi' her to get her into bed. Puir thing. She's fair done up," and Matthew tried to raise up the prostrate figure of his bairn; but sank back too weak, and too overcome to do anything.

"Dinna you trouble yourself, Matthew," said Mrs. Sinclair, gathering the prostrate girl in her arms and raising her up on her knee like a child. "Bring some dry claes. Jenny, an' get some warm watter bottles in the bed. Puir thing, she's in an awfu' state. She's a' tremblin' an' maun hae been awfu' ill," and she worked with and stripped the wet clothes from the girl and soon had her in bed, but in spite of all her efforts Mysie remained unconscious. She then left to get the doctor summoned, leaving the sorrowing parents to look after the girl till she returned.

When she did come back, Matthew was in bed and his condition very much worse. The excitement had been too much for him in his weakened state and he lay exhausted, crying like a child.

Soon the doctor came and did all in his power. At the end of an hour Mysie's eyes opened and she looked about her.

"Where's my faither?" she asked weakly. "Oh, I'm gled I'm hame."

"He's in bed," answered Mrs. Sinclair. "An' you're no' to talk the nicht, Mysie. Jist lie still, like a good lass, an' drink this, an' in the mornin' you'll may be a bit better." And Mysie drank, and with a sigh of happy contentment, she turned her face to the wall, glad she was now at home— home with her wounded spirit and broken life.

The soft easy chaff bed gave her more of rest and satisfaction than if it had been eiderdown. She traced as of old the roses upon the cheap paper with which the box bed was papered, and which had been her mother's pride when it was put on. Mysie watched the twining and intertwining of the roses, as they reached upward toward the ceiling through a maze of woodbine and red carnations, and noted that the curtains upon the bed were the same as they were when she had last slept there.

The old wag-at-the-wa' clock which had belonged to her grandfather, wheezed wearily from the corner and the shrill eerie call of a courting cat outside broke familiarly upon her ear. Thus surrounded by the sights and sounds of old, a glad contentment in her heart, she soon dozed off into a deep sleep.

When Mrs. Sinclair went home just as midnight was striking she found Robert sitting by the fire wondering at her absence. He had just returned from a meeting at a neighboring village, and finding his brothers and sisters all in bed and his mother not in the house with his tea ready for him as usual, he wondered what was the matter.

"I was owre at Matthew's," she replied in answer to the question she knew he was going to ask.

"Is he waur the nicht?" he asked quickly.

"Weel, it's no' him, although he's gey upset too; but Mysie has cam' hame the nicht, an' puir lassie she is in an awfu' state," and she was quick to note the soft blanching of his cheek as she spoke.

"Mysie hame," he echoed with quick interest.

"Ay, puir lassie; but I doot if I'm no' cheated that Mysie'll no' be lang anywhere. The doctor says she's to be keepit quate; for she's gey low. In fact he felt me at the door that he dinna think she could last a week."

Robert sat a long time looking into the fire, while his mother got ready his tea, and described to him all that she knew of Mysie's return and of her sad condition.

"You'd hardly ken her," she went on. "She's that thin and white and faur gane lookin', forby havin' a boast that wad fricht you. Puir lassie, I was vexed for her an' Matthew too is gey upset aboot it. Dae you ken, Rob, I believe they mun be gey hard gruppit. Wi' Matthew being off work, and John deein' an' a' the ither troubles they had this while, I think they canna be ower weel off."

"Ay," he said, "they canna be ower weel off; for they hae had a lot to dae this while. You micht look to them, mither. We are no sae ill off noo, an' we can afford tae help them."

"Weel, Rob, I've been aye givin' them a bit hand, buying beef for soup an' that' an' daein' a' I could. But I'm awfu' puttin' aboot ower puir Mysie. She's gey faur gane, an' wherever she has been she's been haein a bad time of it."

"I saw her at Edinburgh," he said quietly, as she paused to pour out the tea.

"In Edinburgh?"

"Ay," he replied. "Last month when I was at the conference," and Robert told his mother the whole story of his meeting with Mysie and of her disappearance and all that had happened to her from the time she had gone away.

"But you never telt yin o' us, Rob," she said after he had come to the end of the story.

"No, I never telt ony o' you; for Mysie made me promise no' to tell; an' forby she wadna' gi'e me her address. But I was that upset that day that I couldn't collect mysel' an' I minded o' a lot o' things I should hae done an' said after I left her. It was terrible," and he relapsed into silence again, as he went on with his supper.

His mother saw all the pain in his heart that night, though neither spoke much of the state of his feelings for Mysie; but it was evident to her who saw all the cross currents of fate, perhaps more clearly than Robert knew.

She looked at him with furtive pride. There was no showy parading of what he felt, but only the set of the mouth was a little firmer perhaps than usual and the eyes a little softer and glistening. That was all.

"Ay, Robin," she said brokenly, unable to hide her pride and weakness. "I ken a' that you hinna telt me. I guessed it years syne; but I'm sure noo. An' I'm awfu' vexed, laddie; ay, I'm awfu' vexed," and with that he withdrew to his room, more touched with her simple words of sympathy than anything she had ever said to him in all her previous life.

Mrs. Sinclair went to bed, but she knew her laddie had not done so. She heard him in his room and knew that in the silence of the night and in the privacy and secrecy of his own room he was fighting out his battle with fate, and she knew that no one could help him—that only the fiber of his own soul could help him through.

In the morning he rose early and went for a walk, for it was Sunday. Returning, he found his mother with the latest news of Mysie's condition. She waited until the other members of the house had gone out, and then with a sigh observed very quietly but with a world of tender sympathy in her voice:

"Mysie's sinkin' fast, Robin. I think you should gang ower and see her. She canna' last very lang, puir thing, an' she was askin' aboot you when I was ower. I think she wad like to see you. You'll gang ower and see her, Rob," she entreated, a sob in her throat as she spoke. "She'll be awfu' pleased to see you."

"Ay, I'll gang ower, mither," he replied simply. "I'll gang ower efter a wee while."

But it was drawing near to the darkness when he managed to summon sufficient resolution to face the ordeal.

Mysie was lying in the room and he went in to see her—her whom he would have given his own life to restore to activity and health again. A low moan occasionally escaped her as she panted and battled for breath and the color came and faded from her cheeks in quick fleeting waves.

Oh God! Was this Mysie—this faint apparition of the girl whom he had loved? Even in the short month when he had seen her in Edinburgh a very great change had been wrought upon her. The eyes, softly glowing with a quiet radiance as they rested upon his face, were sunk, and the voice faint and weak. A thin white hand lay upon the coverlet and the great waves of brown hair which had been his pride, were tumbled about the thin face framing it in a tangled oak brown frame of deepest beauty.

She lifted her hand as he approached, a sweet smile breaking through her pain, caught him in radiance of love. "I'm glad you've come, Rob," she panted. "I jist wanted to see you again—an'—an' tak' good-by wi' you," and the quick catch in her words gripped his heart as he knelt beside the bed, taking the thin hand between his while the tears started from his eyes and fell upon the white bed cover.

"Oh, Mysie," he said brokenly. His voice refused to go further and he bent his head upon the bed, trying hard to control himself and keep from breaking down before her.

"I'm awfu' vexed, Rob," she said, after a while. "It was a' a mistak' an' naebody's to blame. I ought to hae kent better mysel'," and she paused again for breath. "I—I should hae kent better, that nae guid could come— oot o' it—I was just carried awa'. Dinna ever blame lasses—nor men either, when things happen. They—they canna help themsel's—" and here again she paused for breath, gasping and fighting at every word.

"It's a' a mistake, Rob, an' I think it's a' in the way folk look at thae things." Another pause, while her chest heaved and panted. "Maybe we dinna look at thae things richt," she again resumed. "We—we mak' mistak's and canna help oorsel's; but God dinna mean it as—as a mistak'. It's a' because we think it is. Everything's richt—but we mak' them wrang in the way we look at them. It wad hae—been a' richt—in oor mind, if I had been married afore—afore it happened—but because we werena married—it was wrang. It's a' a mistak' Rob, a' a—" and a burst of coughing nearly choked her and a flood of blood began to gurgle in her mouth.

Robert grew alarmed and lifting a cloth began to wipe the blood from her mouth, looking on her so concerned and anxious that she tried to smile to him to reassure him.

Presently she lay back with eyes closed and her hand limp in his. A wild fear took possession of him as he looked upon the scarcely moving breast, a fear which seemed to communicate itself to the sufferer, and she opened her eyes again, but the voice was weak and very far away.

"Dinna be angry wi' onybody, Rob. It was you I liket, it was you I wanted—but it was a' a mistake."

"I'm no' angry, Mysie," he said stifling his sobs, his tears falling upon the white thin face. "Oh, Mysie, I'm only vexed. I'm only vexed aboot the hale sad business. There now, dearie," he said bending low over her and kissing and stroking the pallid brow and caressing the face so dear to him. "There noo, I'm no' angry. You're mine, Mysie. You've always been mine, an' I'm no' angry. But oh, I love you, Mysie, an' it's breaking my heart to part frae you. Oh, God!" he groaned in agony. "What does it a' mean? I canna' bear it,—I canna' bear't," and a wild burst of grief swept over him as he flung his head and arms upon the bed in a vain attempt to control his sobbing sorrow.

A long pause—then the white hand was raised and crept slowly over his shoulder, working its way among the thick shaggy hair of his head as the fingers strayed from curl to curl, patting him and soothing him as a child is soothed by a mother's hand. It rested upon his bent head and the eyes opened again.

"Ay, Rob, I'm vexed for your sake—but it was a' a mistake." She went on halting and very weak. "It was a' a mistak'—an' naebody is to blame. We are just—driven alang, an'—we canna help oorsel's—it's awfu' to hae— sic feelin's—an'—an' no' hae any poo'er—to guide them richt—it's ay the things we want maist—that we dinna get. Kiss me, Rob—kiss me, as you kissed me—yon—nicht on the muir. Haud me like you—an' I think I can— gang content. Oh, Rob,—ay liket you—it was you I wanted a' the time!"

He clasped her tenderly in his arms as he kissed her mouth, her eyes, her brow, her hair, stroking her and fondling the dear face, catching hungrily the smile that came to the pale lips, and lingered there like a blink of sun upon a hillside after the rest of the landscape is clothed in shadow.

Again there was a pause while he searched the pale face with the lingering smile, noting the veined, almost discolored eyelids, transparent and closed over the tired suffering eyes. Then a burst of coughing again and the blood in thick clots gurgled up from the throat. Then after a little she spoke again.

"Oh, Rob, you hae made me very happy. But I'm vexed aboot you— an'—an' Peter. He tried to dae what was richt; but it wasna to be—I hope you'll—no'—be angry wi' him. He was like me—he couldna' help it."

"Oh, Mysie, I'm no' angry wi' him," he replied brokenly, trying hard to make his voice sound dearly. "I'm no' angry wi' onybody."

"I'm glad o' that, Rob," she said, her hand caressing his head. "You was ay a guid hearted laddie—I'm awfu' glad." Then her mind began to wander and she was back in Edinburgh speaking of her father and John.

"Oh, faither," she rambled on. "Dinna be angry wi' me. There's naebody to blame. Dinna be angry."

Then Robert was conscious that others were in the room, and looking up he beheld his mother and Jenny Maitland and behind them with anxious face and frightened eyes stood Peter Rundell, the picture of misery and despair.

"She's kind o' wanderin', puir thing," he heard the mother say in explanation to the others. "She's kind o' wanderin' in her mind."

It was a sad little group which stood round the dying girl, all anxious and alarmed and watchful. Then after a while she opened her eyes again and there was a look of startled surprise as if she were looking at something in the distance. Then she began to recognize each and all of them in turn, first Robert, who still held her hand, then her mother and Nellie, and Peter. A faint smile came into her eyes and he stepped forward. Her lips moved slowly and a faint sound came falteringly from them.

"Dinna be angry wi' onybody," she panted. "It was a'—a—mistake."

Then raising her hand she held it out to Peter, who advanced towards the bedside and placing his hand on Robert's she clasped them together in her own. "There noo—dinna be angry—it was a' a mistake. It was Rob I liket—it was him—I wanted. But it—was—a' a mistak'. Dinna be—" and the glazed sunken eyes closed forever, never to open again, a faint noise gurgled in her throat, and the dews of death stood out in beads upon the pale brow. A tiny quiver of the eyelids, and a tremor through the thin hands and Mysie—poor ruined broken waif of the world—was gone.

"Oh, my God! She's deid," gasped Robert, clasping the thin dead hands in a frenzy of passionate grief. "Oh, Mysie! Mysie! Oh God! She's deid," and his head bent low over the bed while great sobs tore through him, and shook his young frame, as the storm shakes the young firs of the woods. Then suddenly recollecting himself as his mother put her hand upon his bent head saying: "Rise up, Robin, like a man. You maun gang oot noo." He rose and with tears in his eyes that blinded him so that he hardly saw where he was going, he stumbled out into the darkness under the pale stars—out into the night to the open moor, his grief so burdening that he felt as if the whole world had gone from his reckoning.

"Oh, my poor Mysie," he groaned. "It was all a horrible mistake," and the darkness came down in thick heavy folds as if the whole world were mourning for the loss of the young girl's soul, but it brought no comfort to him.

CHAPTER XXIV
A CALL FOR HELP

It was a quiet night in early April, full of the hush which seems to gather all the creative forces together, before the wild outburst of prodigal creation begins in wild flower and weed and moorland grasses, and Robert Sinclair, who had walked and tramped over the moors for hours, until he was nearly exhausted, his heart torn and his mind in an agony of suffering, sat down upon a little hillock, his elbows on his knees and his hands against his cheeks.

The moor-birds screamed and circled in restless flight around him. They were plainly protesting against his intrusion into their domain. They shrilled and dived in their flight, almost touching the bent head, with swooping wing, to rise again, cleaving the air and sheering round again; but still the lonely figure sat looking into darkness, becoming numbed with cold, and all unconscious of the passage of time.

Gradually the cold began to tell upon him, and he started to his feet, plodding up the hill, through the soft mossy yielding soil. Back again he came after a time, his limbs aching with the long night's tramping; but yet he never thought of going home or turning towards the village.

"Oh, Mysie!" he groaned again and again, and all night long only these two words escaped his lips. They came in a low sad tone, like the wind coming through far-off trees; but they were vibrant with suffering, and only the moor-birds cried in answer.

"Oh, Mysie!" and the winds sighed it again and again, as they came wandering down out of the stillness between the hills, to pass on into the silence of the night again, like lost souls wandering through an uncreative world, proclaiming to other spheres the doom that had settled upon earth.

"Oh, Mysie!" groaned a moorland brook close by, which grumbled at some obstruction in its pathway, and then sighed over its mossy bed, like a tired child emerging exhausted from a long fever, to fall asleep as deeply as if the seal of death had been planted upon the little lips. Occasionally he shifted his position, as his limbs grew cramped, or rose to pace the moor again to bring himself more exhaustion; but always he came back to the little knoll, and sat down again, groaning out the sad plaintive words, that were at once an appeal and a cry, a defiance and a submission. By and by the first gray streaks of dawn came filtering through the curtains of the cloudy east, touching the low hills with gray nimble fingers, or weaving a tapestry of magic, as they brightened and grew clearer, over the gray face of the morn.

Soon the birds leapt again from every corner, climbing upon the ladders of light and tumbling ecstasies of mad joy to welcome the day, as if they feared to be left in the darkness with this strange figure, which merely sat and groaned softly, and looked before it with silent agony in its eyes; and now that the light had again come, they shouted their protest in a louder, shriller note; they mounted upon the waves of light and swooped down into the trough of the semi-darkness, expostulating and crying, not so much in alarm now, as in anger. For with the light comes courage to birds as well as men, and fear, the offspring of ignorance, which is bred in darkness, loses its power when its mystery is revealed.

But even with the coming of the day the still silent figure did not move. It continued to sit until the birds grew tired of protesting, and even the mountain hare wandered close by, sniffing the breeze in his direction, and cocking its ears and listening, as it sat upon its hind legs, only to resume its leisurely wandering again, feeling assured that there was nothing to fear in the direction of this quiet, bent figure of sorrow, that sat merely staring at the hills, and saw naught of anything before him. The things he saw were not the things around him. He was moving in a multitude again. He was walking among them with pity in his heart—a great pity for their ignorance, their lack of vision; and he was giving them knowledge and restoring light to their eyes, to widen their range of vision, so that they could take things in their true perspective. He was full of a great sympathy for their shortcomings, recognizing to the full that only by sowing love could love be reaped, only in service could happiness be found—that he who gave his life would save it.

The great dumb mass of humanity needed serving—needed love. It passed on blindly, wounding itself as it staggered against its barriers, bruising its heart and soul in the darkness, and never learning its lessons. Saviors in all ages had lifted the darkness a bit, and given knowledge, and sometimes it had profited for a while till false prophets arose to mislead.

It was a seething feverish mass, stamping and surging towards every blatant voice which cried the false message to it, rousing it to anger, and again misleading, until it often rose to rend its saviors instead of those who had duped it so shamelessly.

All the tragic procession filed past, and he gave them peace and knowledge. By and by they grew to a long thin stream, feverish and agitated, seemingly all converging towards a point—pain and anxiety in every quick movement, and suffering in every gesture. He looked with still more and more compassion upon them, with a greater love in his breast, but it did not calm them as before, and at last in desperation he stretched out his hands in appealing pity for them, his whole being aglow with the desire to help and pity and love, and he found that the scene changed. He was on the moor, and there was the discomfort of cold in his limbs; but—yes, he was looking at the pit, and there was a long stream of men, women and children, principally women and children, running frantically across the moor towards the pit, and he could hear the faint sound of their voices, which clearly betokened suffering, anxiety and alarm. Something had happened. He must have been looking at that procession for a long time, he realized, and pulling himself together, he bounded to his feet and was off in a long striding race through the moor towards the pit, his heart telling him that something had happened which was out of the ordinary kind of accident that regularly happened at a coal mine. He bounded along, knowing as he went that there was something more of sorrow for his mother in this, whatever it was. He felt so, but could not account for the feeling, and as this thought grew in intensity in his mind, he changed his course a bit, and made for home, to ascertain what had really happened. It was something big, he felt, but whatever it was, his mother must again be called upon to suffer, and his alarm grew with his pace, until he arrived breathless at the house. One look at her face, and he knew his instincts had told him the truth.

She was white and strained, though tearless, but her eyes were full of an awful suffering.

"What has happened, mother?" he demanded, as if he could hardly wait for her to answer.

"The moss has broken in, an' twenty-three men are lost. Jamie an' Andra are among them. They gaed oot themselves this morning, telling me they could work fine, even though you werena there. Oh, Rob! What will I do! Oh, dear! Oh, dear! My bonnie laddies!" and with a sob in her voice she turned away, and Robert was again out of the house, and running through the moor to the pit, as hard as desperation could drive him. His two brothers were down there, and they must be got out. Even as he ran he wondered what strange freak of fate it was, that had kept him out there on the moor all night and so saved him from this terrible fate.

He could understand how his brothers would feel at the chance of working one day by themselves. He had always been their guide and protector. They had gone into the pit with him when they left school, and had just continued working with him since, learning their trade from his greater experience, and trusting always to his better judgment when there was danger to avoid. They would go out that day with the intention of working like slaves to produce an extra turn of coal. Even though it were but one extra hutch, they would fill it, and slave all day with never a rest, so that they could have the satisfaction of seeing approval in his eyes, when they told him at night how many they had turned out, and how well things had gone generally with them in his absence.

He reached the pit, to find that the moss was already rising in the shaft, and that there was no possibility of getting down to try and save these twenty-three men and boys who were imprisoned in the darkness beneath.

He came across Tam Donaldson, who was the last to get up.

"Tell me aboot it, Tam," he said. "Is there no chance of getting down? Do you think any of them will be safe so far?" and a whole lot of other anxious questions were rattled off, while Tam, dripping wet from having to wade and fight the last fifty fathoms toward the pit bottom, through the silent, sinister, creeping moss that filled the roadways and tunnels, stood to give him an account of what had taken place.

"They were a' sitting at their piece, Rob—a' but James and Andra. They were keen to get as muckle work done as possible, an' they had some coal to get to fill oot a hutch, when a' at yince we heard Andra crying on us to rin. Had they a' ran doon the brae we'd a' hae been safe, for we could hae gotten to the bottom afore the moss; but some ran into the inside heading, an' hadna time to realize that their outlet was cut off, an' there they are; for the moss was comin' doon the full height of the road when I ran back to try an' cry on them to come back. So I had to rin for't too, an' jist got oot by the skin o' my teeth.

"I kent fine it wad happen," he went on, as Robert stood, the tears in his eyes, as he realized how hopeless the position was of ever being able to restore these men and boys again to their homes. There was anger in Tam's voice as he spoke. "It's a' to get cheap coal, an' they ought to hae known, for they were telt, that to open oot that seam into long well workings so near the surface, an' wi' sic a rotten roof, was invitin' disaster, wi' as muckle rain as we hae had lately. They are a lot o' murderers—that's what they are! But what the hell do they care, sae lang as they get cheap coal!"

Robert turned away sick at heart. It was certainly a foolish thing, he had thought at the time, for the management to change their method of working the coal; for even though the seam had grown thinner, he felt that it could have still been worked at a profit under the old system. He knew also that the men were all upset at the time by this change, but the management had assured them that there was no danger, and that it would mean more money for the men, as they would be enabled to produce more coal.

This certainly had happened for a week or two, but the rates were soon broken, because they were making too high wages; and the men found, as usual, that their increased output had merely meant increased work for them, and increased profits for the owners.

Was there nothing to be done? Robert wondered, as he paced restlessly back and forth, his mind busy, as the mind of every man present, and anxious to make any sacrifice, to take any risk, if by so doing they might save those imprisoned in the mine. Even while his mind was working, he could not help listening to the talk of those around him. There were strange opinions expressed, and wild plans of rescue were suggested and discussed and disputed. Everyone condemned the coal company for what had happened, but over all there were the white-faced women and the silent children; the muffled sobs, the tears, and the agony of silent wet eyes that spoke more pain than all the tragedies that had ever been written.

Robert could not help listening to one man—a big, raw, loosely-built fellow, who stood in the midst of a group of women laying off his idea of a rescue.

"I'm rale glad to be out of it," he said, "for Jean's sake, an' the bairns; but for a' that I'd gang doon again an' try an' get them oot if there was ony chance o' doin' it."

"Hoo is Jean?" one woman interposed to enquire about his wife, who had been ill a long time.

"Oh, she's gettin' on fine noo, an' the doctor has a hopeful word o' her," he answered. "In fact, I was just feeding the birds the last time he was in, an' asked him hoo she was doin'."

This man, Dugald McIntosh, had one god—his canaries. He read all he could get to read about them, and studied the best conditions under which to rear them, sacrificed everything he could to breed better birds, and this was always a topic for him to discourse upon.

"I was just busy feedin' them when he cam' in, and after he had examined her, I asked him hoo she was gettin' on."

"Fine," he said, "gi'e her plenty o' sweet milk noo, and fresh eggs, an' she'll sune be on her feet again. Fresh eggs! mind you, an' me canna get yin for my canaries! I thocht it was a guid yin!"

Robert turned away; but there was working in his mind an idea, and he ran round to the colliery office to the manager, who was nearly mad with grief and anxiety at what had happened.

"Come in, Sinclair," he said simply. "Can you suggest anything to help us? Whatever is done, it can only be done quickly; for the moss is rising rapidly in the shaft, and even though some of the men are safe in the upper workings, it is only a question of a very short time till the moss will rise and suffocate them, or until the black damp does so. If you have any idea that can help, out with it and let us make a trial, for the inactivity is killing me."

"I have been thinking, Mr. Anderson," replied Robert, "that we might go down the old air-shaft over in the moss there, and run along the top level, which is not far from the surface, and try and blast it through on the heading into which the moss broke."

It might be full of moss too, for no one knew the extent of the breakage in the metals, and even though it were clear, the damp would be lying in it; but surely they might make an attempt on it. Robert remembered working this level to within about nine feet from going through on the heading. If he had plenty of hands, just to go down and drill a hole in anywhere, and blast out the coal with a shot or two wherever he could best place them, he might succeed in getting through to the men. It might be that after the first rush filling the roadways, the flood of moss had drained off, and was not now running so thickly down the heading.

"Let me go and try, sir," he pleaded eagerly. "I think I can manage, if the level is still unbroken. We can work in short turns, so as not to be overcome with the damp. Will you let me have a try? I believe it's the only chance we have, and if we do succeed, look what it will mean to the women in the village. Will you let me try?"

"Yes," replied Anderson, reaching for his lamp, "and I shall be one of the triers too. Go out and pick seven or eight men. I'll get the necessary tools and get off over the moor to the old air shaft. It may still be open. It is a pity we let it go out of repair, but we can have a trial."

Robert ran out, a hope filling his heart, telling his news to those round about, and the first man to step forth, before he had finished, was Dugald McIntosh, the man who had put more value on his canaries than on his wife's health, who quietly lifted up the drills the manager had brought, and slinging them lightly over his shoulder, was off across the moor at a run, with a dozen men at his heels, all eager to get to grips with the danger, and try to rescue their imprisoned comrades.

CHAPTER XXV
A FIGHT WITH DEATH

Robert Sinclair seemed to be the one man who knew what to do—at least, he seemed to be the only one who had a definite aim in view and as if by some natural instinct everyone was just ready to do his bidding. He was the leader of the herd towards whom everyone looked ready for a new order to meet any new situation which might arise. Initiative and resource were a monopoly in his hands. He was silent, and worked to get ready to descend the old air-shaft, with grim set lips. Yet there seemed to be no sense of bustle, only the work was done quickly and orderly, his orders being issued as much by signs as by speech, and soon a windlass was erected with ropes and swing chair fastened, into which he at once leaped, followed by another man. Tools and explosives were packed in and lamps lit and the order given to lower the chair.

Robert felt a queer sort of feeling as he stood waiting on the first motion of the little drum round which the rope wound. He was cool and clear brained—in fact he wondered why he was so collected. He felt he was standing out of all this maelstrom of suffering and terror. Not that he was impervious to anxiety for the men below, not that he was unmoved by all that it meant to those standing round; but after that first wild throb of terror that had clutched at his heart when his mother had told him the dread news and that his two brothers were imprisoned in the mine, something seemed suddenly to snap within him, the load and the intensity of the pain lifted, and from that moment he had been master of the situation.

He glanced round him as he waited quietly in his swinging seat. He felt as he looked, no sense of fear or impending doom. He knew that black damp probably lay in dense quantities down in that yawning gulf below him, he knew that the sides of the shaft were in a bad state of disrepair, and that they might give way at any time as the swinging rope must inevitably touch them, and bring the whole thing in upon him, with hundreds of tons of débris and moss.

Yet it was not of these things he thought. Perhaps he did not think of anything particularly, but a far-off lilt of a children's game which was played at school, kept iterating and reiterating through his brain, and everything seemed done to that tune.

> "Don't take a laddie, oh,
> Laddie oh, laddie oh,
> Don't take a laddie oh,
> Take a bonnie wee lassie."

It sang continually within him and men seemed to move to its regular beat, as they hurried to get ready. He looked at the hills, and noted how quiet everything seemed, their curving outlines gave such a sense of eternal rest. There was a patch of lovely blue sky above him, he noticed where the clouds opened up and a glint of golden glorious sunshine came through; but it looked garish and it closed again and the white clouds trailed away, their lower fringes clinging to the hill tops like veils of gossamer woven by time to deck the bride of Spring. A lark rose at the edge of the crowd of weeping women and children as if unmindful of the tragedy over which it sang so rapturously, and he noted its fluttering wings and swelling throat as it soared in circles of glad song.

All these things and more he noted though it was but a momentary pause.

"Are you right?" came the question from the men at the windlass, far away it seemed and unconnected with the scene.

"Right," he answered with a start, and looking round he seemed to become aware of the white-faced, red-eyed women among whom his mother's face seemed to stand out. She was not weeping, he noticed, but oh God! her face seemed to turn him with the intensity of the suffering in her eyes. He realized that he had not noticed her before, and now with a wild throb of pity he stretched out his hands towards her, a look of suffering in his eyes, as if he were feeling the pains of humanity crucified anew, and the chair began to drop slowly below the surface, swinging down into the darkness and the evil dangers that lurked below. Her face was the last thing he saw—a face full of agony yet calm with a great renunciation coming to birth in her eyes, her lips drawn thin like a slit in her face and all the color gone from them, the head bent a little as if a great blow had fallen upon her—an island of agony set in a sea of despair.

A wild impulse seized him to go back. It was too much to ask of a woman, he felt. Too great a burden of tragedy to heap upon one soul, as he cast his mind back through the suffering years and viewed all the pain she had borne, and the terrible Gethsemane which her life had been; but as the chair swung round he clutched the swaying rope and with the other hand steadied it from crashing against the side of the shaft as they slowly dropped lower and lower into the darkness and the evil smells which hung around.

"Things look bad here," said his comrade as they passed down where at some time a huge portion from the side had fallen out and down into the bottom of the old shaft.

"Ay," answered Robert, "everything seems just ready to collapse," and they dropped lower and lower, swaying from side to side, cautiously guiding their swinging chair from the moss-oozing side, their nerves strained as they listened to the creeking rope as it was paid out from above.

"Holy God," cried his mate, "that was a near thing," as a huge mass of rocks and slimy moss lunged out a little below them and hurtled away in a loud rumbling noise.

Robert pulled the signal cord to stop and looked up to see the white clouds passing over the narrow funnel-like shaft in which they hung. Then he gave the signal to let out again noting how thick with damp the atmosphere was becoming, and having difficulty with his light.

Lower and lower they swung and dropped down into the old shaft and as the rope creaked and crazed above them it lilted:

"Choose, choose, wha' you'll tak',
Wha' you'll tak', wha' you'll tak',
Choose, choose wha' you'll tak',
A laddie or a lassie."

And the memory of the old lilt brought back other scenes again and he found himself guiding the chair from the shaft side steering it off with his hand at every rhythmic beat of the child song.

Soon they reached the bottom of the shaft, for it was not very deep, and found a mass of débris, almost choking up the roadways on either side of the bottom. But they got out of their chair and soon began to "redd" away the stones though they found very great difficulty in getting the lamps to burn. Occasionally, as they worked, little pieces came tumbling from the side of the shaft, telling its own tale, and as soon as Robert got a decent sized kind of opening made through the rocks which blocked the roadway he sent up the other man to bring down more help and to get others started to repair the old shaft by putting in stays and batons to preserve the sides and so prevent them from caving in altogether.

He found his way along the level which had been driven to within nine feet of going through on the heading in which the inbreak of moss had taken place. He noticed the roof was broken in many places and that the timber which had been put in years before was rotten. Strange noises seemed to assail his senses, and stranger smells, yet the lilt of that old childish game was ever humming in his brain and he saw himself with other boys and girls with clasped hands linked in a circle and going round in a ring as they sang the old ditty.

"Three breakings should dae it," he said as he looked at the face of the coal dripping with water from the cracks in the roof. "If only they were here to put up the props. I could soon blow it through," and he began to prepare a place for batons and props, pending the arrival of more help from those who were only too eager to come down to his aid.

It was almost an hour before help came in the shape of two men carrying some props. Then came another two and soon more timber began to arrive regularly and the swinging blows of their hammers as they drove in the fresh props were soon echoing through the tunnels, and Robert set up his boring machine and soon the rickety noise of it drowned all others. He paused to change a drill when a faint hullo was heard from the other side.

"Hullo," he yelled, then held his breath in tense silence to hear the response which came immediately. "Are you all safe?" he roared, his voice carrying easily through the open coal.

"Ay," came the faint answer; "but the moss is rising in the heading and you'll have to hurry up."

Robert knew this, and one of his helpers had gone down an old heading to explore and had returned to say that it was rising steadily and was now within two hundred feet from the old shaft down which he had descended.

"Where away did the roof break?" roared Robert as he changed his second drill.

"Half way doon the cousie brae," came the answer, "an' we're all shut in like rats. Hurry up and get us oot," and again the rickety, rackety noise of the boring machine began and drowned all other noises.

He soon drilled his holes and he could hear them on the other side singing now some ribald song to keep up their courage, while others who were religiously inclined chanted hymns and psalms, but all were wondering whether Robert and his men would be able to break through the barrier in time to save them before the persistently rising moss claimed them.

He charged his shots and called them to go back, telling them the number of his charges, then lit his fuse and ran out of the old level to wait in a place of safety while the explosion took place.

Soon they boomed out and the concussion put them all in darkness; but they soon had the lamps re-lit and were back in among the thick volumes of powder smoke, groping about and shading their lamps and peering in to see what their shots had done to lessen the barrier between them and their imprisoned comrades.

Then the shovels set to work and tossed the coal which the shots had dislodged back into the roadway and soon the boring machines were busy again, eating into the coal; for those tireless arms of Robert's never halted. He swung the handle or wielded the pick or shovel, never taking a, rest, while the sweat streamed from his body working like some mechanical product for always in his mind he was calculating his chances for being able to blast it through the barrier before the moss rose.

"It has only a stoop length an' a half to rise now," reported one of the men. "It's creeping up like the doom o' the day o' judgment. But I think we'll manage. If these shots do as well as the last ones we should be within two feet of them, an' surely to God we can bite the rest of it, if we canna blaw it. Let me stem the shots, Rob, an' you take a rest."

"You go to hell," was the unexpectedly astounding reply; for no one had ever heard Robert Sinclair use language like this before. "As soon as thae shots are off an' if they blaw as well as the others we'll turn out the coal an' then you can gang up the pit, every yin o' you. I'll soon blow through the rest of it, and if you are all up by then it will make for speed in getting the others out. We're going to have a race for it even though we manage as I'm thinking to. So get out of the way and don't talk. Again the air's getting too dam'd thick for you all remaining here. There's hardly as muckle as would keep a canary living," and again he called to those on the other side to beware of the shots, and again ran out to a place of safety while the explosions took place.

Once more the result of the shots was good; but the smoke choked and blinded them and one man was overcome by the fumes. They carried him out the road a bit and after he showed signs of coming round, Robert gave instructions for him to be taken to the surface.

"Oh, Lod, but it's nippin' my e'en," said one as he rubbed his eyes and blew his nose, sneezed and finally expectorated. "It's as thick as soor milk, be dam'd!"

"Well, get him up, and I'll away back and redd out the shots and try and get it through again. The moss is rising quicker noo an' it has only aboot eighty feet to come."

So back he went among the thick choking volume of smoke, tripping and stumbling and staggering from side to side as he scrambled on. Would he be in time to blast the barrier down before the steadily creeping moss rose to cut off his only avenue of escape?

"My God! What's that?" he asked himself as he paused while a rumble and crash behind him told him that the old shaft had caved in burying his comrades in rocks and moss and water.

He ran back but could get no further than within a stoop length of the old shaft. There were hundreds of tons of débris and all was finally lost. For the first time terror seized him and he tore desperately at the bowlders of stone, cutting his fingers and lacerating his body all over with cuts and bruises. He raved and swore and shouted in desperation, the sweat streaming from every pore, his eyes wild and glaring, but he was soon driven back by the moss which was oozing and percolating through the broken mass of bowlders and gradually it forced him back with a rush as it burst through with a sudden slushing sound as if suddenly relieved from a barrier which held it. Back he rushed, his light again becoming extinguished, the flood pursuing him relentlessly, the air now so heavy that he could hardly breathe, but groping his way he reached the first end roadway down which for the moment the flood ran to meet the rising moss creeping up relentlessly from below.

Choking and only half conscious he staggered on with all sense of disaster gone from his mind, with no thought of his comrades on the other side waiting so impatiently to be released, and singing their frothy songs in the hope that all was well, his legs doubling below him, and his lungs heaving to expel the poison which the thick air contained. Down at last he fell, his head striking against the side of the roadway, and he lay still.

The moss might rise hungrily over him now, the rotten roof might fall upon him, all the dangers of the mine might conspire together against him; but nothing they might do could ever again strike terror into the young heart that lay there, feebly throbbing its last as it was being overcome with the deadly poison of the black damp.

He was proof against all their terrors now, the spirit could evade them yet; for though the old shaft might collapse and imprison his body and claim it as a sacrifice to the King Terror of the Underworld, no prison was ever created that could contain the indomitable spirit of man as God. He was free—free, and was happy and could cry defiance to the dangers of the mine, to the terrors of time itself. He could clutch the corners of the earth, and play with it as a toy of time, among the Gods of Eternity.

"Choose, choose wha' you'll tak'," throbbed the young heart and a smile of triumph played upon the lips as the pictures of bygone times flitted across his dying brain. He was again the happy infant, hungry it may be, and ill-clad, but Heaven contained no happier soul. The little stomach might not be filled with sufficient food; but the spirit of him as it was in younger years knew no material limits to its laughter in the childish ring games of youth. Again he was waiting in the dark wintry mornings on Mysie, so that she would not be afraid to go to work on the pit-head; ay, and he was happy to take the windward side of her in the storm, and shield her from the winter's blast, tying her little shawl about her ears and making her believe he did not feel the cold at all.

He was back again at his mother's knee, listening to her glorious voice singing some pitiful old ballad, as she crooned him to sleep; or lying trying to forget the hunger he felt as the glorious old tune seemed to drown his senses while he waited to say his prayer at night.

> "Jesus, tender shepherd, hear me,
> Bless Thy little lamb to-night,
> In the darkness be Thou near me,
> Keep me safe till morning light."

Then there was the "good-night" to everyone and the fond kiss of the best of all mothers, the sinking into sleep that billowed and rocked the weary young spirit of him, crushed and bruised by the forces of the world, and finally the sweet shy smile of a young girl blushing and awkward, but flooding his soul with happiness and thrilling every fiber of him with her magic as she stood upon the hill crest, outlined against the sunset with a soft breeze blowing, kissing the gray hill side, bringing perfumes from every corner of the moor and beckoning him as she rose upward, he followed higher and higher, the picture taking shape and becoming more real until it merged into spirit.

And the creeping moss moved upward, hungry for its prey and greedy to devour the fine young body so fresh and strong and lusty; but it was balked, for it claimed only the empty shell. The prize had gone on the wings of an everlasting happiness and the spirit of the moor, because there is no forgetting, triumphed over the spirit of destruction, so that in the records of the spirit he shall say:

> "I shall remember when the red sun glowing
> Sinks in the west, a gorgeous flare of fire;
> How then you looked with the soft breeze blowing
> Cool through your hair, a heaving living pyre
> Fired by the sun for the sweet day's ending;
> I still shall hear the whirring harsh moor-hen,
> Roused from her rest among the rushes bending
> I shall remember then.

"I shall remember every well-loved feature,
How, on the hill crest when the day was done,
Just how you looked, dear, God's most glorious creature,
Heaven's silhouette outlined against the sun;
I shall remember just how you the fairest,
Dearest and brightest thing that God e'er made,
Warmed all my soul with holy fire the rarest,
That vision shall not fade."

But pain and tragedy forever seem to have no limit to their hunger; and in the clear spring air above the place where the bodies of her boys lay, Mrs. Sinclair's heart was again the food upon which the tragedy of life fed. All the years of her existence were bound up in the production of coal, and the spirits of her husband and of her sons call to-day to the world of men—men who have wives, men who have mothers, men who have sweethearts and sisters and daughters, stand firm together; and preserve your women folk from these tragedies, if you would justify your manhood in the world of men.

ABOUT THE AUTHOR

During the whole literary journey, Gertrude Atherton wrote over 40 novels, several short stories and genuine essays ended up with a successful career. She was majorly known for her prolific contribution to literature during the late 19th century. Born in 1857, she grew up and brought up in San Francisco California in a wealthy and socially stable family. In both countries, the United States and Europe, she completed her education with a vivid understanding of a broad cultural base. She wrote epic genres including novels and short stories and essays. Wide predictions and explanations of diverse themes and styles helped her to become notable at a rapid pace. She often dived into the social and cultural norms of her time and staggered critiques of society. Atherton was well known for her collaboration and association with the greatest literary figures of her time which includes H.G Wells and Ambrose Bierce. However, her popularity slowed down during the 20th century and her interest in her work was acknowledged by her peers and most of her scholars appreciated her for her major contribution to American literature.